I0739499

THE Scent OF Apple Tea

VALERIE IHSAN

WILLOW BENCH BOOKS
SPRINGFIELD, OREGON

The Scent of Apple Tea
Copyright © 2016 Valerie Ihsan.
All rights reserved.
Printed in the United States of America

Cover Design: Paperandsage.com

Willow Bench Books
796 Kelly Blvd.
Springfield, Oregon 97477

ISBN: 978-0-9975810-0-3

*To my wild man, my one and only nose-mate:
I'm so happy we belong to each other.*

*To my awesome teenagers:
Thank you for being your unique selves,
and for teaching me to be the best I can be.*

OTHER BOOKS

Other books by this author:
(Available at valerieihsanauthor.com)

Smell the Blue Sky: young, pregnant, and widowed
(Written under the name Valerie Willman)

How to Grieve: Even when you don't want to
(Written under the name Valerie Willman;
free on website.)

For free downloads, please go to:
valerieihsanauthor.com.

Kathryn

BEFORE KATHRYN GREW HERBS IN THE WILLAMETTE Valley, when she still had red hair and courage—without being in any other way remarkable—she unintentionally communicated with a dead Scottish ancestor. Flora started appearing in the silent realm where dreams come from when Kathryn was a young mother, forty years ago.

All her adult life Kathryn had been afraid of dying alone, though she didn't know it. She didn't know the phobia was trapped inside her heart, behind the wall of the pericardium, stuffed inside the vessels and capillaries, hidden.

She'd carried the fear for years. For Flora. Mentally aching and bleeding from a memory that wasn't even hers.

Kathryn wondered how her life would've been different if she hadn't suffered that dormant fear by proxy, what decisions she might've made without the terror shackling her ankles.

Perhaps she wouldn't have fought with her daughter as much. Maybe she would've encouraged Heather more when they'd had the time, instead of holding her close at home—so certain that if Heather had left, the terrifying sorrow and blankness of being alone, old, and useless would bleed into her lungs so that when she died in fearful paralysis, it would be as if being buried alive.

Heather

Heather walked the pathway around the perimeter of their front yard. She wondered, idly, why they still had a quarter-acre lawn. Why hadn't they put it to better use? A little field of lavender might look nice there. She inhaled large breaths of nature and fresh warm August air.

She enjoyed the serenity of the front. The back bustled with the frenzy of weeding and harvesting. In front were remnants of fairy houses and vignettes she and her mother had made when Heather was a child.

Thirty years.

Thirty years they'd been in this house. On this land. No wonder her mother was so attached. Though, wasn't it funny that while her mother felt more and more cemented to this place, Heather was so ready to leave she felt like a wound up Jack-in-the-box *waitingwaitingwaiting* for the lid to pop. She loved her home, but adventure was serenading her, though not in a loving way. It felt more pressured—as if she were running out of time. The pea gravel crunched and rolled under her feet. She sniffed.

After her circuitous walk, Heather's outlook improved. She sat down at her desk with a ubiquitous cup of tea and began the end-of-month accounting.

After an hour, the invoices and online banking forms blurred. She was so bored she wanted to bang her head on the computer screen.

The trouble was she just didn't feel inspired to do that last hour of accounting work. Scotland came to mind again.

She typed Scotland into the Google search bar on her browser's homepage. VisitScotland.com was the first link to seduce her mouse's cursor. After only five minutes of skimming the tours under the Travel tab, she homed in on the most interesting one: the Highlands and Whiskey tour. "Authentic Scotland," the website boasted.

A ten-night stay. A tour of a whiskey distillery and the Highlands—where her ancestors were from. The more she browsed the tourism webpage, the more excited she got. At the end of her "accounting" hour, she had downloaded three mobile apps on her iPhone, perused the "Practical Information for Travelers" section on the website, and devoured the pages on "The Highlands" and "The Kingdom of Fife."

She refused to research the cost of the trip.

Yet.

This vacation was something she really wanted to do with her mother. Heather didn't know why it was so important to her. It just was. Maybe it didn't matter why. Heather's head began to hurt and she felt a familiar and sinister morsel of fatigue edge toward her consciousness.

Startled, she hurried to the back door. She rushed through the sweet potato harvest, panic rising, and barely made it to the pantry with the potatoes before the fatigue hit.

Fatigue was too sedate of a word.

The Wave.

That's what it was. A tsunami of exhaustion. Maybe that was what bears felt before collapsing into hibernation. Except when Heather felt the Wave, she felt scared. Afraid that somehow, if she lost consciousness, she'd never wake up.

The hot shower she'd planned for after the garden chores would need to wait. She couldn't stand up any longer.

Heather stepped out of her shoes and stumbled to the bed. Leaving her clothes on, she fumbled with the blanket and managed to get under it, rolling to her side. She closed her eyes and surrendered to stillness. She wasn't especially sleepy, but her body felt as if it were filled with heavy sand. Moving was not a possibility. Tears leaked out and dripped over the bridge of her nose.

This had happened before—twice—but never as fast. Heather wondered how long the Wave would last. The first time, it went on for only a day. She'd attributed it to depression. It was right after she'd broken up with Kyle, earlier in the year, and when her mother had first pushed her to take over the farm management and the retail herbal business.

The second time, the Wave lasted a whole week. She'd had the flu a few days prior, so thought it was just a particularly stubborn case that she wasn't bouncing back from.

But now, in her bed, in the middle of the afternoon, she realized that it wasn't depression; it wasn't the flu. Something was not right. Normal people didn't collapse after digging up sweet potatoes and surfing the Internet for travel plans. She sniffled and wanted to wipe her face but couldn't.

"Heather?"

Kathryn called through the house. "*Heather?* Are you in here? You left the back door open."

Heather heard footsteps and mumbling. "The flies will be terrible," Kathryn said. "Heather?"

Kathryn walked into the bedroom. Surprise and then concern dripped from her mouth, her words. "What's happened? What's wrong?" She sat on the edge of the bed and adjusted the coverlet away from Heather's face. She smoothed Heather's hair back and wiped the tears from her face.

"What is it?" Kathryn asked quietly.

"The Waves are here, Mama," Heather whispered.

"The waves? What are you talking about?"

"Tired."

"You're tired?"

Heather could hear that her mother was trying to understand.

The tired was wrong.

"Waves of tired. Like last time." Heather forced out the phrases, breathing hard between each one. Fear crept up her spine.

Kathryn stroked her daughter's forehead.

"Does anything hurt?" She uncovered Heather and started massaging her arm, her hand.

Heather tried to shake her head.

Kathryn rubbed Heather's body with slow, firm, reassuring strokes, moving to her back and neck. She covered Heather with the blanket again, smoothed her hair back once more and kissed her forehead.

"Maybe it's time to see a doctor."

Alarm rippled through Heather and she blinked rapidly. But …

Mama was right.

At least Heather would know if something was really wrong.

3

Kathryn

Loch Dochfour whispered and lapped the edges of the shore, mixing soil with its waters and teasing out the magic needed for the native plants to thrive. Early summer's sun was just beginning its ascent when Flora picked her way around the water's edge, through foliage and dankness, searching, searching.

Flora didn't see it at first, but gradual lightness pointed her to the white star-petaled plant just past the water's edge. She reached in, water splashing up to her ankles, and grasped a red stem, and then another and another, until she had a handful. She smiled. She would bring them to Her. *To Kathryn.*

As the sky brightened, Flora ran through the fields adja-

Valerie Ihsan

cent to River Ness, the bouquet of bogbean in her fist. She laughed then, stopped and spun around, opening her plaid wrap like wings. She did a jig in bare feet, red braid flopping, and looked to the sky, searching, searching again. Her blue eyes alighted on one particular spot of the heavens and she lifted her bogbean skyward.

KATHRYN WOKE FROM ANOTHER FLORA DREAM AND stretched in bed, dislodging her little Westie, Janet. Janet stood up and shook from nose to tail then sat, expectant and prim.

The dream was a reoccurring one—the first of the Flora dreams. Sometimes Flora sent reruns when she didn't have anything to say but still wanted to stay in touch.

Kathryn smiled in the pre-dawn darkness and proceeded to fumble with her slippers and robe.

Years ago, when Heather's mental illness worsened in college, Kathryn had danced in the living room in feverish frenzy—exorcising her own demons so that she could help with Heather's—and then recovered under a blanket with a chai in her hands, eyes glossy with despondency.

Today, she was less likely to dance despite her troubles and more likely to reach for that cup of tea, but that didn't mean she ever backed down from hard work.

Kathryn moved quietly through the living room and turned on the light in the kitchen, which smelled of bread and caramelized onions from last night's dinner. There was an undertone of sandalwood incense and kombucha left too long to brew. She set the kettle on medium heat, slipped on the Crocs waiting at the back door, tightened her robe, and stepped outside.

No one would see the hot-pink chenille at six o'clock in the morning. Only the rooster, who was already making a racket. She walked into the large coop—more like a shed—and opened the chicken door.

"Good morning, my lovelies," Kathryn crooned. The plump hens, scrawny teenage pullets, and the nasty rooster fluttered down from their perches and scurried across the ramp to scratch and revel in the fresh morning air. Kathryn eyed the rooster and stood at the ready should he once again attack her shoes. He strutted and paced behind the hens until they were all through the door, and then he followed after.

Kathryn hurriedly replaced their water and added crumble from rat-proof bins to their trays. It was stupid to be afraid of the rooster, but—she laughed—if shielding herself from Spade, a New Hampshire Red, was the only distasteful thing to her days, then she had a pretty great life. Later, she'd come out with some grapes. Her chickens freaked for grapes. Apple peels, too.

Kathryn collected the eggs from the nesting boxes and gently laid them in a basket lined with soft chamois. She scooped out chicken manure into a bucket and fluffed up the bedding, adding a handful of fresh straw here and there. She swept out the floor, tossed the manure into the chicken run, and moved on to the rabbits.

She made sure they had fresh water in their bottles and added timothy hay to their feeding area, but this early in the morning the rabbits still slumbered in their hay burrows—unlike the early-rising chickens.

Later, after breakfast and checking the greenhouse starts, Kathryn would let the rabbits out into the Bunny Fields—allocated places for them to jump and frolic. Sometimes she even opened the adjoining door to the chicken run and the rabbits would play alongside the chickens. Most of the time, the two species co-existed peacefully, but Kathryn only let them out together when she felt confident that Spade wouldn't be a dick and attack a rabbit. Maybe she should just eat him. She could get her chicks by mail order like a lot of folks did these days.

At the mudroom—a converted back porch—Kathryn kicked off her Crocs. Inside the house, slippers back on, she poured the hot tea water into her favorite ceramic mug from St. Vincent de Paul. It was brown and blue and obviously handmade. It fit her hand perfectly.

With Early Morning Chores over, she enjoyed her tea and journaled until it was time to get dressed to head out to Late Morning Chores, which would dovetail into Gardening Time. Kathryn always named things with capital letters because they were alive for her, had distinction.

When Kathryn closed her journal and took the last sip of her tea, she had resolved not to worry about Heather. She'd been getting that restless look about her recently and, selfishly, that made Kathryn nervous. She didn't want Heather traveling alone again. The last time was disastrous. She swallowed down the anxiety and rinsed out her cup in the sink.

She wanted Heather to find happiness and love, especially when a bout of depression sank its claws into her, but traveling alone was dangerous for her, and Kathryn couldn't go anywhere right now—the end of August being their busiest time. It was the middle of harvest season and there were a million-and-fourteen things to do on the farm. Plus, there just hadn't been a man yet that had had the chutzpa to stick around and help Heather take responsibility for her meds.

If she stayed on them, Heather functioned completely normally. But if anything upset that chemical cocktail, her depression took an even darker turn and scooted toward the edge of something else—unable to work, hiding in her room for months at a time.

Kathryn often struggled with her hopes for Heather and her own fears of what would happen if Heather *did* fall in love and leave.

Kathryn would be alone then and that would be unbearable.

4

Heather

HEATHER REGISTERED THE SUN THROUGH GAUZY curtains and burrowed deeper under her cotton blanket. It was probably seven in the morning, but she still wasn't getting up. A rooster crowed outside and Heather grumbled into her pillow.

Please don't let it be one of those days.

Visions of other places full of adventure and newness wove through her drowsy mind. However, rather than eliciting muscle relaxation and the sigh of pleasure one might expect when dreaming of beaches or rainforest hikes, the visions made Heather scowl. She wasn't there. She was still on the farm—her prison.

When Heather did sit up, even the sight of whimsically painted bedroom furniture, a collection of Frank Baum *Oz* books, and all her potted vines couldn't cheer her up. In fact, the whole room seemed decidedly outdated and childish this morning, which only made her mood worse.

Heather was tired of her malfunctioning brain. The depression used to be seasonal. She'd even had one of those sun lights that helped with the persistent darkness and rain of Willamette Valley winters. But then one time in college she'd holed up in her dorm room for three weeks and stopped showering.

Since then, she's been medicated. College hadn't worked out, and she's worked on the farm ever since. At first it was fun. Her mom had officially hired her for the bookkeeping and marketing of Herbal Junction Farm and surprised her with an enormous antique pedestal desk. It was a magnificent piece of nineteenth century art: solid mahogany construction, leather top, and brass pulls. And it was hers. Her mama had also given her the title of Office Goddess.

She flopped her arms by her side, and a waft of summer morning air circled in and danced past her nose. She didn't like taking the pills. But she didn't like apathy reaching its cold fingers into her mind either. She'd been taking her meds regularly, but something was different these days. The depression felt different. Black days gripped her more often. Maybe her prescription needed to be changed.

She slid her feet into fuzzy, fake cheetah-fur slippers and pulled on a thin robe with two dime-sized holes in it. It was ugly and she hated it, but somehow she couldn't make it to the department store to get a new one.

She drank from the water glass on her turquoise bedside table and decided she wouldn't let the day get the better of her. Maybe she'd take a luxurious bubble bath instead of her usual shower. Heather sighed. But that would only put off work longer. She wished, once again, that they had a hot tub. She'd gladly race through work for the reward of sinking into 104-degree water with a new novel. Even if it *was* ninety degrees in the afternoon.

Her mom thought hot tubs were environmentally tragic—draining chemically laden water onto the land every three months, filling it up again, heating it with electricity every day, *yada yada yada*. Heather had heard it all before. Somehow, though, she could conveniently justify it. The heat was *therapeutic*—to both body and mind.

A small luxury like that might distract her from dwelling on the annoying fact that she—an adult—still lived with her mom. It was not what she'd envisioned for her life. She thought she'd be married by now, living a whirlwind life in Barcelona, or London.

Heather hurried through her morning routine and then went in search of caffeine and food before dealing with the computer. Kyle and Jill were coming over that night. She hoped her foul mood and her bellyache, which had returned, would shift by that time. Thank god for Costco-sized bottles of ibuprofen and Tums, or she'd never get any work done.

"TONYA AND BAILEY ARE COMING OVER FOR TEA TIME

today," Kathryn said that afternoon. She arranged the leftover cinnamon rolls from breakfast onto a tray. "But they'll be leaving early. They're going to the library. Did you know that Fern Ridge Library has a book club every Wednesday for kids? Bailey's in it. Isn't that cute?"

Heather smiled weakly. She sat at the table and reclined as best as she could in a dining room chair. She was tired and her belly still hurt. Bailey was a sweet kid, but she sure talked a lot. Heather felt sorry for Tonya—a widow with a ten-year-old daughter. *Imagine!*

She tried to engage with Tonya whenever she came over to visit with her mom, but Heather still didn't think they had anything in common, even though they were basically the same age and had been neighbors for nine years. Sometimes talking with her was draining; it was hard for Heather to keep up her portion of the small talk. After nine years, why didn't they have more to say to each other?

Heather wondered again why Tonya had clicked with Kathryn instead of her. It didn't really matter though. Tonya was her mom's friend, and Heather was glad that Tonya and Kathryn could fill that role for each other. Perhaps they connected because they'd both suffered in life—Tonya in losing Doug and raising Bailey by herself, and Kathryn in dealing with her daughter.

Heather frowned and played with her fork. Her illness threatened, snapping at her again. She could see its black curling edges in her peripheral vision. She didn't want to be something her mother had to *deal* with.

Her mother walked over and tapped her on the nose.

"I'm glad we still do Tea Time," Kathryn said and smiled.

Tea Time originally began when Heather was four years old. The story went that Kathryn had been sick and tired of playing yet another round of Candy Land, so she gifted Heather with her very own tea set—two pretty cups, with two pretty saucers, and a wee teapot.

They weren't toys so Heather couldn't keep them in her room then, but Kathryn would get them out whenever Heather wanted to use them. When this became multiple times a day, Kathryn implemented Tea Time. With her capital Ts. The times changed throughout the years, what with violin lessons and school and play dates and after-school sports or jobs, but somehow Tea Time stuck around, and truthfully, Heather would miss it if it were gone.

"Why don't you ever invite Kyle over anymore?" her mom asked. She organized mason jars, filled with dried tea and herbs, in a line on the countertop while they waited for Tonya and Bailey.

Heather shrugged. She eyed the cinnamon rolls in front of her and fought the urge to nibble before Tea Time officially started and their guests arrived. It was three o'clock—just when mere mortals ached for a break from work and for a chance to load up on sugar and caffeine to carry them through the rest of the day.

Their tea—as in the years before—was still served in pretty cups with saucers.

"I liked him," Kathryn said, crouching over a jumbled drawer.

"Kyle's just a friend now, Mom. I like him, but …" She laughed over the welling sadness. "It's better if we're just friends. Less pressure for him." She gave in and pulled a cinnamon roll to her plate. "I'm too much trouble," Heather said, pretending it was a joke. She ripped the roll into chunks, dropping them on her plate.

Kathryn snapped up and closed the drawer, apparently giving up the search.

"That's absolutely not true, Heather. You're capable and you work hard," she said. She gripped the counter. "*Sometimes* you need help remembering to take your medication, but that's just because it works so well that you convince yourself you don't need it." She cracked her knuckles. "That's *not* too much trouble."

Kathryn sat down at the table.

"Is that the only reason you're not seeing him anymore? Because you think you're too much trouble for him? You broke up with him?" Kathryn's blue eyes searched hers.

Heather dropped her gaze back to the carnage on her plate. She wouldn't think about Kyle right now. Arguing about her job would be a safer conversation topic. For the truth was, she did want something different, more exciting. Managing the business and marketing side of Herbal Junction just wasn't doing it for her. And she had to tell her mom. But how? Kathryn was always against hiring extra help. She couldn't understand why though. Something about "Flora," she guessed.

"I don't want you to die alone," her mom blurted out.

"*What?*" The non sequitor startled her. She'd obviously

missed something. Heather made a mental note to stay with the conversation.

"I'll be going first," Kathryn said, matter-of-factly, her face flushed, mottled and maroon. "Who will take care of you when I'm gone? You should rethink Kyle. I bet he still likes you."

"*Mom*!" As if she'd go begging back to him. He wouldn't stick around once he saw her as she really was, naked without her medicine. He'd never stay. No one else had. Why would he?

"I'm just saying," her mom said, "give it a little more effort. It could work. You're such a lovely girl." Kathryn reached for Heather's face but Heather pulled out of reach.

Why couldn't she have even *one* conversation with her mom without rolling her eyes or clenching her fists? It was like a tic that only happened around her mother.

A knock signaled the arrival of Tonya and Bailey. Kathryn got up and let them in. Heather steamed in her own juices. She wanted to rage against her mom who went from one sentence extolling Heather's capabilities, to another suggesting that she needed to be taken care of. *The nerve!*

But because Tonya and Bailey didn't need to witness her wrath nor her sudden rude departure to her bedroom—which she vastly preferred at that moment—she bit the inside of her cheek and smiled at Bailey's blond cowlick.

Kathryn let Bailey light the candle on the table and they all recited:

Blessings on the blossoms
Blessings on the fruit
Blessings on the leaves and stems
And blessings on the roots.

"Bon appetit! Now we may eat!" Bailey piped. Tonya giggled.

The three of them ate and talked and laughed while Heather watched. Her mother's face was now rosy cheeked and lit with delight. Kathryn *was* a beautiful woman. Heather had to give her that. Her eyes were still bright blue and she was a *young* sixty-four. She'd stopped using henna dye years before but, even still, Kathryn's long gray hair looked striking next to her almost wrinkle-free skin, different than the invisible look some women got in their crone years.

Heather's anger subsided enough to hope that she would keep her own youthfulness as well as her mother had. And then, because it was a practice that helped with her blacker moods, she added up the things in her life that she was grateful for.

There were lots, actually. She met up with Jill and Kyle every Tuesday night at Sam Bond's Garage for brews and bluegrass, bringing her banjo to jam with. She ran for pleasure … sort of. More like, she had bought the shoes and Lycra running pants, but still. She liked being active and hiking all the waterfalls she could find in the surrounding area. And she loved her home, despite her restlessness.

Heather sighed and returned to the conversation at the table. Things would get better. They never stayed as horrible as they seemed in any given moment. This "moment" had passed fairly quickly. She was still gray inside, but the battle of blackness had been avoided this time around.

Maybe she was just worried about seeing Kyle tonight. She *had* been missing him. He and Jill were coming over to play music. She set her shoulders straight. She would be lighthearted tonight and not pine for something she couldn't have. But … maybe her mother was right. She usually was. Though did it hold true that if her mother was right, then Heather was wrong? What if they were both right? What if she were both a perfectly capable person needing help taking her meds once in a while, *and* too much trouble for a man to love her?

If she'd looked outside before Kyle and Jill had arrived that evening, Heather would've seen the silver sky. A silver sky meant that a circumstance requiring delicacy was approaching. But because she didn't know of its metallic heralding, or see the clouds trolling past, Heather couldn't prepare for the speed at which her life would change.

Jill breezed in and hugged Heather, her guitar sliding foreword and bumping against Heather's shoulder. Heather breathed in Jill. Jill was her very best friend. They connected in all ways. Heather joked once that if she'd been a man, she would've totally seduced Jill into dating her, which was backwards because if Heather had been a man, then Jill, a lesbian, certainly wouldn't have fallen for her. Jill loved women but wasn't the man-hating type, courtesy of a fabulous father who instilled in her a general faith in the male population.

Jill and Kyle had been friends for years, more years than Heather had known either of them. In fact, Heather had only known Kyle for less than a year. They'd hit it off really well and were inseparable within two weeks. But after three months, Heather had shut down. She had felt the black sorrow descending and didn't want Kyle to witness her at her worst, so she called it off.

He had to have been hurt, but somehow—probably because of Jill—they were able to transition into a soft friendship with occasional bouts of wild flirting. Kyle always instigated, and she wondered if it was his way of hinting at what she'd lost by dumping him.

On good days, she chose to think of his behavior as his way of saying that he was still interested if she ever wanted to try again, rather than think he was deliberately attempting to spite her. And, truthfully, on those good days, she did wonder if she might like to try, but mostly her black moments kept the distance between them palpable. She was too much trouble for a long-term relationship. Flings were okay, but unfortunately they weren't as satisfying as they used to be. And a fling with Kyle wouldn't be possible. They'd already tasted a closeness that prevented such casualness.

Heather took their coats and they forewent the dining room table, opting for the living room's squishy couch instead. Heather and Jill flopped down with their banjo and guitar, respectively. Kyle pulled up an ottoman and made himself comfortable. All jammers needed an audience and Kyle was an avid supporter of his newly discovered bluegrass aptitude.

"Why don't you start playing something?" Jill asked Kyle.

He shrugged.

"Chicken?" Jill taunted.

Kyle laughed.

"No. Just doesn't burn inside me. I wouldn't do the music justice." He smiled at both of the women. Jill rolled her eyes, but Heather ducked her head, emotions swimming.

Why does he still do this to me?

He wasn't doing anything, Heather corrected herself. She was just being stupid. They hadn't been together like that for eight months now. It was over. She shook it off and plucked at her strings, "Shady Grove" picking its way out. Jill grimaced but played along on her guitar anyway.

Kyle lent his voice to some of the lyrics, and Heather felt shiny and new by the end of the song. Kyle clapped.

"Thank you. I love that song," Heather said.

"Check this out," Jill said. "I wrote a new song." She sat up and balanced on the edge of the couch.

Kyle dragged the ottoman closer to Heather.

"There," he said. "Now we're both the audience." He winked at Heather.

Oh brother. That was about as subtle as the old arm-behind-the-shoulder-while-stretching-and-yawning thing guys did in movie theaters when they were sixteen. There would be *no flirting* tonight. Irritation burned in her fingertips. She hated that being around Kyle still affected her. She didn't want to like him anymore. She shifted the banjo in between them, if only for the illusion of separation.

As always, Jill's songs brought tears to Heather's eyes. She felt stupid for forgetting. She sat up and settled her banjo onto her lap. A prop. A distraction. She didn't want Kyle to see her cry. She couldn't be vulnerable with him. It would trigger something she wasn't ready for. Jill sang on, nodding at Heather. She knew what effect her songs had on Heather.

Jill and Heather played for an hour, Kyle singing along in places, until they were spent. Kathryn made hot chocolate for them, as if they were young children fresh home from a snowball fight, and said goodnight, slipping into her room. When the hot chocolate and visiting were finished, Jill yawned and stretched.

"I'm beat," Jill said.

They all stood up and the three of them exchanged hugs.

"See you next Tuesday, Heather," Kyle said, looking into her eyes and holding them there. Heather's breath quickened and so did her thoughts.

She needed to get away for a bit. The farm was a little stifling. Or maybe it wasn't the farm, just the monotony of her life. She needed some stimulation. Scotland would be the perfect distraction. She'd never been, even though all her relatives grew up there. Except her mom. Mom was the only one of her siblings that hadn't been born in Scotland. It would be the perfect adventure to close out Herbal Junction Farm's harvest.

Kyle squeezed her hand.

"Hello?" He laughed. "Your eyes just came into focus." Kyle looked over at Jill, who shrugged. "See you next Tuesday," he said again.

He dropped Heather's hand and he and Jill left the house, leaving Heather with a sense of otherworldliness. Where did she go just then? She had been so trussed up in her thoughts that she hadn't spoken a word of farewell to her best friend and the man who, unfortunately, had wedged himself behind her sternum and wouldn't leave.

She sighed and turned for her room. She was too tired and depressed now to brush her teeth tonight. She climbed into bed fully clothed and waited in the darkness for sleep to envelope her. She wouldn't have to think of her shortcomings if she could just sleep.

Her mind spun for a little while, but eventually agreed to let go. The curtain of somnolence fell precisely eighteen minutes after she'd lain down, and ravens cawed in her dreams.

5

Kathryn

Tears had rained down on another wee grave behind the homestead that day. Flora fell back on the bed and saw terror in her husband's eyes, acknowledging Flora's sickness and his own powerlessness. Flora could smell his fear. It came out his pores and filled the small, over-heated room with the stink of it. Flora's spirit raged and crashed into the corners of her rib cage, distraught and restless, devastated that her love for her children hadn't saved even one from the fevers. She felt her eyes grow too large for her face, and her breath grow too hot for her lungs. She knew she wasn't long for this world, and she was terrified of leaving her poor man alone.

He would be alone.

 Valerie Ihsan

FLORA'S SOUL SCREAMED UNTIL KATHRYN AWOKE, THRASH-ing and sweaty. It was the only time Flora had ever sent a *memory*—let alone a nightmare. The memory was shadowy, gray. Not like the golden-tinted dreams that Flora sent.

Kathryn blinked sleep from her eyes, heart pounding. It was the time of morning before the sun rose, before the rooster crowed. She coughed, untangled herself, and sat up on the side of the bed. The air in her room felt creepy now, like there were bugs crawling up her neck. She opened her window wide and shook herself, releasing the black negativity that followed her from the dream world.

Janet, the Westie, did the same.

KATHRYN PUT OUT THE BEST PLATES AND SILVER—USED only for Tea Time and special occasions—and checked the gluten-free, dairy-free lemon bars in the oven. She had started to wonder if Heather's fatigue might be caused by a dietary sensitivity. If gluten made her foggy, perhaps dairy did, too. She hoped that Heather wouldn't have to eliminate more and more foods.

She sat down at the table and let Heather pour her a cup of tea. The lemon bars needed to cool. Tea Time would run a little late.

Heather's hair was loose today—red and bright. She seemed to be choosing more comfortable clothes lately. Today she wore a black sundress made of soft, stretchy tee shirt-like fabric.

Kathryn had been trying all her usual remedies

and tinctures for boosting immune system function on Heather, and even plied her with extra supplements like iron and vitamin D, but it wasn't seeming to have any effect on Heather's fatigue. Kathryn frowned. Maybe it was time for Heather to get a blood test done, just to see if they were missing something—the dream from that morning still skittering through her consciousness.

Heather's round green eyes blinked and crinkled at the edges of her soft smile. Strangely, she looked relaxed that afternoon, rather than tired. The dark shadows under her eyes were minimized by the afternoon sun shining through the dining room windows. Heather sipped her tea and they both waited and smelled the warm lemony steam drifting to their noses.

"It might be nice to have Bailey come over after school a couple of times a month to do a little more work," Heather said. "She loves coming over and taking care of the rabbits—though she does get too attached to them. I wonder if part of the reason I hate butchering day so much is fearing Bailey's disapproval and outrage."

"She even names one or two of them each year. Did you know that?"

"Really?" Heather's face twisted into a frown of pity. "That's horrible. Poor Bailey. To have her friends ritually killed off for our eating pleasure. It really is so macabre."

The sweet smile left and Heather was distressed again.

"I know it bothers you that we aren't vegetarian," Kathryn said, "I just don't think I could do it. Go ahead if you want to, but I'm getting older and settled in my ways. I don't want to give up my rabbit stew."

An awkward pause ballooned, and then diffused just as quickly with their laughter.

"That sounded pretty crotchety, didn't it?" Kathryn said.

Heather reached for the plate of treats.

"Lemon bar, Mama?" Heather's smile returned.

After finishing off way more lemon bars than was socially acceptable, Heather pushed back from the table and smoothed her dress, making sure there were no crumbs.

"How about I play a little for you today?" she offered.

"I'd love it," Kathryn said.

Kathryn put the remaining lemon bars in an air-tight container, and wiped down the table. She even hand washed the rest of the dishes, just so she could listen longer.

The twangy and fun yet strangely forlorn sound of Heather's banjo filled the house and spilled out of the open windows. Kathryn's shoulders relaxed. Maybe the herbs could hear her, lifting their leaves in salute, twisting to point at the house. In the same way they followed the sun, they could follow Heather's music.

Kathryn

Summer insects buzzed and droned, slow, in the heat. The village children gathered around Flora. She sat on a fallen tree. The mothers waited under the shade of oaks and rowans, murmuring in the background. Some stood and watched; some sat, eating bread and cheese.

Flora chose a wooden dowel rod from the basket beside her and dipped it in a honey pot. She handed it, the end now smothered in golden food, to the closest child, who licked the dowel with a solemnity bordering on fervor. Flora repeated the act with great ceremony, a smile playing at her lips.

The sun warmed Flora's uncovered head. She skillfully tucked a strand behind her ear with only her wrist, careful not to get honeyed fingers in her hair. She picked up another *dowel, dipped, and handed the treat to the next child.*

The mothers smiled in relief at this respite, the silence of sated children a boon to their normally hard days.

Flora wiped her hands on her apron. She lifted her eyes to Kathryn and nodded—her smile back.

WHEN FLORA FIRST STARTED VISITING KATHRYN IN dreams—when Kathryn was a new mother—she'd had that same dream, once a week, for six months.

And the funny thing? Many years later, when Kathryn was feeling the effects of single parenting on a particularly difficult day, she drew on that dream. She remembered the nod, and that Flora had looked directly at her *through* the dream.

Once, when Heather was young, Kathryn had wiped her daughter's crying eyes with a cooling washcloth and given her a spoonful of sticky honey from the hive in the backyard. Kathryn had reveled at the silence, tension melting from her shoulders. At the same time, she had felt the hair prickle at the back of her neck.

It was just like in the dream.

That was the day Kathryn had wondered if Flora was trying to communicate with her.

SATURDAYS WERE FULL OF YUMMINESS AND GOOD FRIENDS. Kathryn checked on the cobbler and made sure the tea water was hot. Sometimes she encouraged Heather to invite her friend Jill over, but ten o'clock on Saturday was mostly reserved for Tonya and Bailey.

Tonya's husband, Doug, had passed in a car accident

four years before, and since then, Kathryn had taken to inviting Tonya and Bailey over for brunch on Saturdays.

Kathryn removed the bacon strips from the paper towels they were draining on and transferred them to a pretty platter for the table. She'd wait until the guests got there before frying any eggs. Cold eggs were rubbery and gross.

She disliked purchasing disposable products like paper towels, preferring washable ones, but she made the exception for paper towels used solely for the purposes of draining bacon and cleaning up pet messes in the house—though sometimes toilet paper worked just as fine for those.

Bailey had just turned ten and loved the bunnies in the back so much that Kathryn *graciously* allowed her to play with them and clean out their cages and get them fresh food and water after breakfast on Saturdays.

All the grown-ups were as equally satisfied with this arrangement as Bailey was.

The knock at the door sent Janet barking like the guard dog she thought she was.

"Get out of the way, furball," Kathryn said. She used her foot to gently move Janet out of the path and opened the door. Janet jumped and wagged and danced in front of Bailey, who fell to the floor cooing and petting, much to Janet's delight.

"I never know what to bring you, Kathryn. I can't bring flowers or food or wine or tea. You have it all already. I can't even knit you anything, since you're the one who taught me." Tonya laughed and handed Kathryn a chocolate bar. "You don't make these, do you?"

"No. And this is a perfect gift. Thank you." Kathryn chuckled and walked backwards to let Tonya pass her.

"And guess what, Bailey?" Kathryn asked, while stashing the chocolate bar in a cupboard near the stove.

Bailey looked up from her doggie giggle fest. "What?"

"We have some new babies outside..." Kathryn left the surprise hanging in the air.

Bailey scrambled to her feet and jumped up and down in place.

"Bunnies? More bunnies?"

"No." Kathryn smiled secretly. "I was going to wait until after breakfast, but seeing that you're not able to wait that long…" Kathryn looked up at Heather, who'd just walked in the room. "Heather, could you show Bailey our new tenants?"

Heather smiled and the two tromped outside in pretty floral skirts, the sun surprising them that day.

"What are they?" Tonya asked Kathryn. She poured herself a cup of tea and sat at the table.

"Ducks." Kathryn smiled and turned on the burner for the frying pan.

"Ducks? Babies this late in the year?"

"Spring is the normal time for chicks and ducklings, but there's a reputable breeder online that does mallards all year long. Well, into the autumn anyway."

"Doug's brother lives on a farm in Montana and loves his ducks. He's a farmer through and through and believes all animals on a farm are for either working or eating. But his ducks are his babies."

"I've read that they live a long time, get depressed if left alone, and make a lot of messes. Just what I need, but—you know how I love chaos."

Tonya laughed.

"You must, because it follows you everywhere."

Kathryn turned the eggs over and shut the burner off.

"I suppose it's not really chaos, just busyness," Kathryn said. "I wanted to try them, but the thought of learning how to adjust to ducks and bonding with them *in the spring* when I'm doing all the planting and such was just too much. Even I'm not that stupid."

"Not stupid. Just a glutton for punishment."

They both laughed and Tonya ate a piece of bacon.

"The eggs are ready."

"I'll go and tell them. I want to see these ducklings, too," Tonya said. She wiped her hands on her jeans and took a last sip of tea before heading out the back door.

"Oh!" Tonya said, stepping back as Bailey barged in at a gallop.

"Heather fell down!" she said, running to the table.

Kathryn made to stand up, startled at the child's outburst, but then Heather came limping in.

"What's happened?" Kathryn said.

Tonya held Heather's arm and led her to the table to sit down. Kathryn got up and bustled at the freezer, getting ice ready for whatever was hurting Heather.

"I don't know," Heather said, shakily. "I just..." She shook her head. "...lost my balance?"

Tonya scooted Bailey out of way while Kathryn added the ice to Heather's ankle and went to get the arnica out of the first aid kit. Kathryn's heart rate bounced up with her alarm. Heather never *lost her balance*. She had always been enviably graceful. *Kathryn* was the round hippie who bumped into things. Heather, on the other hand, had inherited her absent father's spatial superiority.

"Thank you for telling us about Heather's fall, Bailey," Kathryn said. "Could you pour Heather some lemonade from the pitcher? She might want to take a pain pill."

Heather nodded and covered her eyes with her hand. Bailey scampered off with gusto to perform her Very Important Task.

Heather

Heather looked out her bedroom window. Burnt umber and red leaves shivered in the autumn breeze. The neighbor's house was visible through the pines, vine maples, and the one oak tree clustered between their properties. She leaned her forehead on the windowpane. It was cold. She touched the tip of her nose to the window's smoothness and breathed a fog onto the glass. She went in search of a warmer robe; it was time to switch to terry cloth. The mild ache from her fall two weeks before had sunk deep into the ankle, past sinew and tendon and bone. It distracted her, making her restless and uneasy.

On her dresser lay the travel brochure for Scotland. She'd read through the visitor's website and felt strangely

Valerie Ihsan

excited on some days about the prospect of going, but she knew that in order to secure her mother's agreement, Heather would have to sway Kathryn with a traditional paper catalog—not the cold blue glow of a computer screen—so she'd ordered one.

In the bathroom, Heather knelt down to the cupboard under the sink and pulled out yet another package of pads. She sighed with something uncomfortably similar to defeat.

She'd have to call Planned Parenthood again. This was the second time she'd have to cancel her Pap test. She was getting more and more irregular.

She shivered into a fearful mood and went to the kitchen to see if her mama was still in the house. She needed her comfort today.

"Hey you," Kathryn said, turning over a crepe at the stove.

"You always seem so chipper in the mornings." Heather smiled. "How do you do it? I bet you've been up for hours with the animals—" The dog propped her front paws up on Heather's shin. Heather ruffled her ears and made kissy noises.

"—And fed Janet. *And* made breakfast from scratch again," Heather said. She shook her head. "I can barely get out of bed in the mornings." She kissed her mother's cheek. "*You* are a brilliant woman."

"Ah, well. I just wanted you to have a bit of wholesome goodness in your belly before going to the doctor's," Kathryn said.

Heather sat down.

"I'm going to have to cancel again."

Kathryn turned with a spatula in hand. "Why?"

"My period started again." Heather swiped her hand across imaginary crumbs on the table. Her eyes filled with tears. "What's wrong with me?" she whispered.

"Oh honey." Kathryn strode to the table, spatula still in hand, and giggled. "Baby. It's just the change. You're going through the start of it. My period was crazy for three years before it stopped altogether. You're fine."

Heather stared at her mother, a giddiness shifting from belly to throat.

"I'm perimenopausal?" She laughed, but it was truncated, cut off. She wiped her eyes and sniffed. "I'm so stupid. I never thought of that." She took a deep breath and nodded. "Perimenopause. That's all."

"But Mama, you'll have to leave the farm sometime," Heather said a week later. The kitchen was warm with frustration. "Why won't you just hire another farmhand and cut back on your workload? Then you could go to Scotland, too. Take a vacation, for God's sake. *Jesus.*"

"Don't be dramatic, Heather. Why do you want me to go to Scotland so bad? If you want to go, go. Take someone else. Take Jill. I already said, I'm not interested. *And,* if you'd just help out with the chores, I could do less. Anyone can do the web stuff you do. Let's hire someone to do *that,* and I can teach you more about Herbal Junction."

Heather squeezed her ceramic mug.

"*Mother,*" she said through clenched teeth. "I don't need to learn about Herbal Junction. I grew up here. I know how it works; I just don't want to be a farmer."

"I don't want to hear it. This farm has always been for *you*." Angry splotches dotted Kathryn's cheekbones. "This land is in your blood. How can you throw that away?"

Heather took a centering breath and squeezed her eyes shut. *This is her dream. Don't crush her.* She opened her eyes and took a sip of tea, holding her anger in check.

Kathryn sniffed and wiped her nose with a linen handkerchief that had been ripped from a stained shirt.

"Mama. I love you. I know this is your dream life, your calling, but it's not mine. I'm sorry if I disappoint you, but I'm not going to take over Herbal Junction for you. Ever." She smiled weakly and reached for her mother's hands.

Kathryn pulled them away and stood up, her expression like plaster.

"We'll always take care of each other," Heather said, pleading. "But I can't be a farmer."

Kathryn turned her back to Heather and walked away from the kitchen.

"Please," Heather said. "Hire someone to help you. I worry about you."

Kathryn scoffed.

Heather gulped the last bit of her tea and went for her banjo. *Fine!* She closed the door of her room, opened the window wide for the fresh air, and played for two hours before she felt sane enough to endure her mother's company again.

This farm is going to kill her.
Or me.

8

Kathryn

An old Flora made her way to the door of her home. A distraught villager woman waited there for her. Flora handed her a small fabric bag and gave her instructions on how to use what was inside. Kathryn couldn't hear but saw her lips move. The woman held the parcel to her chest—her relief palpable. Flora smiled with warm eyes and squeezed the woman's arm in compassion.

When the woman left, Flora clopped to the fireplace—her cane aiding her, but in the way at the same time. She stooped to poke the fire. She spoke, as if to the flames, but turned her head to look at Kathryn.

"This is why," she said.

  Valerie Ihsan

And Kathryn, once again, saw the villager's relief.
"This is why."

ANOTHER RERUN. KATHRYN ROLLED OVER AND WENT BACK to sleep, questions embedded in her slumber. Why was Flora sending her reruns these days? It was almost like Flora was starting from scratch. Did *that* mean something? Was Kathryn supposed to start from scratch on something?

"MOM, JUST LOOK AT THE BROCHURE."

It was a foggy autumn day in early October. The mums and Russian sage were still prolific, and Kathryn had put some in every room of the house. But this morning, even cheery colors on the kitchen table weren't enough to banish what was blowing in just now. Heather thrust the glossy catalog at Kathryn.

Kathryn wanted to eat her toast and pear hazelnut jam in peace. Heather had ruined her breakfast. Once again, she was spouting off about leaving the farm.

"Can we talk about this later? I'm eating, Heather." Kathryn closed her eyes and violently chewed her next bite of toast. If her eyes were open, undoubtedly she'd see Heather roll hers or give her one of those death glares from her teenage years. For some reason, they'd been making a comeback lately.

She heard Heather walk away. Kathryn slitted her eyes and peered through her lashes to make sure she was really gone. Upon spying the cursed brochure on the table, Kathryn huffed and snapped her eyes closed again.

A WEEK PASSED UNEVENTFULLY AND KATHRYN HOPED THE issue had self-resolved, but she was accosted again while bringing in the groceries from Ray's Place.

"But I don't understand why you'd not want us to go—for *me* to go. It's *Scotland*, Mama. Where *Flora* was born."

"You leave Flora out of this. This has nothing to do with her," Kathryn said. "It's just you being selfish."

Heather's face contorted into an incredulous grimace.

"I can't leave the farm for a *month,*" Kathryn said. "We've got orders to fill, the garden to put to bed, and all our winter projects to sort through. I'm sixty-four. I need you here."

Heather crossed her arms and set her jaw.

"I don't need your permission to go. And if you feel the need to pull business rank, fire me. I'd love it." She stalked out of the room.

Kathryn thought of several uncomplimentary names she wanted to call Heather right then. Instead, she finished bringing in the groceries, put them away, and ate an entire dark chocolate bar. She went outside to watch the chickens free-range for forty-five minutes before she could face the world without anger again.

It took Heather much longer, she noted. Heather didn't leave her room for the rest of the day, except to use the bathroom. She even refused dinner.

After Kathryn ate dinner alone, she put the chickens to bed and took a book to her room. She would've preferred the immersion of a movie, but she didn't want to risk running into Sourpuss in the living room.

The book didn't hold her attention, and sleep proved elusive. She flipped around, tangling herself in the sheets and her flannel pajamas for nearly an hour, until she finally drifted off to sleep.

The next morning forced her out of bed and into her chores. Heather slept in. This used to be charming—her royal daughter not appearing until nine o'clock in the morning, while Kathryn started work at six thirty. Now it was irritating. Heather should be working with her. This was *their* farm, together. She didn't want Heather to be just an employee doing bookkeeping and marketing. She wanted a partner who loved the land as she did.

It was more than love, really. It was duty and honor and respect. Duty sounded authoritarian, but that wasn't the way it felt. Kathryn did her work out of love. The soil she dug in was part of her body. They were made up of the same material—cosmically and physically. Matter was matter. Energy was energy. Little bits of divine embedded in all living things.

How could Heather not see that?

When Kathryn let the chickens out, the rooster charged at her boot and pecked the toe of it. Kathryn sighed in what felt very much like defeat. She eyed the poopy bedding and wondered if the world would end if she didn't tidy the coop today.

Maybe if Heather went to Scotland, she'd feel that same kinship with the land and her ancestors that Kathryn felt in Veneta, Oregon. Maybe Heather going would be a good thing. But she couldn't go by herself. Not after Cairo.

And if Heather didn't commit to Herbal Junction Farm, what would become of the land, to Kathryn's connection to Flora?

Inside the house, Kathryn found a note on the kitchen table. "You have tour at 1:00 p.m. Eugene Waldorf School. 3rd grade."

Hating to start the day with sadness, Kathryn made a quick decision. She telephoned Tonya next door, knowing she'd be up getting Bailey ready for school, and asked her if she'd like to go have coffee and pastries at Sweet Life Patisserie that morning. She also asked if Tonya could possibly help with that afternoon's tour.

"What a wonderful surprise. Sounds better then what I had planned. I'll drop Bailey off and then come over. And yes, I'd be happy to help with the tour," Tonya said.

Kathryn made a sufficient enough dent in the Morning Chores that she didn't feel guilty driving off. The rest could wait. She needed an eclair.

"Mama? Are you all right?" Heather pushed open Kathryn's door the next day.

Kathryn sat at her vanity table. She cleared her throat and closed her eyes.

"You go if you want. It might be fun for you. But I'm staying here," Kathryn said, knowing that it was an empty offering. Heather couldn't go by herself. She'd get caught up in her fun and wouldn't take her medication.

"But I want to go with *you*. It would be a fun thing for us to do together."

Years and years later, Kathryn would pick this moment

in time to regret. If only she'd responded differently that day.

A rooster crowed from afar, and Kathryn leaned back in her vintage cane dining chair—the original bench seat for the vanity table long since discarded for its broken and wobbly legs.

"I don't want to go by myself, Mama. You know I can't. I want *us* to do it. I thought you'd be excited, too. Don't you want to see Scotland again? You've never taken me. *I* want to see it before I die."

Kathryn looked up sharply.

"Don't be ridiculous," she said.

Heather marched out of the room and into her own, closing the door with what Kathryn interpreted as resounding disappointment.

9

Heather

With the closing of October, most days offered a biting chill that drove Heather into wearing tights with her skirts and layers under her sweaters. But there was no rhythm or reason to October weather in the Willamette Valley. Three days of blissful sunshine preceded a day of dreary gray and rain, with a foggy morning that burned off to blue sky by three in the afternoon.

Mother Gaia was saying good-bye to the last of her summer kin and—at the same time—welcoming the death that autumn brought. Leaves fell, flowers shriveled up, and the potatoes and garlic were harvested. Rows of onions dried from their tops hung in rafters in the yurt they used for drying, and Mama started roasting root veggies and making stews and soups.

Despite the onset of the cold that bothered Heather more and more, autumn was her favorite season. Even though it was the end of one thing—harvesting—it was a beginning in another sense. A beginning of awareness. An opportunity to take stock. Did she do everything she'd wanted that year? What did she want to plan for in the upcoming one?

Not-so-strangely, she felt that fall was the beginning of the year in some ways. After all, the Celtic new year was Samhain. Halloween. And October was sacred in a secretive way, too.

Long ago, maybe seventeen years before, Heather had ended a life by choice. She wasn't proud of it, but she didn't regret it either. It was the result of a one-night stand with a boy-man she'd met at a bar that didn't even exist anymore. Now it was a retail shop for handwork supplies—wool and knitting needles and kits for hand sewing dolls.

No one else ever knew.

She'd never told anyone.

It wasn't that she was ashamed. More embarrassed. She'd done something foolish, didn't want to raise a child with her mother, and so had ended it before it had begun.

But she remembered every October.

It brought pensive moments and *what ifs*, but it also brought a sense of rightness. She'd made a mistake and she'd been scared and sad, but when it was done, she'd walked to the banks of Blue River and sent out a delicate paper box with a white Japanese anemone flower nestled inside. Letting go, saying sorry, and beginning again.

Heather touched her hair and the contours of her face in the privacy of her bedroom. Despite the earliness of the afternoon, the room had grown shadowy while she sat on her bed and thought about the past, but most of all about beginnings.

Life certainly hadn't turned out quite like she'd imagined it. She still lived with her mom. No husband. No children. Sometimes she thought she wouldn't have been able to have these things anyway, with her depression. How could she have cared for her own children and raised a family, if she could barely care for herself?

She stood up and flipped on the light.

Beginning again. Every day.

Other times she thought of Kyle and knew that love couldn't be completely out of her grasp. Surely she was worth it. Maybe Kyle would love her despite her brokenness. But it didn't matter anyway; she didn't have the courage to try. She traced her fingers over the trinkets and jewelry on her dresser top and chose a chunky red set of earrings and a silver pendant for tonight's show.

Tonight would be another new beginning, and she was sick with the anxiety of it.

Jill's band, The Juniper Berries, had invited her to sit in on a few songs with them. They were opening for Betty and the Boy at Laurelthirsts in Portland that night.

Heather held her head, closed her eyes, and inhaled full and slow deep breaths. She spun around and smiled into the emptiness. If you didn't keep smiling, you wound up bitter and angry. Boring even. Or a weepy mush.

At least they hadn't asked her to sing. She just had to keep up on the three songs they'd practiced together. She could do that. And she knew that she'd feel great when it was all over. She just had to make it through the first part.

Heather carefully chose her outfit. It had to be trendy enough, yet still unique. It had to be comfortable, because she was doing something *un*comfortable, but it also had to enhance her shape and not be dowdy or frumpy.

She settled on a long and full brown corduroy skirt, with tights underneath. A pair of burgundy cowboy boots to finish the look would be perfect tonight. She paired the skirt with a crocheted lace sweater over a creamy turtleneck and tied her hair back in a ribbon.

There. Practical and *romantic.*

"Mama!" Heather called through Kathryn's door. "I'm almost ready. You?"

"Just about." Kathryn opened the door. She was fastening an earring to her lobe. A dangling gypsy one.

"I fed Janet and made us a couple sandwiches to eat before we go," Heather said. "I don't want to subsist on bar food when I'm nervous like this." She pressed her hands into her abdomen and then shook them out as if repelling dust from a rug.

Kathryn smiled.

"You'll be fine. You're going to do great. What an adventure!" She squeezed Heather's elbow and whooped. "This is so exciting."

10

Kathryn

THERE WAS HER GIRL. ON STAGE! HEATHER HAD never dreamed of being a musician, but she sure had taken to the banjo and to her musician friends.

I'm glad she's got something in her life all her own, separate from me and the farm.

Maybe Kathryn was being unrealistic. If Heather wasn't into the farm, she wasn't. But every time she thought that Thought, goose bumps crowded on her arms and neck, and she felt sick to her stomach.

If Heather didn't help her with the farm, what would become of it? In another ten years Kathryn would need some serious assistance. She knew a lot of farmers who worked until their midseventies, but they had help. Maybe it *was* time to hire a young person around the farm. A sodden weight settled in her chest. This wasn't how she'd imagined her future. But then Heather hadn't imagined a future with major clinical depression either.

What will become of us?

Kathryn loved Herbal Junction. If Heather ever married or decided to go off for good, Kathryn couldn't keep up the place by herself. But the mortgage was paid off, so what did it really matter? Even if she had to give up farming, she'd still have the house.

But I'd be alone.

Cold sweat collected under her hair and she shivered. The audience clapped, bringing Kathryn back to the bar. Heather was smiling bigger than … well, it seemed to have been a while since her baby had smiled that completely.

She knew she hadn't been helpful in that area. Heather had brought up Scotland again and Kathryn had turned her down. Again. It was quite annoying really. She just wanted them to stay at the farm as long as possible.

She knew. Even without Flora hinting at it. Kathryn knew—though she didn't really know why—with that niggling tickle at the base of her skull, that if they didn't make the most of their time at the farm now, together, then they wouldn't have the opportunity later. She shrugged it off as best she could and focused on the concert.

After an hour of chatting with Heather's friends and sipping a glass of wine, Kathryn found herself genuinely having a glorious time. She was proud of her daughter. She felt so much love for her, she just wanted to hold her up high above her shoulders and give her anything she wanted, if Heather would only be happy.

For *Kathryn* had been happy. Happy and content with her life and how it had all worked out. She was proud of her accomplishments and of who she was. She was imperfect, sometimes bossy, and liked having her own way, but overall she liked herself pretty well.

And she only wanted that for Heather. And for that smile to stay.

"Mama." Heather found a seat next to Kathryn. She gripped Kathryn's arm and laid her head on Kathryn's shoulder. "I'd like to go. Can I stay in your hotel room tonight?"

"Sure. But I thought you wanted to stay with your friends," Kathryn said. Heather had made plans to stay in The Juniper Berries' suite of rooms.

"No." The smile was gone. "I'm just tired and worn out. I think if I stay any longer I'll just make myself sick and ruin their night. I need to sleep."

Kathryn touched Heather's cheek like she would've when she was a little girl.

"Of course. The stress of the evening has probably gotten to you. Let's go."

She stood up with Heather and they gathered their things. They said their good-byes and endured Jill's surprise at them leaving so early.

In the van, Heather leaned her head against the passenger side window and closed her eyes. The silence on the way to the hotel was palpable. Almost wet, like a heavy fog.

Kathryn took her eyes off the road more than once to look at her daughter.

Heather

Early morning light shone through the windows of the Rose City Inn. Heather heard her mother rummaging around at the sink, opening little packets of things. The coffeemaker gurgled. Heather sighed and stretched. Her sleep had not refreshed her.

"Darling?" Kathryn whispered upon approaching the bed.

Heather opened her eyes and rolled over to see her mother with a mug in hand. A tea tag fluttered in the breeze of Kathryn's movement. She offered the beverage to Heather.

Heather cleared her throat and managed to prop herself up on pillows before accepting the warmth and aroma.

"I think this should be the other way around. Don't you?" Heather said. "Why am I so tired?"

"You had all the stress of performing. You've worked really hard for this. I just watched." Kathryn winked at her.

A soft knock sounded.

Heather sipped the hot tea. She was cold and wanted to snuggle back under the covers but was curious about the visitor all the same. Funny that she could want to have visitors *and* want to hide away from the universe at the same time.

It was Jill.

Oh. And Kyle. Heather sighed and pushed her hair away from her face.

"Hi," Heather said.

"She texted me," Kathryn said, gesturing her head at Jill. "I invited her to join us for breakfast before we drive home." She widened her eyes in what looked like an apology. "And you know I can't leave Portland without stopping at Powell's first. You guys can visit while I shop."

Heather closed her eyes and balanced her mug on her sternum. Warmth seeped in, spreading to her shoulders, and a flush of heat rose up the back of her neck. She smiled through her sigh.

"Are you up for it, Heather?" her mother asked. Heather could sense confusion and worry in the question.

Instead of answering, Heather opened her eyes and directed her words to Jill.

"The concert was fun last night. Thanks for inviting me to join in." She gestured to the hotel bed she still occupied. "It seems to have kicked my ass though. I'm quite tired, but brunch and books sound lovely." She smiled at them all to reassure them and felt strangely maternal for doing so.

Kyle coughed into his hand. When every pair of eyes turned toward him, he looked startled.

"Um. I'll just … wait outside then."

"Yes." Kathryn stepped forward. "We'll finish getting ready and meet you in the lobby downstairs."

Heather looked at the sheets tucked around her waist, the weight of *best behavior* sitting on her shoulders now. She wished that just Jill was coming, or that she and Kyle didn't have any baggage between them and could just enjoy friendly time together.

When she started primping in the bathroom, she stopped in a huff of disgust. She wouldn't get gussied up for him. She wasn't trying to *snag* him again, or anything. She settled for a braid down her back and lip gloss—what she would've worn at home.

After a hearty breakfast at The Olive Branch Bistro—chosen for its decor and dietary allowances—they moved on to the mandatory trip to Powell's for her mom. Heather and Jill wandered for fifteen or twenty minutes and each chose a couple things to bring home. Kyle, thankfully, wandered off on his own mission. Jill purchased a bright-yellow bumper sticker sporting a girl in glasses and the phrase "Reading is Sexy." She also bought a copy of *Motorcyclist* for her dad and a book on country-charm home decor, which surprised Heather.

Though she'd been known to load up on travel magazines and journals with adorable computer-graphic owls on the covers, Heather's choices ran more literary this time.

Her mother would be shopping for another couple hours, so Heather, Kyle, and Jill sat at a smooth and rustic wooden table at Powell's coffee cafe. Heather rubbed her palms across the table, happy with her selection of books and that she was currently enjoying an almond-milk mocha latte—something she rarely indulged in back home. Mocha lattes were a Powell's-only drink. The high sugar content usually wrecked her with a headache for two days afterward, but it sure was melty-warm-yummy-goodness while she drank it.

Kyle sat across from Heather with his index finger threaded through the mug's handle. He looked at Heather and smiled. Smiled with his eyes. With his pores.

"You look content," Heather said.

Kyle winked. Heather rolled her eyes, but a half smile slipped out. She frowned then, angry at herself.

"You sounded great last night," Jill said. "I wish you could've stayed over with us in the band room. Why didn't you?"

"I told you last night. I was tired and not feeling well. I didn't want to spoil anybody's night."

Jill sat up straight. "But you wouldn't have spoiled our night. We would've taken care of you." She quite obviously kicked Kyle's foot under the table. "Right, Kyle?"

"Jesus, Jill," Kyle said, grabbing at his coffee cup. "Good thing there's a lid on this."

"I doubt that I could've recovered as well as I have

with The Juniper Berries tramping around me, high on their obvious success. *Your* success."

"You were successful, too, Heather. You played great last night, babe," Kyle said. His dark chocolate eyes smiled over the edge of his coffee cup. Heather's eyes lingered a little too long. She looked down and swirled the mocha's contents in her cup and thought she heard a breathy secret laugh from him. Her face burned.

"Don't call me that," she said.

Regretting the mocha, Heather rubbed her temples—a headache quickly forming. She just wanted to go home now. Another nap was in order. She couldn't believe how much the trip had affected her.

Heather leaned into Jill, listening to her and Kyle banter about the show. Her head was really throbbing now.

"Jill," Heather whispered.

Jill reached around Heather in a hug.

"My head really hurts. Do you have any Advil?"

"No. I'm sorry." Jill looked to Kyle, who shook his head.

"Will you find my mom and bring her here?"

"I'll go." Kyle hopped up.

"Look at that butt. How could you break up with that butt?" Jill said as Kyle hurried away. "I only date women and even I like that butt."

Heather smiled but didn't move her head from Jill's shoulder.

Jill's tone shifted to worry. "Are you okay? You're really in that much pain?"

"It just came on suddenly. Overdoing it again maybe," she mumbled.

Kyle arrived with Kathryn. They conferred and Kyle went to purchase pain killers. Kathryn hurried through the decision-making process over which books to buy and went to the cashier.

Jill helped Heather to the car, holding her elbow.

"I'm sorry we're leaving early, Mama." Heather felt miserable and embarrassed. More and more often she seemed to have weird sudden pains or illnesses that ruined plans and made extra work for her mother.

Another reason to get a farmhand.

"Don't be silly. You've got a headache. Nothing to be sorry about. In fact," she flashed Heather a smile, "you've probably just saved me fifty dollars. I know I would've found more books if I'd stayed longer."

Kyle found them by texting Jill. Heather was already in the front seat buckled in, with the window down, trying not to throw up from the pain. He knelt by the window and ripped open the ibuprofen. He knocked three into his hand and whispered Heather's name.

Heather's eyes fluttered open and Kyle handed the pills to her through the window. He handed her his open water bottle and she swallowed the pills. The water refreshed her enough that she could thank him properly.

"Of course," he said. He kissed his thumb and touched her bottom lip. His fingers brushed the underside of her jaw. They were warm, and she suddenly wanted to crawl into his arms until the pain went away.

"Feel better, babe."

Irritation welled up and she jerked her face away, her brain sloshing in her skull. The nausea rose higher. She breathed sharply in through her nose.

"Don't call me that," she said fiercely. But it was only a whisper.

12

Kathryn

Waves crash into the surf, salty to the lips, sun silver in the dawn. The air is tepid and the roar of water dizzying.

There is a pause in the universe.

Then, blackness tunnels until the ocean is only a pinprick.

A room appears, rising out of shadows. An ordinary room, with a desk and a sofa, and a potted plant. It stays in perpetual twilight. Dim. It has a feeling of dreariness.

And then the ocean, raw, crashes through the bleak room with disturbing waves.

The waves and the darkness competed, back and forth, until Kathryn woke up, on edge but wiser.

Heather's waves of fatigue and her dark depression were separate issues.

The dream had felt sticky. It left a residue under her skin that couldn't wash off. Flora wasn't in this dream, but it was from her just the same.

Heather was thirty-nine and should've been perfectly capable of finding her own doctor, but the fact was that she wasn't. That last Wave, as they had taken to calling it, and the headache at Powell's had hit them both hard. It had been frightening to see Heather so incapacitated.

Kathryn got up before the sun and pulled on her robe. Before any chores or tea, Kathryn looked up chronic fatigue syndrome on the Internet, but it didn't seem especially like what Heather was going through. She sighed and turned off the monitor. Janet wanted outside and Kathryn could hear the chickens getting restless in the coop.

She didn't really expect to find a cut-and-dried answer. People lived on spectrums. Everything from ankle sprains to autism had *ranges*. People weren't all one thing and not the other. They were a mishmash of traits blended together to create unique individuals.

She knew she was stepping on Heather's toes, but really, the girl wasn't taking care of herself and far be it from her to stand by and watch Heather fall apart. It was time to step in.

At breakfast, Heather disagreed.

"I'm fine, Mama. Just a little sleepy, that's all." She smiled, but only with her lips. Her eyes stayed dull. "I think my period is about to start." She placed her hand on her lower abdomen. "That's probably why I had the bad headache. Just hormonal shifts." She lowered herself into a dining room chair.

Kathryn eyed her.

"I made you an appointment with a naturopath. Her name is Denise. She sounds really cool and won't try to shove more pharmaceuticals down your throat."

"Honestly Mama. If it could make me feel like myself again, I'd pop it."

Janet's tags jingled against each other. She sloppily drank her fill and dripped the rest onto the floor, four feet away from her bowl.

"But I'm fine," Heather said. "Everything's normal. I just get a little worn out sometimes. *Maaaybee* ..." Her eyes twinkled above the dark shadows under them. "... I should go on a vacation." She smiled with her eyes now. "Let me show you what I found. It's an app." She looked behind her at the desk in the living room where her phone sat, charging.

A surge of alarm pinged like a pinball against Kathryn's spleen and rib cage.

"Oh but first," Kathryn rushed, "let me finish about the doctor."

Heather turned back around in her chair and held her head up with her hand.

"You know, *Flora* might like it if you went," Heather mumbled.

Kathryn ignored that.

"I just wanted to let you know that the appointment is two weeks from now. Almost. It's for next Friday. She'll want to do a complete blood work up, so you'll have your blood drawn that same day."

Heather grimaced and suddenly appeared to Kathryn like a sullen teenager.

"We've got to start somewhere. Don't you want to know if there's something wrong?"

"Well, sure. But nothing's wrong." Heather looked around their small homestead from the vantage of her dining room chair and changed the subject. "What are you working on today? Do you need my help for something?"

And so they moved on with their day, Heather moving a bit slower than Kathryn was used to seeing, and Kathryn knowing that she'd distracted Heather from Scotland again. And whatever app she was talking about.

KATHRYN'S EYES FILLED AND SHE BIT HER LIPS. *Why am I resisting Scotland so much? It's just a place.* She was propped up in bed, pillows stacked behind her. A water glass sat on her side table, along with the book she wanted to read before going to sleep. *Maybe it's resistance to* Heather *going. But why? She'd be fine there, as long as a friend goes with her.*

And there she was again. Back full circle. Why didn't she want to go to Scotland with her? And, anyway, so what? So what if she didn't want to go? *Heather* wanted to go. And it didn't seem like her request was idle. She'd been on Kathryn about it for months.

The harvest *was* over. If there was any time in a farmer's life when she could possibly go on a vacation, it would be now.

She blinked and flicked away errant teardrops before they fell on her journal pages. Her shawl and flannel pajamas felt soft against her skin under the down comforter. She'd promised herself a long time ago that whenever she felt uneasy about something, she'd write until it made sense. Or at least until the "next step" showed itself.

She wrote for thirty minutes, and nothing. Kathryn stared at the ceiling.

That night Flora visited her again—and it was such an odd experience. There was always joy at meeting, but a sense of mission, too, something that needed to be accomplished within the dream—for Kathryn knew they were dreams, even as she dreamt them. And the missions came with urgency. Plus, it was all a puzzle. Flora never said, "Here's all your answers." It was more like a Name That Flower game show.

THE LIGHT WAS GOLDEN, AS IT OFTEN WAS IN DREAMS. FLORA walked through a field of tall grass. The sunset shone golden through copper clouds and contrasted with the purple outlines of the Highland hills. Flora smiled. Kathryn reached out to her, but Flora turned away. Kathryn followed behind her until she saw the street Kathryn's family had lived on in Inverness, Scotland. And then Flora was beside Kathryn, handing her a large broccoli head.

Kathryn

BROCCOLI?

Kathryn lay awake and stared at the ceiling. Janet wiggled next to her, indicating that she really ought to be fed—*Spit spot.* Sometimes Kathryn imagined Janet as an old upper-class British woman from the early 1900s. Set in her ways. Curmudgeonly. But lovable.

Like Dame Maggie Smith, or an older Mary Poppins.

Kathryn moved her legs under the sheets. For as down-home and hippie as she was, she allowed herself the secret pleasure of fine Egyptian cotton sheets. She once imagined that satin sheets were the ultimate in luxury and bought herself a set. Embarrassingly, her cracked and callused feet had caught on the fibers and made snaggy ripping sounds when she moved under them. Hardly sensual at all.

The high thread count of her current set of sheets caressed her calves. Her flannels hiked up just enough for the tease of the sheets. She sighed with delight and contentment and stretched.

Time to get up.

"Yes, Janet. I know. Breakfast time!" She ruffled the doggie's muzzle with little fingertip scratches. Janet wagged and licked approvingly.

Sliding her feet into slippers and adding a warm terry cloth robe over her flannels, Kathryn visited the bathroom first, then opened the back door for Janet.

Such an old lady name for an old lady dog.

What had prompted her to name the squirming short-legged puppy *Janet?*

Kathryn grinned. She put the kettle on low, unloaded the dishwasher, and fed Janet.

Broccoli?

Flora had never shown her vegetables before.

Kathryn found some thick socks and an old wool sweater to pull over her flannels and prepared for Early Morning Chores. The rabbits and chickens wouldn't wait while she sipped tea. When she returned, the water would be hot enough to enjoy while she compiled her daily To Do list.

It was frightfully nippy for so early in November, and Kathryn wished she'd thought of gloves. The early morning air permeated her pajamas as if she weren't wearing any at all.

"*Brrrrr!*" she said aloud.

Janet barked, startled at Kathryn's outburst. She giggled out visible puffs of breath.

The chickens were happy to see her and fluttered down from their roosts. She replaced the rabbits' water, too, and added fresh timothy hay and a few greens she'd brought with her from the kitchen. She'd come out later in the day, when it was warmer, and put the rabbits in the run, too. And bring them a veggie lunch that they'd like.

She always fed her animals real food, along with the kibble pellet stuff she picked up at Diess's Feed Store on Highway 126. She shivered and finished up quickly. Apologizing to the bunnies for her rush and promising to return to play later, Kathryn fled back inside, stripping off her work boots and coat, and put on her robe and slippers that she'd left at the back door. She left her knit cap on for the moment and poured herself that tea.

Sighing, she warmed her hands around the mug while Janet lapped up water and then lay down on her mat.

Broccoli?

14

Kathryn

GOD, I HOPE I DON'T REGRET THIS IN FIFTEEN SECONDS.

"I've been thinking about something," Kathryn said. She wanted Heather to be happy, and there really didn't seem to be a reason not to go, just a bad feeling.

Heather collected a forkful of their pot roast dinner.

"Yeah?" She tried to catch her mother's eye, but Kathryn didn't look up from her food. "What's that?" she asked, suspicion in her tone.

"Maybe I *will* go to Scotland with you."

"What?!" Heather banged on the table. Her eyes widened and she grinned, balling up her cheeks into little flushed apples. "*Mama!* That's brilliant!" She stood up and shimmied and jumped up and down until she landed, out of breath, back in her chair.

"Excited?" Kathryn asked.

THE NEXT DAY, KATHRYN PUSHED HER CART THROUGH the aisles of the feed store, her mind wandering. Heather was over the moon about the Scotland trip, but Kathryn couldn't shake that creeping sensation up her neck every time she thought about going. Why *had* she changed her mind?

Stopping at the magazine and book section, she scanned the titles to see if anything called to her, but they were all Beginner Books designed to teach people how to keep backyard chickens or to persuade folks to grow organic food. She was already on that wagon.

On her way back to the farm, she remembered the broccoli from her Flora dream. Broccoli wasn't in season right now. Was she supposed to buy it anyway? Why did Flora show her broccoli? It wasn't even an herb.

Kathryn drove down Highway 126 heading west. It was about time she went back to Scotland anyway. She hadn't visited for fifty years. She might not have been born there, but she was tethered to its land in ancient ways. Kathryn had never questioned why Flora came to her in dreams. Truthfully, she'd been thankful. It was a connection to Scotland that her sisters couldn't share.

By the time she'd pulled into her driveway, she felt the stirrings of anticipation and excitement.

15

Kathryn

KATHRYN AWOKE. HER BREATHING AND HEART RATE were normal. The room was dark; it was still late. Her clock read twelve thirteen in the morning. Why was she awake? She shifted to her side and adjusted the pillow above her shoulder. She licked her lips and swallowed a couple times and then closed her eyes. Behind her lids, a snapshot unfolded.

The earth. Loose rich soil. Weathered hands. A mother's hands. They were Flora's. She was harvesting a plant. A basket with a handle stood close by. A blue plaid ribbon was tied to the handle and flecks of dirt clung to the edges of the basket.

What plant was it?

Kathryn looked closer.
Her eyes opened wide in the night of her bedroom.
Broccoli.
She laughed and went back to sleep.

THE NEXT MORNING, KATHRYN MADE HASH FROM A POR-
tion of the pot roast they'd eaten the night before. She
added two eggs on top and covered the whole thing with
a lid.

After checking once and adding salt and pepper,
Kathryn determined everything was done; she brought
them to the table.

"Brunch is on!"

Heather emerged from her room wearing the new
yukata Kathryn had sewn for her birthday, black and
white with pink blossoms. She wore it even though a
heavier robe would've been warmer. This made Kathryn
smile. She'd made it in secret while Heather attended the
bluegrass jams on Tuesday nights.

"Oh. I forgot the fruit salad." Kathryn went to the
fridge and came back with the brunchy dessert.

"Mmm. Blueberries. Where did you get those? They
aren't local, because they aren't in season." Heather arched
her eyebrows at her mom.

Kathryn felt sheepish. She had insisted they try to
eat local, no matter how uncomfortable, but sometimes
it was just too hard to pass up fresh fruit in the gray of
late fall, for gosh sake. Poor Mama Gaia. The fruit salad
would've tasted much better had Kathryn's conscience
allowed it.

After a few forkfuls of the hash, Heather startled Kathryn with the knowledge that she wasn't the only person in the house that had dreamt of broccoli that night.

"What?! Broccoli? I had a dream about broccoli, too." Kathryn's arm hair stood at attention and a worm of creepiness moved down her spine.

"Don't look so freaked out, Mom. It was just a dream."

"Yes, but I *also* dreamt of broccoli last night, *three times* last night, as a matter of fact. *And* a couple nights ago. It's Flora. She's speaking."

"Broccoli?" Heather smirked. "That's a little unusual, isn't it?" She grimaced and caught her breath. She pressed her left hand into her lower abdomen.

"What is it?" asked Kathryn, alarmed. She was already wigged out about the weird dreams, and by the fact that *Heather* had dreamt of the same thing, too. Kathryn stopped.

Heather just had a Flora dream.

Far from being overly protective of the Flora dreams, Kathryn was suddenly mortified by what it meant that Flora had visited them both in the same night. Repeatedly.

What was so damn important about broccoli?

Heather inhaled sharply.

"What?" Kathryn said again.

"I don't know," Heather said. "Must be some angry gas pains."

"You're going to the appointment I made for you, right?" Kathryn said.

"Sure." Heather shrugged.

"Don't ignore this, Heather." Kathryn had a niggling feeling that Heather was going to cancel the appointment and fall into her pattern of denial and avoidance. She gritted her teeth. Heather was forty years old now. She ought to be taking better care of herself. *She* should be the one making the appointment, not ditching it.

"So if we're really going to Scotland on this trip of yours—" Kathryn crossed her arms. "—How are we going to take care of the farm while we're gone? Not to mention the paperwork and administration part of things," Kathryn said.

Heather absently rubbed her belly and forked up another bite of hash and eggs. She nodded, then took a sip of her peach rose hibiscus tea.

"I'll start up a list of duties that need taking care of while we're gone and then we can delegate." Heather sat up straighter. She looked shiny from the inside out.

"This is going to be so great! I'm ordering our passports *today*," Heather said. She tucked a chunk of hair behind her ear and shoveled her food in her mouth.

Kathryn chuckled. Clearly, Heather had other things she wanted to be doing right now. Kathryn waved her off, and Heather left so quickly for her spiral notebook that she didn't rinse her dishes in the sink. Kathryn rolled her eyes.

Heather returned with note-taking implements. She popped a strawberry in her mouth and furrowed her brows. Thinking. The off-shore drilling kind of Thinking. Kathryn could actually see Heather's mind whirling and dashing and slogging.

Kathryn shook her head again and gathered the dishes.

"Thank you, Mama," Heather murmured without looking up.

16

Heather

It took five anxious weeks waiting for them, but the passports finally arrived on a dark afternoon in early December. Despite a bellyache that had spanned two days, Heather did a little circle dance in the wet gravel until she was dizzy and had to lean against the mailbox.

When her insides stopped lurching, she skipped down the long driveway—indifferent to the fact that she was forty years old now. She was bursting with the physical evidence in her hand. She could leave. She could adventure. She could explore.

Kathryn wasn't nearly as excited as Heather. In fact, she looked decidedly cross. Heather didn't want to know what Kathryn's attitude was about. If she asked, Kathryn might

　　　　Valerie Ihsan

give her some made up reason to cancel the trip. Heather knew exactly where she wanted to go and what she wanted to do, and she didn't want anything to wreck it.

After comparing prices and dates and airlines, Heather finally made her purchase. Seven weeks away seemed like *forever*, but she contained her impatience by going out and buying every single travel guide for Scotland that Barnes and Noble carried.

SO COLD.

Heather's teeth chattered in the dark tent of her bed linens. This flu was kicking her ass. She'd been sick for three days and she wasn't getting any better. How come her mom never got sick? And Jill only ever had an occasional cold. Heather felt like a wimp.

The muscles in her shoulders knotted and hunched forward, rigid. She yawned through her tremors.

She had no idea what her temperature was, but it didn't feel like the kind of fever that she could just ride out. The undersides of her eyelids were swollen, her lips hot. She raised herself up on a shaky arm and turned down the blankets. Her head pounded so fiercely that she instantly felt dizzy and queasy.

The thought of walking the four or five paces to her door without the warmth of her robe was not compelling her to get up for the Advil. Sitting up, she tugged at the quilt, intending to wrap herself in it for the trek to the bathroom, but she just didn't have the strength.

A rush of warm frustration rose from her core and spilled out of her collarbone. Now sweating, she started to whimper and cry. Like a newborn blind kitten, Heather felt her way to her robe and clumsily put it on. She had to try three times to get her left arm through the sleeve. When she opened the bedroom door, a rush of frigid air accosted her and she almost cried out.

Advil. I need Advil.

She shivered and shuffled to the bathroom where she consumed three pills of the fever reducer, when normally she allowed herself only one. She made it back to her bed and burrowed under the blankets, her robe still on. Her clothes and linens twisted around her uncomfortably, but she didn't care, and she suddenly wished for her mother's hands—touching her back, smoothing her hair, tucking her in. What an odd thing to wish for. She was far too old for that.

She cleared her throat. Waves of violent shivering crashed through her.

There was no way her mom would hear her if she called out, but she wanted to try anyway. She felt frightened but couldn't understand why.

"Mama?"

She closed her eyes. Her head hurt, and all her muscles screamed. She breathed in and out through her nose and thought of roses and sunny summer days. She thought of camping with her friends. Of traveling to Scotland soon.

And then, there was her mother.

"Darling? What is it?"

Heather felt Kathryn kneel by the bed and reach for her forehead. It must've been a mom thing—instinctively knowing to feel for fever in questionable moments.

Kathryn gasped and Heather's eyes opened wide in the dark room.

"You're so hot, dear!"

"Cold," Heather said. She reached up to her face to wipe the tears away, but most were already evaporated. She sniffed.

Kathryn rallied, wide awake now, and tidied Heather's blankets.

"There now. I'll get the thermometer. Do you want anymore water? Can I get you anything?"

"My knit hat. I'm sorry I woke you."

"I'm your mama; that's what I'm for. I'll be right back."

Janet leaped up onto Heather's bed. Janet always slept with Kathryn, but the snuggly dog was a welcomed heat source. She curled up behind Heather's knees.

Kathryn returned with the thermometer and a hat. It wasn't the one that Heather wanted, but it was warm enough, and she was grateful for it.

"Maybe some tea?" Heather said. She felt terrible for asking. She didn't want to be dependent on anyone—least of all her aging mother. And in the middle of the night.

"Sure. But let's get a temperature reading from you first, before you drink anything." She poised the digital thermometer at Heather's mouth.

"But I just took some Advil. With water."

Kathryn faltered.

"Then I'll just take it under your arm and add a degree like I did when you were a baby." She pulled the shoulder of Heather's robe and pajamas down so she could get to her armpit.

When the thermometer beeped, Kathryn drew it back to read it, and Heather buried herself under the blankets again.

"*Jay-sus*, Heather. It's 103.9 degrees. I'm glad you took that Advil. How much did you take?"

"Three."

Kathryn nodded and then eyed the clock.

"I'll be back in half an hour to check your temperature again."

"I'm sorry," Heather said from the depths of all her blankets. Stacked one on tope of the other were a feather blanket, the quilt her mother made her, a thin cotton blanket, the bedsheet, and finally Grandpa's tartan blanket. Kathryn had brought the tartan blanket in with the hat.

"Just go back to sleep, Mama. I'll be fine now. I'm sorry I woke you up." Her head felt like it was being cored out with a giant wine bottle opener.

Kathryn touched Heather's knee through the blankets.

"Good night," Kathryn said, and she quietly closed the door behind her. Then she opened it again, poking her head through the gap.

"I'll just leave this open a crack, and mine too, in case you need to call me again."

Heather hummed in response. Talking hurt her brain.

Kathryn

KATHRYN SAT ON HER BED. JANET NOSED OPEN THE door and hopped up next to her. She petted the dog absentmindedly.

She was tired but strangely awake. Heather's fever was too high this time. She'd have to wait at least twenty minutes, though thirty would be better, before checking her temperature again.

Oh the tea!

She kissed the top of Janet's head. They went to the kitchen together and Kathryn lit a comforting oil lamp. When the tea was made, Kathryn tiptoed to Heather's room and set the mug on the bedside table.

She kneeled beside Heather's bed, her knees uncomfortable on the wood floor, and looked at the clock again. Only thirteen minutes had passed. If the fever had gone down even a little bit—even just two-tenths of a degree—she'd know the medication was doing its trick.

She made a note to herself to add her Immuno-Booster tincture to Heather's echinacea tea tomorrow morning. She would get the herbal star treatment.

Her heart pounded and her hands shook.

Why was she scared?

It's just a fever.

Heather had had it for several days though, and it was much higher now. She'd seen the naturopath on Friday and was taking a homeopathic remedy, but nothing had changed yet. Kathryn decided that if Heather's temperature was still high at its next check, she would take Heather to the emergency room.

One time, when Heather was seven years old, she was so sick she couldn't keep anything inside her. She threw up everything. Even water. The urgent care doctor had given her suppositories to suppress the vomiting, so she wouldn't get dehydrated. Heather's little heart had beaten so fast that Kathryn had sat by the bed and put her hand on Heather's chest, trying to imbue healing and love through her fingertips. She had sat there for twenty minutes, until Heather had fallen asleep. Only then had she given herself permission to leave the room.

Kathryn shifted to a squatting position, hesitant to disturb her sleeping daughter but too anxious to wait. She touched Heather's forehead. The room was a tad lighter. She could see Heather's eyes flicker open and close.

"It's time to take your temperature again," Kathryn whispered. "Open your mouth."

Heather complied and, in less than a minute, Kathryn found the same 103.9 degrees on the read-out screen.

She bit her lip.

She went back to her room, set a timer, and tried to get some rest.

Why was she so worried?

Within the course of two hours, Kathryn had taken Heather's temperature four more times and given her three more tablets of Advil. But the thermometer now said 104.3 degrees.

It wasn't working. Kathryn pulled on a pair of jeans and added socks and boots. She pulled a sweater over her pajama top and ran a foamy toothbrush through her mouth.

She went and started the car so it could begin warming up inside. She went to Heather's room and turned on the bedside lamp. If Heather noticed, she didn't flinch, just kept breathing in and out her open mouth. The air was heavy with illness. Kathryn went to the dresser and tried to pick out something that would be both warm and easy to get on Heather.

Kathryn pulled down the bedcovers. She murmured and smoothed and moved Heather's limbs and assessed how to get her clothes on. Perhaps Heather wasn't too sick to help.

"Heather? We need to leave now." Kathryn nodded when Heather blinked open her eyes.

"Mama?"

"I'm taking you to the hospital. Your fever is just a bit too high." Kathryn decided to leave Heather's silk long johns on and pulled a pair of yoga pants over the top of them. Then she put socks over Heather's bare feet.

"You must sit up, dear. I'll help."

Heather whimpered but acquiesced.

THEY WAITED AT THE EMERGENCY ROOM IN A CURTAINED-off bed. Heather was given Tylenol right away since the ibuprofen wasn't working. A nurse started an IV to give her fluids and took a blood sample.

Kathryn worried a hand through knotted hair and rubbed her face. She knew she looked a frazzled mess. She was good in a crisis, yes, but still exhausted with worry and adrenaline overdose.

They waited for a terrifying hour, a nurse checking on them every once in a while, with Heather's temperature hovering at 105 degrees. A doctor finally admitted her to the acute-care floor and ordered an ultrasound. Heather's bellyache was back again and the doctor wanted to rule out appendicitis.

Kathryn gathered their things and followed the CNA wheeling Heather up the seventh floor. As they navigated the corridors, Kathryn admired the art and architectural design. They were as peaceful as the hospital's name—Riverbend.

Reassured that someone else would make the decisions for a while, and that information would be coming soon, Kathryn allowed herself to just be with Heather.

She fell asleep twice in the chair before the achingly

young hospital doctor arrived with Heather's imaging results two hours later.

He looked at the clipboard in his hand.

"You don't have appendicitis, Ms. Gordon. Just that nasty flu." He paused, still staring at the clipboard. He cleared his throat. "During the ultrasound, we saw that your right ovary was enlarged, so we took a closer look."

He looked up at Heather and back to the clipboard with a flicker of movement, his knuckles white on the prop.

"You have at least one mass on your right ovary."

Kathryn gasped, her hand to her throat. He took a steadying breath. He really was so very young. He moved closer to Heather's bed. Her face was white, her eyes big. He gentled his voice.

"I need to run a few more tests to see what we're dealing with. I've ordered a CT scan and a couple more blood tests." He shuffled brochures and papers under the clipboard, then seemed to think better of something and paused.

"I'll send in a nurse," he said. He touched Heather's foot through the blanket. "I'll be back before you're discharged."

Kathryn and Heather held eye contact, neither one breathing.

A mass. Kathryn saw the same thought in Heather's face.

18

Kathryn

Stunned. Stunted. Each breath a stab to her heart, to her lungs. Kathryn held Heather and they cried. *A mass.* Heather, her skin still too hot to the touch, trembled in Kathryn's arms.

"*Might.* You *might* have cancer," Kathryn said. "We don't know if the mass is even a tumor, *or* if it's malignant." The last word came out in a whisper.

Heather sobbed and snuffled.

"I hate my brain. My *brain* gave me cancer," she said.

Heather balled up her fists and struck herself over the head. Again and again. Alarm jumped and raced in Kathryn's temples. She reached for Heather and pulled at her wrists.

"Stop! You're distraught," Kathryn said. She released Heather and fluttered her own hands, walking in a circle. "*I'm* distraught."

Heather's nostrils flared and her eyes widened so much, Kathryn could practically see them becoming bloodshot.

"*You're* distraught? Fuck off, *Mama*." Heather turned her face away.

Kathryn flinched at the verbal slap. Heather clenched her fists and released them, over and over, but didn't hit herself. Kathryn pressed a hand to her own chest and blinked back her wretchedness. The nurse on duty came in to intervene and led Kathryn into the hallway.

"You're both worried," she said in a low tone. "Give her some space. I'll be in in a few minutes to take another blood sample. Her CT scan is scheduled for two hours from now. Why don't you take a coffee break while you wait? It'll be okay." The nurse patted Kathryn's arm, which was ridiculous because the nurse was a good twenty-five years younger than her.

Kathryn nodded and walked back into Heather's room to get her purse.

"I'm going to get some coffee and make some calls. I'll be back."

Heather didn't respond or even look at her.

Kathryn fought the knee-jerk reaction to say something mean in return. She left the room and cried in the elevator.

She called Tonya and told her the news.

"Oh no, Kathryn," Tonya said.

"We don't know anything yet. There are still more tests … "

Tonya and Kathryn's mutual pauses swelled into shocked silence.

"What can I do for you right now?" Tonya finally said. "Do you want me to make you dinner? I can bring it to the hospital, or I can just leave it in your refrigerator for whenever you want it."

"Oh." Kathryn hadn't even thought of food. "Um. Yes. That would be great, actually." Her throat grew taunt. Compassion from others made her want to cry. *How strange.*

After hanging up, Kathryn made another call to the part-time farmhand, Jack, who helped during harvests and with the heftier jobs that required a strong back and longevity. He agreed to go over to the farm once a day to do a walk through and make sure nothing was falling apart in her absence.

Kathryn was pretty sure they'd be home tonight though, if they were lucky.

Lucky? Kathryn snorted with cynicism.

She walked the long stretch of hallway back to Heather's room, a coffee from the hospital's Starbucks in each hand. *What's going to happen?* She bit her lower lip and forced oxygen into her lungs. Whatever it was, she would be strong for Heather. She was the most important thing in Kathryn's life. After all, she'd just handed her farm over to Jack, and *she didn't even care.*

It was "Heather First" now.

Kathryn set her shoulders and walked with purpose.

Heather

Janet met them at the door, woofing a greeting. Tonya was there, too. She'd let herself in to drop off a chicken enchilada casserole.

"I bet you're glad to be home," Tonya said, taking bags and travel mugs out of Kathryn's hands and stepping aside to let Heather pass. "How are you feeling, Heather?"

A surge of electricity shot from Heather's feet to her chest. She swiveled around to face Tonya.

"How do you *think* I feel?" She dropped her belongings on the floor, deliberately stepped over them, and stomped to her room. She was still feverish but down to a manageable 102 degrees.

Inside the low light, she slid onto her bed, smelling

her sheets, her pillows, her blankets. She'd been gone for less than thirty-six hours but had still missed the human smell of her room. Hospitals were sterile. As they should be, but still. She was glad to bury her face into the feather pillow and close her eyes. Mentally exhausted, Heather didn't know how she was going to wait until the biopsy.

When the doctor had returned that afternoon to share the results of the tests, he'd said that there was a strong indication of advanced epithelial ovarian cancer. An appointment with a gynecologic oncologist was next and then biopsy surgery.

She'd been a dick to Tonya, she knew. But *honestly*, what a stupid question to ask someone who just found out she had *cancer*.

"*Maybe* cancer," she whispered.

She momentarily escaped the news and Tonya's unintentionally cruel question in sleep. When she awoke from her nap, Tonya had gone home, and Kathryn was at the table.

"I'm sorry I was so rude to Tonya," Heather said, walking toward her mom. Her ears popped and her face stretched into a grimace. There was no warning, only a sudden catch in her lungs, and then slobbering all over herself.

"Oh honey." Kathryn pulled Heather into her soft arms.

Heather sank in, relieved, then stiffened. She sniffed and pulled away. She wiped at her tears in quick, broad swipes and shook her hair away from her face, blinking rapidly.

She hoped her "I'm totally fine now, thank-you-very-much" mask was on. She laughed at herself, her *falling-apartedness*, but it was fake. Maybe her mom wouldn't notice.

"I've been doing some reading," Kathryn said, in a let's-make-a-plan voice. "While we wait for the biopsy and results, we can start you on a tincture of … "

But then Kathryn trailed off.

She took one look at Heather and pulled her to the kitchen. Kathryn rummaged in the refrigerator and emerged with a half-eaten eclair from Sweet Life. She took a bite and handed the rest to Heather.

Heather hesitated and then snarfed it down, quick, with anger and depression spiraling around her. *Even in the face of death, there are always eclairs.* She hiccuped in hysteria.

There was a chocolate smudge above Kathryn's lip and custard dotted her fingers. She licked it off but the chocolate left a coating over her middle finger, so she got up and retrieved a cloth napkin from the drawer. Janet clicked after her, hoping for eclair, no doubt.

Heather didn't bother with a napkin.

Kathryn

LATE DECEMBER SUNLIGHT SHONE FEEBLY THROUGH the window in the kitchen. Kathryn had a rare craving for coffee and schlepped out the coffeemaker from the Pantry of Useless and/or Extravagant Kitchen Appliances.

Heather was on week three of recovery from her biopsy surgery.

Biopsy surgery, my ass.

Her surgery had lasted two hours. They didn't just take the ovary out. Once they were in there, the surgeon had to take both ovaries, the fallopian tubes, and her uterus. They also had done something called debulking, had taken out a few regional lymph nodes, and some fatty tissue that started with an "O" that Kathryn couldn't remember, and had scraped a layer off of her liver, checking to see if the cancer had metastasized past the pelvic area.

Her diagnosis was Stage III, Grade II ovarian cancer. Kathryn still struggled with what that really meant, but she knew it was bad.

She nearly dropped the coffeemaker—what if the immune boosting herbs she was giving Heather were actually *feeding* the cancer cells? Maybe it was time to start researching on the computer. Kathryn welcomed all the help she could get, whether it came from computer or dead relative.

Besides, Flora and her ridiculous broccoli dreams hadn't been much help anyway. Kathryn didn't mean any disrespect, but *what was Flora thinking?*

Still. Flora had never steered her wrong. It wouldn't hurt to look into it. Or maybe she should just honor their unspoken agreement and accept whatever Flora sent her with blind faith.

Kathryn was pretty good with Blind Faith—though she sometimes worried that it made her look simple. People frequently rolled their eyes at Kathryn. As a recourse, she'd started prefacing her opinions and ways of life by joking about her "hippie woo-woo ways." It made people laugh, relax in their judgements, and take her less seriously. She'd rather be seen as fanciful, or even *eccentric*, than bat-crazy.

She found the coffee filters and pulled the coffee beans from the freezer.

Broccoli?

Maybe she could force-start some broccoli seeds. A lot of farmers' markets were closed this time of year. The ones that stayed open year round didn't have broccoli now, and Kathryn didn't like to buy produce from the grocery stores. Even if she could get organic, she knew that it was shipped from far away. Hardly sustainable.

While the coffee was percolating, she turned on the desktop computer. What were the healing properties of broccoli? Other than the nutrients it provided you, like iron and such, she couldn't see anything special about it.

Heather was still in her room. She'd been holing up since the surgery. Kathryn couldn't blame her but was at a loss as to how to offer any comfort. Heather had lost so much. Her health, her fertility, and her dream of Scotland delayed—maybe permanently. Kathryn's heartbeat sped up. Hot tears pooled in her eyes. She blinked and they spilled out.

With shaking hands, she googled "Broccoli, Healing Properties."

She stared at the clock. She'd gone through two cups of coffee and one hour on the computer, reading. Flora was definitely on to something. Kathryn had skimmed countless articles, starting with "Broccoli: A Potent Tool Against Osteoarthritis and Cancer." It turned out that broccoli contained something called sulforaphane, which supposedly killed cancer stem cells.

"Specifically, it appears that broccoli contains the necessary ingredients to switch ON genes that prevent cancer development, and switch OFF other ones that help it spread. Research has shown

that fresh broccoli sprouts are FAR more potent, allowing you to eat far less in terms of quantity. Sprouts consistently contain 20-50 times the amount of chemoprotective compounds found in mature broccoli heads."

That was it! With growing excitement, Kathryn hurried out to the potting shed and found last year's seed packets. She'd alphabetized them. Broccoli was right in the front.

She'd sprout them. She didn't need to grow them at all; she'd just keep the sprouts going consistently. She could even dedicate a section in the kitchen just for sprouting.

Kathryn collected the items she needed and set to work. She moved faster and faster, as if to beat the cancer cells in a mad race.

It *was* a mad race.

Maybe she wouldn't tell Heather about it yet. But that was stupid. They were both going to try absolutely anything to beat this cancer. And she really, really hoped that Heather would consider using alternative means to fight in addition to the conventional ones the doctor had outlined. There wasn't any reason why Heather wouldn't, given their history. Kathryn had always gone with herbs first.

There was a place for Western medicine, of course. Like when you break an arm or have appendicitis. And she was all for using life-saving antibiotics for when a person *truly* needed them, like for advanced cases of bacterial infections, or scary ones, like staph infections. You could die from those. Cancer, too.

But ear infections? Come on. Garlic and mullein oil in the ears worked fine for that.

She pulled a sieve from a bottom drawer and retrieved a large shallow baking dish from the cupboard. She washed the seeds in the sieve, watching closely to make sure that none escaped through the holes.

Lacking a seed sprouter, she used what she could find in the kitchen and from her garden supplies. She started a list of useful items to get at Down to Earth, the home and garden store in Eugene. Veneta lacked stores like that.

Broccoli took about five days to sprout. If Heather ate them every day, and with every meal—well, maybe not breakfast—it would be best to have more than one sprouter going at the same time. Perhaps she'd get two sprouters from Down to Earth.

Kathryn put the newly cleaned seeds in a jelly jar and covered them with water. They needed to soak overnight. She'd have plenty of time to go in town and purchase the rest of the supplies, among them, more broccoli seeds—if she could find them.

She hurried through her chores and checked in with Heather before she left for town.

"I found some cool things on the Internet about diet and nutrition and how much of a role it plays in fighting cancer."

Heather didn't respond. She was sitting up in bed, only having left it a couple of times that day to use the bathroom. Although she was unwashed and pale, with dark smudges under her eyes, Heather was somehow more beautiful to Kathryn than ever.

"I'm so sorry, my baby." Kathryn choked up again. "We'll fight this. I promise. We'll figure something out."

Heather kept her eyes on the corner of her room.

"I'm going into town now. Can I get you anything?"

No answer.

"Okay. I love you so much. I'll be back soon."

She started to close the door again but decided against it. Janet might go in and keep her company, and besides, the room needed some airing. Kathryn worried, while gathering her coat and keys, that Heather's depression would sink so far in that she wouldn't be able to fight this war.

For that's what it was. And she could see herself in full armor with her standard raised high, blowing in the wind, leading the charge against the toxic evil that was threatening her daughter's life.

She would fight this. And if Heather couldn't, or wouldn't, help herself along the way, Kathryn would do it for her. She would be the strong one.

But that was okay because Kathryn had always been the strong one.

And with Flora's continued help, she knew with every fiber of her being that the land would save Heather—the earth they walked on, the soil they plowed, the food sown from it. And there her bravado ended.

But what if I lose her?

She couldn't think of that.

Wouldn't.

There would be *no space* in her soul for that.

But it snaked in, persistent. And if she dwelled on it,

or even *looked* at it for a mere ten seconds, she despaired.

Without Heather, Kathryn would die alone. Like Flora's husband. When Flora had died in the famine of 1625, she left the poor man all alone. All of their children had died before her. It had been a terrible dream to watch. The only nightmare that Flora ever sent Kathryn.

Sticky tar-like fear oozed circuitously around Kathryn's brainstem, like a cat rubbing figure eights at her ankles. She drove toward Down to Earth, her breathing forced into submission.

When she got there, she walked into the soothing fertilizer smells of the gardening department and felt her blood pressure lower.

The broccoli will work.

Heather

Heather's sense-numbing depression faded one evening when her phone emitted a strange-sounding chirp. She rolled over in bed and picked it up from the side table. The skin around her eyes felt puffy and stretched, and fresh pain bored deep behind them. She needed water and fresh air and to get out of bed, but she couldn't seem to muster it.

A red sunset crept through her window beneath the curtains. Her mom's slow-cooking rabbit stew permeated the house, each air molecule coated in simmering juices of homemade love and attention.

Heather knew she'd behaved badly, isolating herself in her room and engaging with no one. She'd answered no calls and her cell phone was packed with Facebook notifications and texts that she'd never read.

Poor Mama. She's grieving, too.

Heather curled up into a ball in her bed—the phone limp in her hand—and let the tears come again. Or maybe for the first time. She actually couldn't remember if she'd cried before, but she must have.

She cradled her belly. A hysterectomy meant no children. Ever.

What if … ?

What if I have ovarian cancer because of what I did all those Octobers ago?

Heather's chest thudded like a freight train and she felt sick. Her hands were cold and sweaty. She breathed deliberately and slowly. Yoga breathing.

At forty, she was pretty much past her childbearing years anyway, though she'd known some women who'd had their first (or fourth) child at forty-two. It could be done. But really, that was beside the point. Who would date her now?

Who dates a person with *cancer?*

No one.

The facts were: she was romantically alone, she lived with her mother, and she was forty years old, with no guarantee that she'd see fifty.

Or forty-one, for that matter.

She wasn't ever going to have children anyway. Certainly not now. If it had been meant to be, it would've happened fifteen years ago.

She wiped her nose with her hand and dried it off on

the sheets. She looked up the notification that had come in on her phone. It was a note to herself. "Do I have all the clothes I need for Scotland?" *Scotland.* What day was it? She looked to her phone again.

Only three weeks until the trip began! How could she have forgotten about Scotland? *Damn depression.* It fucked up everything.

Despite being snug and warm in her blanket cocoon, Heather allowed the plaid promise of Scotland—not to mention her rank and fear-saturated pajamas—to lure her into a bath. The first one after her pelvic surgery.

While the water ran hot into the tub, Heather gathered the books she'd been reading last week, along with her journal and a pen, but then sighed and left them all on the bed. She was too tired to do anything in the bath but wade through the washing.

She certainly couldn't keep her eyes closed for much longer. She knew she'd have to make some decisions.

But not just yet.

A bath first.

And a fresh set of sheets.

Leaving her bedroom, Heather saw her mother setting the table. Kathryn stopped but Heather scooted into the bathroom before her mom could approach. They made eye contact once before Heather closed the bathroom door.

She sank into the hot water an inch at a time. It was a little bit too hot but somehow cathartic. Washing anew. Preparing the body for the onslaught. The fight.

Would she win? What if this was it? The gynecologic

oncologist had said they'd have to see after the chemotherapy, but if she responded to the treatments, there was a good chance of survival. Another five years, at least. But what was five years? So she'd die at forty-five years old instead of forty?

Slowly and carefully, Heather lowered her head into the water and let it permeate the oil on her scalp. When she emerged, she let her skin cool before adding shampoo. Lather. Rinse. Repeat.

With the loofah, she made circles on her flesh, careful to avoid the incision site. She scooped and rinsed off the suds and the body oil until she felt a little less like a caged and neglected animal.

Not that she'd been neglected by anyone but herself. *What did I do to contract cancer? How did I let it in?*

She closed her eyes and gently wiped the tears away, even while more flowed. She stroked her own hair away from her forehead, like how she petted Janet. Her fingertips smoothed down her neck muscles, and she allowed her arms to cross over her chest into a hug.

She filled her lungs, then let the air all out. She didn't want to postpone Scotland. She would go there first, and *then* do the chemo. She'd push that out just a little bit longer.

When the bath water had cooled and she felt not quite new, but like she could at least change the sheets on her bed, she emerged from the bathroom.

And there was her mother.

With a hug.

Heather fell into her arms and cried and cried. They

both did. They sank to the floor and Kathryn rocked her like a little baby. Janet, ever helpful and loyal, sat solemnly beside the mourning and witnessed it as only a faithful pet could.

Afterward, Kathryn brought them both a box of Kleenex.

"I feel like I need another whole bath," Heather said. They both giggled a little and blew their noses.

Heather got up from the floor, using the wall for support. She couldn't believe the discomfort she felt from just getting up and down. She retrieved two washcloths from the linen closet, wetted them with cold water from the bathroom tap, and handed one to her mom. Heather covered her face with it and gasped at the difference in temperature. She wiped her tears and snot away.

"I made some stew. Do you feel up to joining me tonight?" Kathryn's face, always readable, didn't fail to display her hopefulness. All her recent worrying had etched new lines in her face.

Heather touched her own face.

Will I get those lines now, too?

"Dinner, yes," she answered. "But first I want to change the sheets on my bed. They're gross."

"I'll help." Her mother rushed to lend a hand.

Heather looked at her mother's rough hands flapping open the sheets and her strong body edging around the mattress, tucking here and there. Kathryn was always in control of something.

Since cancer wasn't something anyone controlled, Heather supposed that changing the bed linens would have to do. An alarming urge to laugh rose up her throat, but she swallowed it before she had to explain her new, apparently black, sense of humor.

Heather knew changing the sheets wouldn't be enough for her mother to feel in control of in the face of Heather's illness. How could it be? But Heather left her to it and put on clean, warm pajamas and her robe.

She moved slowly back to the bed, hunched over and shuffling like an old crone. But she didn't mind too much. She preferred physical pain to emotional any day. Kathryn and Heather changed pillowcases in silence and then Heather opened the window. She closed the bedroom door to keep the cold outside air from getting into the rest of the house while they ate dinner.

Heather sat down at the table and Kathryn ladled out the stew into their bowls.

"I didn't realize the trip was so close. We've got to get packing," Heather said.

The ladle clanked against the stew pot. Heather kept her eyes down and pressed her hands into the table on either side of her bowl.

"No." Kathryn's face was granite. "That's *not* happening."

"What do you mean, 'No'?" Disbelief rocketed to her fingertips. Heather twisted her hands, palms up, in the air—speechless.

"You're too sick to *travel*, Heather. What about the chemotherapy?"

"I'll do the chemo when we get back. It's just a few extra weeks." Resolve burned in Heather's face. Her instincts said, "Now or never." The surety of it rolled in her belly and burned in truth.

"I don't believe this," Kathryn said. "NO." She sloshed stew into her bowl, flecks splattering on the tablecloth.

"How do you know how sick I am? How do you know what I can handle?"

"I'm your mother. Of course I *know*."

"You never let me make up my own mind." Heather flung her hand out accusingly. "It's not your decision this time! If I'm going to die, I want to see Scotland first." She stood up, the chair scraping loudly on the floor.

Kathryn's eyes widened.

"You're not going to die," Kathryn said, her mouth gaping like a fish out of water, frantic to breathe.

Heather picked up her stew bowl.

"I'm eating in my room," she spat out.

SHE FINISHED HER STEW IN A HUFF.

How dare she presume to know anything about how I'm feeling right now and what I'm capable of. I've let her push me around for far too long. I'm deciding what's right for me from now on—and I should've done it years ago.

Her scalp tingled and her lips itched. Too much oxygen to the brain.

Her eyes landed on the travel brochure for Scotland. She got up from the bed and picked up the brochure from the top of the dresser. The dresser was dinged up in a couple of places, and the trim from the lowest drawer had fallen off and was propped up against it. But it was her favorite piece. She'd found it at a thrift store and bought it herself with her first paycheck as a seventeen-year-old. She'd worked at Orange Julius at the mall in Eugene. Not super glamorous, but it had been the first time she'd worked anywhere but the farm.

She flipped through brochure pages that she'd already looked at fifteen times and wished that she could get on the computer to look at more Scottish stuff. Her laptop was in the living room. She suddenly had an aching need to plan the trip itinerary.

It was true—what she said to her mom. If she *did* die, she wanted to be able to say on her melodramatic death-bed that she had lived and traveled and *done something* with her life. She flung the thick brochure away from herself. It fluttered to the ground and *thwapped* on the floor.

She went for her phone, ignoring the texts once again, and examined those Scottish apps she'd installed months ago.

Forty-five minutes later, she *really* had to pee and the apps couldn't hold her attention any longer. She *really really* didn't want to see her mom though. She listened at the door, but heard nothing. She cracked it open and peered through the slice she'd created. There was her mom. At the table. Head in hand. Staring at her bowl and playing with her spoon. Her food must've been cold by then and Heather knew that she hated cold food.

Heather felt a smidgen of guilt waft up to the back of her neck and she shivered.

She'd been a jerk to her mother.

Heather sighed. Her mother looked up and eyed the door. Heather closed it, caught spying. She felt ten and grounded. She frowned and pseudo-kicked her toe at the oak floorboards. *Grade-A Jackass.* That's what she was.

She picked up her stew bowl and left her room. She walked purposefully to the kitchen.

"Sorry about before, but I really don't want to talk right now," Heather said. "I need to be alone for a while longer."

She didn't look at Kathryn as she passed. She filled her bowl to soak in the sink, then hurried to the bathroom and then back to her room—grabbing her computer bag on the way.

Sitting cross-legged on the bed, she went to her messages and sorted through the frantic texts from Jill and Kyle.

She really wanted to call Jill but knew Kathryn would be—*could be*—listening. A text would have to do.

Her heart thumped. With a dry throat, and sticky mouth, she typed with two thumbs:

```
Wanna go to Scotland with me? I've
already got the tickets. I'm NOT going
with my mom. I'll explain later. Please
say, Yes. It's selfish, I know, but I
could really use your camaraderie and
support right now. We'd leave next
month!
```

She hit Send and waited.

And waited.

To occupy her mind, she made a list of sights she wanted to see and wrote down the contact info for the tour she was most interested in.

Finally the "delivered" message status changed to

"read," and Heather's breath quickened. She held the iPhone in her hands, lightly, like a bird's nest.

After five minutes of ridiculous stalker-like waiting, Heather took a huge breath and recognized a truth.

Heather needed Jill because she didn't *want* to need her mother. Did she really want her best friend as a pleasant travel companion? Or was she just using her? The truth was, Heather didn't want to travel alone in case she took a turn for the worse.

Heather grabbed the edge of the quilt and blankets with one hand and rolled them around herself like a burrito.

Soon enough, she was asleep.

When she awoke, a text from Jill awaited.

`Hell yes.`

21

Heather

A GLORIOUS WEEK OF SECRET PLANNING AND PACK-ing passed. She refilled her pain medication prescription and her antidepressants. She hid her packed carry-on under the bed. Heather felt stronger and more sure of herself than she had for twenty years.

She and Jill would have the time of their lives and the euphoria from the vacation would carry Heather through the not-so-great days after that. But there she stopped. No use thinking about the chemo now. Scotland first. Thank goodness that Jill still had a passport from a Habitat for Humanity stint in Panama she did three years ago. It saved Heather from having to dwell on what she would've done if Jill hadn't had a passport.

When the day of Heather's follow-up appointment came, Kathryn insisted on coming along, so they rode in Heather's car together. Heather hoped that she wasn't really sick enough, after the tumors had been removed, to warrant a speedy chemotherapy treatment plan; maybe they'd say she didn't need chemotherapy after all.

At any rate, she'd wanted to discuss postponing it all until she was back from Scotland. Heather squeezed her lips together and backed out of the driveway. Now she'd have to wait on that discussion. Maybe she'd talk her mom into staying in the waiting room while Heather talked to the doctor. She wasn't *twelve*. She didn't need her mommy along. She turned on the CD player so she wouldn't have to talk to her.

The oncologist's office at Riverbend's campus looked like the same generic doctor's office in any city, in any building. The walls were white, the furniture light blue and mauve, the prints on the wall hotel-like in their sameness. It was depressing really. She checked in and sat next to a fake ficus tree in the corner.

Heather quickly set her purse in the chair next to herself, effectively barring Kathryn from fussing at her, or holding her hand. She didn't even want her mom's *arm* touching her right now. She just wanted to get this over with and finish packing for her trip.

Kathryn flipped through a *Good Housekeeping* magazine dated six months prior, until Heather was called back. Kathryn stood up, too.

"Mom. You don't have to come back with me. I can do it by myself."

Kathryn looked annoyed. "But I came all this way with you. I didn't do that to sit in the waiting room."

Heather looked at the nurse and back to her mom. Heather's face warmed under their collective gazes. She swallowed the embarrassment down and tried for one more surge of independence.

"I didn't ask you to come," she hissed under her breath, pressing her bag to her chest.

Kathryn glared and Heather looked back at the nurse, who raised her eyebrows and gestured at the hallway of consult rooms. Heather followed the nurse, hoping her mother would take the hint and wait for her there, but no such luck. Kathryn marched behind them, exuding self-importance.

How would she talk to the doctor now?

After taking Heather's vitals, the nurse told them to wait again. Heather kept her eyes on her cell phone, but without the *Good Housekeeping* magazine, Kathryn kept trying to start conversations. Perhaps she was feeling guilty about her interference.

The gynecologic oncologist came in and shook hands. She looked at the chart notes on the computer and asked Heather how she'd felt since the surgery.

"Fine actually," Heather said. She plastered a fake smile on and stopped herself from saying, *"I don't know what all the fuss is about."*

"That's good," the doctor said. She began typing notes as she talked. "So here's how it'll work: on the way out today, you'll make an appointment for a pelvic exam and a CA-125 test with me for two months from now—"

Kathryn began taking notes with what looked like manic desperation.

"—and you'll need to do those every three months throughout your treatment, or less, depending on how you're responding to the chemotherapy."

At last, Heather and Kathryn made eye contact.

Chemotherapy.

Kathryn maintained that proper nutrition, supplements, and the right herbal remedies could cure anything. Even cancer. Kathryn had seen the documentaries. Though, when real life showed up, Heather had seen her waffle a little on her theories.

Heather was generally more pragmatic and wanted to make sure they'd gotten all the cancer out with the surgery, but the idea of *six months* of chemotherapy and vomiting and losing her hair in clumps was, quite frankly, terrifying. And she still hoped that the doctor in front of her would say, *"Never mind about all that chemotherapy. You're fine now."*

But instead, she said, "We have you set up for the chemotherapy treatments to start in two days."

"Okay then," Kathryn said, starting to get up.

Here was Heather's chance!

"Except I want to ask a couple private questions," Heather said. She screwed up her courage, stuffed her embarrassment, and turned to her mom. "Mom, please wait outside for me in the waiting room."

Heather turned and kept her eyes on the doctor, knowing that the doctor's presence would prevent anymore bossiness from her mom. When Kathryn left, Heather smiled in apology and the doctor rolled her chair closer.

"Dr. Chattel, I want to wait and schedule the start of treatments for the end of *next* month," Heather said.

The doctor tilted her head. "Excuse me?" she said.

"I'm traveling and won't be back until next month. I'd like to have a chance to settle in and unpack and rest up a bit before starting chemotherapy." This all made perfect sense to Heather.

Several facial distortions flitted over the doctor's face. Heather imagined Dr. Chattel siphoning any condescending remarks into a run-off vessel before speaking out loud. But that was perhaps an ungenerous perception. She'd been nothing but polite and helpful since they'd met.

"Ms. Gordon. *Heather.*" She raised her eyebrows. "You have *advanced* ovarian cancer. The surgery got most of the cancer cells out, but we didn't like the look of the liver biopsy results. This isn't an elective treatment ..." She corrected herself. "... Unless you want it to be."

"I *know* this is serious, Dr. Chattel. But I've booked a flight to Scotland for next week, and I'll be gone for three weeks." Heather looked down at the chair legs next to her and adjusted her sweater. Maybe truth was best right now. It *was* her life they were talking about, after all.

She leaned forward in her chair and looked into Dr. Chattel's brown eyes. "I feel very strongly about this trip. I need to go on it. And what if I don't have another chance?"

"There is no guarantee with cancer, Ms. Gordon," Dr. Chattel said. "If you delay the chemotherapy for even a *week* at this stage, there is no telling where the cancer could return. I strongly urge you to reschedule your trip until at least after your first round of treatment."

Heather set her jaw and leaned back in her chair.

Dr. Chattel cleared her throat and frowned. They held a long look. Dr. Chattel looked away first.

"On the way out, please make a follow-up appointment for immediately after you return from your trip." She turned away and rolled back to her computer, signaling the end of the appointment.

Heather walked to the front desk but Kathryn waved her over.

"I've already scheduled your next appointments." She handed Heather an appointment card.

Heather took it with a shaking hand, feeling violated. She looked down at the handwritten dates, two of which were ones during her Scotland trip.

"I have plans with Jill on those days," she said. She turned to head back to the scheduling desk and heard Kathryn get up from the chair.

Heather whirled around and pointed at the empty chair, her eyes boring into Kathryn's.

"I will make my own appointments, Mother."

Her heart raced. Livid, Heather canceled the appointments and said she'd reschedule at a later time. She avoided her mother's eyes, and they made their departure in silence—one that continued all the way back to Veneta, and into the night. Neither one ate dinner. And when Heather got up in the middle of the night to use the bathroom, she saw that both of them had worn their clothes to bed.

Kathryn was asleep on the couch.

Heather

"*WHAT?*" DISMAY ROCKED THROUGH HEATHER.

"I'm so sorry, Heather." Jill kicked her car tire.

They were in the parking lot of Sam Bond's Garage. The January night was dark and rainy, but Jill had wanted to talk privately so they were out in the drizzle. Now Heather knew why. This was *terrible*.

"I *have* to go, Jill." She grabbed Jill's wrist. "You *know* why."

Heather hadn't let Jill tell anyone else about her cancer. Only Kyle knew, and that was because Jill told him before Heather could swear her to secrecy. And, of course, Tonya knew. Heather's stomach soured. She didn't want *all* the people she knew pitying her. It was embarrassing enough.

She just wanted to go on vacation, come home for chemotherapy, and be left alone to heal. No one needed to know. She wouldn't be treated any different.

She'd go on this vacation—alone if she had to. She could manage her antidepressants on her own and take charge of life. *I'll be a better person.*

Once she returned from Scotland, she knew for certain that the travel bug would sink its parasitic claws in her and she'd fill up her passport within five years. Mama would just have to hire someone else to do the books. Heather had made it clear she didn't want any part of the farm anymore. She knew that before her cancer diagnosis, but having her life hang so precariously made her know it in her marrow.

The wind blew a heavier cloud in and the rain intensified, driving Heather and Jill shrieking back inside.

Jill looked at her, dripping, her face hangdog miserable.

"My chef has pneumonia. He's in the hospital. I'm the only one left that can cook. I can't close down the restaurant."

"Can't you hire a temporary replacement? It's 2010. We're in a recession. There are plenty of skilled chefs that would gladly take the job," Heather said, frantic.

"I can't leave my restaurant to a stranger to run." Jill's lip curled. "Besides, there isn't time to train anyone. There are only five days left before the flight."

Heather covered her mouth with her hands and counted to twenty. She wiped her hair back from her face and fluffed it up. Water droplets flew off and landed on the wood floor, adding to the small puddle collecting at her feet. She wasn't really mad at Jill. Jill wasn't responsible. It was unfair of Heather, but there was a part of her that felt a dagger of betrayal. *She should've chosen me over her job.* Now Heather'd have to go by herself. A heavy dread filled her head and her hands were wood.

What if Cairo happened again? She'd had so much fun in the whirlwind of sightseeing that she'd forgotten her meds a couple of days in a row. She'd felt deliciously clear without the cloying stagnation of the antidepressants and decided not to take them for just a little longer. She'd spiraled into such a dark place so fast, she still got chilled thinking about it.

In the end, her mom had had to *go to Egypt* to get her. Heather was so embarrassed afterward that she'd never traveled alone again. But this time it would be different. More was at stake.

"I'm sorry. I really wanted to go," Jill said. "I'll pay to have the ticket changed to someone else."

Heather took off her coat in the heat of the room. There would be no more conversation tonight; it was too loud to talk anymore. Fiddles and guitars warred against one another in song and then coalesced into foot-stomping harmony.

"Don't worry," Heather shouted. "I'll just go by myself."

Jill's eyes opened wide and her lips parted.

"It'll be fine," Heather said. She slung her coat over her arm. "It's too late to ask anyone else anyway."

Heather decided a beer was in order and scanned for the bartender. There were three people ahead of her in line.

She couldn't think about this right now. She resolved to stuff it until she got home and could think in a quiet place.

"You *can't* go alone," Jill said. She knew about Cairo. Heather had told her, one melancholy night over wine and chocolate.

Heather spotted Kyle, just back from a graphic design conference in British Columbia. He had the ski tan in the shape of goggles on his face to prove it.

A beer in each hand, he slid through and around the people congregating in front of the bar. He made eye contact with Heather and smiled, raising one of his glasses in a wave.

"You guys gonna play tonight? They're already jamming," he said. A bar patron jostled him from behind.

"Oh hey. Sorry," the man said, but beer had sloshed out of Kyle's cup already and landed with a splat on Heather's sweater.

"*Shit,*" Heather said.

"Sorry, sorry!" Kyle said, taking a step forward, and then one back. He stared at Heather's wet sweater, his face red.

"Dammit." Heather feebly stomped her booted foot. This night was just *terrific*.

Jill grabbed Kyle's upper arm with enough surprised force that more beer sloshed out of his cup.

"Take Kyle!" she said.

"What?" Kyle looked at Jill, then Heather.

"*No,*" Heather whispered, lethally. She wished she could shoot laser beams out of her eyeballs. Being alone with Kyle for three weeks would *not* keep her heart safe.

She succeeded at keeping her emotions neutral only because she saw him when Jill was there, too.

"I'm leaving," she said. She stuffed her arms into her coat. "Excuse me." She slid past Jill and Kyle into the main room to pick up her banjo. She was taking her beer-soaked, cancer-ridden, sorry ass home. She'd have a beer there. And another hot bath.

Once home, she opted instead for hot chocolate with a hefty dose of peppermint schnapps, and the whole five hours of BBC's *Pride and Prejudice,* in a quilt, with Mica the cat, on her lap.

She had to salvage the day *somehow.*

TWO DAYS LATER, WITH NO OTHER LEADS, SHE MET KYLE at Vero Espresso on Pearl Street in Eugene. Sweat collected under her arms and her face flushed. Kyle smiled at her.

"My treat. What can I get you?" he said.

She asked for chamomile tea. It would settle the flutters.

Kyle looked hopeful, his eyebrows puppy-dog alert but somehow elegant at the same time. His dark hair and eyes always slayed her, and she thought maybe he knew it, too. Knew his worth. He wouldn't beg for more than she offered, but perhaps he waited for her to change her mind. To come back to him.

She dropped her bag on the floor next to the table. Once seated, Heather took off her coat and sweater, straightened the rings on her fingers and tossed him a mouth-only smile. She pushed her sleeves up, and then, turning cold, immediately pulled them down again.

Kyle's hair was longer in the winter. To keep him warmer, he said. She liked it long. His curls came out. She stuffed a compulsion to move a stray lock away from an eyebrow. She liked him. A lot. Maybe even loved him still. They'd had some fun together, but it would be cruel to dangle more than she already did—that smidgeon of friendship.

And that made what she was about to do to him *evil*, and she hated herself for it. She lifted up her sticky tongue and swallowed twice. She wiped her palms on her jeans. Not that he'd be interested anymore. Not with her being even sicker than before. Clinical depression *and* cancer?

What a catch.

"What's up? You look—"

"Don't say 'terrible,'" she said and laughed to hide her discomfort.

Kyle held onto his mug like he wanted to put his hands elsewhere.

"I was going to say 'scared.'"

His eyes. She choked on a breathy sob.

"Water," she said and left the table quickly. When she came back, she was resolute. She sat down and sipped her tea, recognizing the stall, despite her moments-old resolution.

"What is it?" Kyle asked, worried. He touched her hand.

She jerked back.

"Shit. This isn't going to work. I'm sorry to waste your time." She hopped up again and fumbled with her coat.

She shoved her sweater into the felt bag she had been using as a purse.

She couldn't let Kyle see her fall apart. Her hands shook and she bumped into the table when she turned to leave.

"Wait wait wait," he said, rushing it all into one word. He stood up and grabbed her coat sleeve. "What's going on?"

He started to gather her into a hug, and she stiffened. *Shitshitshit.*

Don't let me cry. And don't let me hurt this lovely man, she prayed.

He dropped his arms and shuffled backwards, looking down.

"I'm sorry," she whispered. "I was going to ask you a favor, but I've changed my mind. I need to go now. Please forgive me." She pulled her bag onto her shoulder again and hurried away. She shook her head, trying to dislodge the Truth that hung on to her in self-righteous smugness. *It wasn't him she was protecting.* It was her. Reality stared, steely-eyed, into her solar plexus.

She held her breath and counted her steps to the car. She would not cry. She would be strong.

What was she thinking? He could do so much better than her. He was too good a man to be stuck with the likes of her. She was a mess.

Was Scotland that important after all? Which did she have the strength for—going alone, or risking a broken heart?

She opened the car door and Kyle was beside her again, his hand on her arm.

"Wait. There's something wrong. I know it. Would you please just tell me? We're friends right? Let me be your friend."

The drizzle above them morphed into fat rain. It dripped down the collar of her coat and, now without her sweater on, she shivered.

"Let's get in the car." Kyle gestured.

Inside the closed car, Heather felt a mild bubble of hysteria bounce around in her torso, like a pinball. She sighed. Apathy approached. This was too intense to deal with right now.

"Sorry to make this sound so mysterious. It really isn't." If she closed her eyes, she could get everything out in a rush and be done with it. "I'm going to Scotland for three weeks. My mom doesn't know. Jill was going to go with me. I have the tickets already. We were going to leave in less than a week, but now Jill can't go. I thought I could go by myself, but…"

She faltered. She followed the dark swirls and patterns behind her eyelids. She imagined being transported into a different time and place. A safe place. What kind of life would she have there in that existence? Would she be happily married with children? Would she be a travel writer, seeing the world?

"… but I'm too scared to go alone." She fake chuckled. It sounded insane to her own ears.

"Jill thinks I should ask you to go, but …" She dropped her shoulders in defeat. "I'm scared of that, too."

She opened her eyes, feeling soggy and wrung out. It wasn't what she'd meant to say at all, but it was what passed her lips. Kyle's previously stricken facial expression shifted to a slow, irritating smile. Like he knew he was having an effect on her.

"*Because,*" she hurried on, "because of this!" She gestured to his sexy grin.

"I am *only* your friend, Kyle. That's all. That's all we would ever be. If you come to Scotland with me, it is *only* as a fill-in for Jill."

Hope remained firmly attached to Kyle's face and Heather felt like a shit. He was totally going to make more out of this traveling-together-thing than there was.

But worse than that, what if *she* did?

Kathryn

"HELLO. MS. GORDON? KATHRYN? THIS IS KYLE. Heather's friend." Kyle's crisp voice traveled through the phone. Kathryn still used a landline and had found a funky turquoise rotary telephone at an antique store.

Antique, my foot.

Since when was thirty years ago "antique"?

Kathryn was perfectly willing to be Retro. And even Funky. But not Antique.

"Yes, of course I know you, Kyle. What's up? I don't think you've ever called this line before. Are you looking for Heather? She's grocery shopping." Kathryn's heart fluttered happily. *Maybe they'll get back together again.*

"No, ma'am. I just … I have something to tell you but …"

Kathryn pinched her eyes together, suspicious.

"I'm listening," she said.

"A couple days ago, Heather contacted me about going on a trip together—"

Kathryn gasped, knowing what was coming.

Or maybe she didn't. She forced herself to wait, to hear exactly what Kyle had to say.

"Ms. Gordon?"

"Yes, yes. I'm here. Go on."

There was another pause and then, "We're going to Scotland in three days."

"Three days!" Kathryn steadied herself at the counter. Her heart thumped. This explained the secrecy at the doctor's office.

"I don't know what went on between you two," Kyle said, "and I certainly don't need to know. I just somehow didn't like the idea of you not knowing until after we were gone."

Kathryn wrapped the phone cord around her finger, bending and unbending it, watching her skin blanch out and then redden over and over.

How could she do this to me? To herself! What if she gets worse there, and I can't get to her in time?

It was completely irresponsible—making Kathryn come fetch her from around the world if she had another spell. Well, Kathryn wouldn't have any of it. She wasn't going to drop everything and fly to Scotland. What about the farm? It was too much to handle by herself.

Heather was just immature and selfish. She was being a brat. That's what.

Kathryn's heart rate sped up and she angrily swiped at a hair tickling her forehead.

"So you're going with her," Kathryn sneered.

"Yes. And I promise to take care of her, Ms. Gordon," he said. "I won't let anything happen to her while we're gone. She'll start chemotherapy when she returns," he said. Kyle faltered. "Also…"

"What?" Kathryn snapped. She wanted to be off the phone so badly that she turned a blind eye to her own rudeness. She felt a headache coming on.

"The only reason I could rationalize snitching on Heather—"

Kathryn stiffened at the word "snitch." As if she didn't have the right to know what her own daughter was up to. Kathryn saw herself from the outside and shook her head, breathing deeply. *Calm yourself. She's an adult.*

"—is because I wondered if you could give me, or tell me how to get, any herbs or remedies that will help Heather if she, you know, *feels weak* while we're away."

"Why don't you ask Heather this?" *Jay-sus, this was terrible. Maybe I should just go with her.* She pulled the phone cord taut and sat in a dining chair.

"What about something from Flora then?"

Kathryn went numb, ice crystallizing under her fingernails and in her bowels.

"Flora?" She *told* him about Flora? Kathryn slowly rose from her seat.

"Yes. Heather says she knows all about herbs."

Flora's story and how it entwined with her own was special. Only Heather knew about Flora and about Kathryn's … *gift*. How could Heather do this? Sorrow pooled in the back of Kathryn's throat, gagging her.

"I don't want to ask Heather," Kyle said. "I just want to give her a drama-free vacation. Let me just give her that."

Kathryn coughed and sputtered and dropped the phone on the floor, spitting the sorrow into the kitchen sink. In its place a burble of anger grew, warmed by Heather's betrayal, hatching like a dragon's egg, in a torrent of fire.

Heather was completely *unreasonable* and *irresponsible* to go on this trip. There was no Get Out of Jail Free card called Scottish Vacation. She returned to the phone then. Kyle was still talking to her. She interrupted him.

"You don't want to ask Heather? You don't want to talk to her about her risk, her health, how many problems she could get into over there? Has she even packed her antidepressants? Do you even know about those?" Venom filled her mouth like saliva.

She was building to a rant. She had to get off the phone. Kyle didn't deserve to be yelled at by anybody, plus he *did* let her know about this *fiasco*.

"This trip is a terrible idea. I need to hang up now. Good-bye." Kathryn slammed the phone down.

She paced the house, talking to herself. Janet looked at her, Westie ears perking up. She jumped off the back of the couch and trotted around the living room, following Kathryn. They both looked to the window more often than was necessary, impatient for Heather's return. How long did it take to go grocery shopping for two people anyway?

She stomped around a little more and then found some work outside to try and calm her nerves. The headache did indeed come on full force though, so she had to retire to the bedroom for a rest. She knew she wouldn't be able to sleep.

Traitor.

Tears welled up and her breath hitched. Heather's betrayal far exceeded any hurt she'd ever caused Kathryn before. Heather knew how important Flora was to her, to Herbal Junction. She was why they were so successful. And Flora was her friend; she was family. Heather hadn't just betrayed Kathryn, she'd betrayed Flora, as well. Kathryn stared at the ceiling, breathing hard.

What if Flora stops visiting me now? Would she do that? Stop coming because Heather told? Kathryn's heart sped up. When did Heather do it? When did she tell Kyle? Kathryn squeezed her freezing hands, twisting her fingers, and curled up into a fetal position. *Why* would she do it? Flora was sacred. And not Heather's secret to tell.

The sorrow was back and leaked out of her tear ducts. Maybe Heather felt she had to. She wouldn't have said anything otherwise. Not Heather.

Kathryn's thoughts tripped and fell over one another, like dominoes.

What if Heather died over there? Feeling lightheaded now, Kathryn rubbed clammy palms on her sleeves. The bedroom walls closed in on her. All of a sudden she needed to see Heather. She went back to the living room and looked out the window again.

Still not here.

She waited on the couch, knees drawn up. Heather would die over there and Kathryn would be alone. Kathryn rocked herself, hugging her knees. If Heather wanted to go so badly that she'd sneak off without her, then Kathryn would've gone with her, like they'd originally planned. But with the input of the oncologist, *in conjunction with her treatments.*

Kathryn yelled out, punched a couch pillow, and dissolved into tears. *Heather will die and Flora will go away, too.*

Despite her horrible sadness and fury, she felt strangely proud. Kathryn sniffed and wiped her nose with the back of her hand, little sob spasms hiccuping through her lungs. Heather—in the face of her own death—actually did a rather brave thing. She'd stood up to Kathryn, who admitted to herself—through tears and laughter—that she could be pretty controlling sometimes, and Heather had done something she felt passionate about. She had made a decision—albeit a dangerous one—and stuck to it.

A fourth emotion beat wings against the inside of Kathryn's skull. Fear. Frightened for Heather's safety and health—that was understandable; *but why am I scared?*

She looked out the window again. If Heather would only wait a little longer. Scotland would still be there after the chemotherapy. Cold foreboding prickled at her scalp, and she rubbed at the base of her skull furiously, drowning out the little voice that said, maybe *Heather* wouldn't be there after chemotherapy.

When Heather returned from the store, Kathryn's panic subsided as fast as it had begun—anger blooming once again. She hid in the bedroom while Heather made her trips back and forth to bring in the groceries, not budging to help. If Heather was *fecking* going to Scotland without her help, she could bring in the god-damned groceries by herself.

Kathryn

Two nights before Heather and Kyle were to leave for the Portland airport, Kathryn wrote up an extensive list of instructions for them and taped their itinerary to the refrigerator.

Kathryn found the name and phone number of the nearest hospital in every town they were visiting and added that info to the list of herbal remedy instructions. She also added Dr. Chattel's phone number and Riverbend's urgent care number, *with* the country codes. That way Kyle could call from out of the country if he needed to.

Kathryn still disliked using the computer but had done the Google searches and found everything she'd looked for.

It was just a magic metal box with a card catalog inside. Kind of like Mary Poppins's bag.

The Dewey decimal system wasn't needed anymore, that was for sure. What a shame that the hours spent in elementary school learning about it were all for naught. Useless.

Never mind though. Computer searches were much faster. And they did help her with the broccoli thing.

She gathered all the dried herbs she could and double-packaged them in waterproof bags with copious amounts of tape. The tape was hardly necessary, but somehow it made Kathryn feel better seeing the secure bundles in a neat pile. She labeled them all with what was inside so that Kyle could prepare the steeped concoctions that would boost Heather's immune system.

Yes. She'd hung up on Kyle when he'd asked for her help, but she couldn't resist. The need to be *doing something* to help her daughter live far outweighed Kathryn's pride.

On a ridiculous whim, she'd also packed a sprouter and the broccoli seeds. The computer said the broccoli seeds were the *best* out of all the vegetables at suppressing the cancer cells. She still didn't know if that was true or not. You couldn't trust everything you read. But she didn't want to take any chances.

After surveying the contents on the dining room table, Kathryn slumped her shoulders cartoonishly. There was so much, it would all need its own suitcase. Heather would surely complain. Kathryn pressed her lips together. It didn't matter; Kathryn would pay the extra bag fee. It was important that they had these things. This was not the time to pack light. Kathryn shook out her shoulders and stretched her neck.

She went to the hall closet and found an old upholstered bag that had been her mother's. The leather handle was cracked and peeling, and the tapestry was faded in color, but Kathryn still loved it—and not just because it had been her mum's. She went to empty its contents and was delighted to find both Heather's christening gown and her first pair of shoes. She hadn't thought of those items in years.

She rewrapped them in tissue paper and smiled, even as tears leaked out the corners of her eyes. She hummed and continued dusting off the bag and emptying it of the crumbs that always seemed to be at the bottoms of all her bags.

You'd think I carry open bags of crisps with me everywhere I go.

Kathryn returned to the dining room and loaded everything from the table into the bag, including her instructions.

Drat! I should've made two copies. What if she loses this one?

Worried now that all her work would be for nothing, and, more important, that Heather would be without instructions, Kathryn wondered if she had time to take the list to the copy place. Or she could handwrite a second copy.

Stop.

Kathryn placed both hands on the table and took two shaky breaths.

Get ahold of yourself, Girl.

Heather was an adult. And she'll have another adult with her.

We'll be in contact while she's gone.

She'll be okay. Kathryn blinked.

Suddenly dizzy, she stood up straight, slowly,. She waited until the darkness behind her eyes cleared and went to put the kettle on.

26

Heather

THE NEXT MORNING, HEATHER HURRIED THROUGH the last of her packing.

A fire crackled in the living room, and Heather's door was open to enjoy its warmth. Her laptop played a Scottish folk playlist she found on Spotify. It was moody and depressing but strangely uplifting at the same time, somewhat like a movie soundtrack with a penchant for crescendos at odd moments, balanced out with lulls of flutes and harps. Regardless, it set the mood for Scotland and packing, and Heather felt passion and excitement rising within her. She would be leaving for another part of the world in less than two hours.

Eying the overflowing, yet still-too-small suitcase, she

changed her mind and took out the bulkiest items and decided to wear those on the plane to save room. Her black wool felted hat would be worn, too, as it would be crushed in the luggage.

Kathryn leaned in the doorway with a spiral notebook in her hand.

"Do you have a moment?"

Heather eyed her mother. Would she start lecturing? Heather couldn't handle that right now.

"Maybe," Heather said. She turned down the music and pushed the suitcase over and sat down.

Kathryn came in and squatted beside her and held out the notebook.

Kathryn cleared her throat violently and sniffed. Her face was angry, but somehow her words and tone were not.

"Since I won't be there to help you, and you insist on going right now *before*—" She closed her eyes and flicked her hand dismissively. "I thought you might not object to following this plan I've made up for you. It'll boost your immune system, and these vegetables and supplements specifically support cancer patients' systems."

Heather read through the items. The top of the page displayed a grocery list of eighteen different veggies, including the sprouted broccoli seeds.

"You don't have to eat *all* of those every day. Just make sure you eat *something* from the list every day. And not just a couple servings. A lot. Put them in everything. Make a smoothie in the morning full of kale and arugula; use a banana to sweeten it. Eat broccoli with dinner. Have cabbage soup. Whatever. Just make sure you eat tons of what's on that list."

Heather nodded. This wasn't her mother just being bossy. This made sense. And it was doable. It wasn't radical. Frankly, *not* going through with the doctor-ordered treatment plan right away, and letting the cancer cells multiply while on vacation was radical. This plan would just keep her as healthy as possible while doing it.

Under the vegetables was another list—one of tasks.

- Drink green tea every morning with breakfast smoothie.
- Smoothie should have: green tea extract, veggies listed above, multi-vitamin powder, and liquid vitamin D drops.
- At midmorning, take reishi mushroom capsule with raw juice if you can find it.
- Lunch: Steamed broccoli with whatever you are eating. Or a big salad with the greens listed above.
- Tea Time: More green tea, of course. If you are worried about the caffeine this late in the day, drink the herbal tea I packed for you for evening. And while not eating sugar for three weeks sounds horrific to me, remember that eating it actually suppresses your immune system. Be super mindful of when you eat sugar. *Make good choices, Poppet. I love you!*
- With dinner, eat extra of the veggie servings. In fact, it would be best if that's all you ate. What if you stir-fried ALL of the veggies on the above

list in avocado oil and added a little nutritional yeast? It would probably be delicious. Though maybe you wouldn't eat it every day for three weeks. Haha.

Heather smiled at the personal notes mixed in with the instructions and looked up at her mom. Kathryn smiled back, clearly on autopilot, because then she looked vaguely uncertain, like she didn't know why she was smiling.

But the hostility wasn't there anymore, and that was all that mattered to Heather. She breathed in her mother's love and breathed out her own relief that they were on speaking terms before she left for Scotland. In the back of her mind she recognized that it was only herself that had been doing the cutting off. No matter. The cooling-off period had been necessary for both of them.

She was proud of her mother's attitude. Kathryn had accepted Heather's choice to deal with the cancer on her return. Though, secretly, Heather wondered if she was making a terrible and foolish mistake.

What if I die out there?

Heather impulsively leaned over and hugged her mother. Kathryn tilted off balance and her knees made ominous cracking noises as she steadied herself.

"That's all I need. Me hurting myself just as you leave. Who would help me while you're gone?"

They both laughed nervously—the unspoken double meaning behind her question standing out like the sharp angle of a coffee table.

Kathryn

"CALL EVERY TWO DAYS OR SO TO LET ME KNOW about your health … and how much fun you're having!" Kathryn added. Her knuckles whitened on the steering wheel. Her shoulders positively ached from the tension she'd endured for the past week. She breathed into them and forced them down from her ears. She moved her hands to the bottom of the steering wheel and gripped it with her thumbs.

Heather sat next to her in the passenger seat. Her window, like Kathryn's, was lowered two inches.

"Mom."

Kathryn couldn't see Heather's eyes, but she knew they were rolling back in her head. If Kathryn sounded overbearing and slightly frantic, it was because she *was*. On both counts. She knew it though. Self-awareness had come with old age, but then so had entitlement. She might be driving her daughter crazy, but it was allowed.

Who wouldn't feel partially deranged at the thought of watching her terminally ill only child fly to a different continent, away from everything she knew, including medical treatments that would save her life, if only she'd *do them*?

Kyle, wisely, had his iPod turned on, earbuds in.

Kathryn took a deep breath and tried for a more adult course of action. "I hope you enjoy yourself. I really do. Now that you're leaving, I wish I was going, too. And not just to baby you." She moved her hands back up the sides of the steering wheel and switched lanes to avoid getting stuck behind a behemoth trailer.

"I've written down the name of a woman who was related to an old neighbor of my mother's, God rest her. A granddaughter. I've never met her or even talked to her. I only know her name because I still get an occasional Christmas card from her mother. She started sending them after Granny died. Anyway ..." She flicked her hand. "If you've a mind to it, you could perhaps get an insider's view of certain places. Go where the locals go. That sort of thing."

Heather touched Kathryn's shoulder.

"Thanks, Mom. That's a cool idea." Heather turned and looked at Kyle, now snoozing in the backseat.

Kathryn caught Heather's soft smile out of the corner of her eye. *This American Life* came on NPR just then and

Kathryn turned it up. They rode in comfortable silence for the next twenty minutes, listening to the program. Then Kyle woke up, stretched, and asked if they were close to the airport because he had to use the facilities.

"Sorry. Too many iced teas."

When they approached the airport, Heather spoke up again.

"Mom, you can just drop us at the curbside. There isn't any need for you to come to the ticket counter with us." She put her hand on Kathryn's shoulder again. "And thanks a lot for driving us to the airport."

"Yeah thanks, Ms. Gordon," Kyle said.

"Oh." Kathryn deflated. "But I wanted to walk you to the security checkout and everything."

Heather sighed and looked out the window.

"It's *really* not necessary, Mom." Her voice sounded clipped.

Kathryn's face heated up. Was she embarrassing Heather? Was she being annoying? She swallowed.

I don't want her to go. What if I never see her again?

She steeled herself. *Come on.* She was only going for three weeks—the cancer wouldn't kill her in three weeks, if it even *did*. The tumors were technically gone. It would be fine.

Fine.

She'd be fine.

Everything would be fine.

But if it wasn't, she didn't want their last conversation to be a petty argument.

"Well." Kathryn swallowed again and veered toward

the road for the departure gates. "I guess I don't have to come inside. There won't be much time for last minute visits if you're going through security. And it might be more complex since you're on an international flight, as opposed to a domestic one."

"Exactly."

Kathryn wanted to wipe the smirk off her daughter's face. She didn't have to be rude about any of this.

At the curbside, Kathryn turned the engine off and helped them get all their bags out of the trunk. Kathryn hugged them each once and let go with a forced lightness. Inside, her heart vibrated like a hummingbird's wings.

Heather and Kyle balanced the smaller bags on top of the larger wheeled ones and strapped their carry-ons onto their backs. Smiling, they waved their giddy farewells, and Kathryn watched them walk through the revolving door, swallowing them whole.

They were gone.

Kathryn got back in the van and drove away.

In order to avoid thinking of how quiet the house would seem without Heather there, and about how she hoped it wouldn't be a portent of things to come, Kathryn stopped halfway home and had a piece of pie and a coffee at a generic diner in a shiny strip mall.

All in all, it was a depressing drive home, and the grayness followed her into the house. At least Janet and Mica were glad to see her.

28

Heather

On the first leg of their trip, in Blair Atholl, Heather went to bed one night at the Atholl Inn and couldn't get up the next day.

"Don't tell my mom. I'll be better tomorrow. I just overtired myself."

Kyle gave Heather her herbal treatments.

"Maybe we could do a little less walking tomorrow?" Heather's self-disgust settled in her throat like thick mucus. She sipped at the smoothie Kyle made with the blender her mother packed. She'd bent over laughing when she saw it, along with the British BS-1363 outlet adaptor and the voltage convertor her mom bought at, strangely enough, Radio Shack.

She sipped again and glared around their beautiful tartan room. When Heather and Jill had made reservations, they'd opted for quainter accommodations than a generic hotel and had tried for a bed-and-breakfast type of place where their pocketbooks allowed it. Not the intimacy she wanted with Kyle though. It would give him the wrong idea. She wondered if it was too late to change the lodging arrangements in the next town they'd be in.

If she didn't pull her head out of her ass and pace herself and stop *ignoring* her cancer, she wouldn't get to enjoy Scotland at all. Why did she have to have cancer *now*? Why couldn't it happen at the respectable age of eighty-four? That's when cancer should show up, if it had to.

She leaned her head back against the wall. Kyle gathered a book from his suitcase.

"I'm going to do some reading. I was thinking of doing it down in the common room, unless you'd like me to stay with you. I can read here, too." Kyle looked around and smiled. "It's a sweet room."

"I'm sorry, Kyle." Heather gestured at herself. "For being sick on our vacation. I wanted to forget about it for just a little while longer." Panic fluttered between her diaphragm and rib cage, and she felt Mad Hatter mad.

"I don't want to be sick, Kyle," Heather whispered through the rising hysteria.

Kyle sat on the edge of the bed and grabbed Heather's hand. He pulled it to his chest.

"Breathe." Kyle breathed with Heather, who nodded when her panic lulled. "You are just jet-lagged. Rest. I'm tired, too." He held up his book. "That's why I'm going to take it easy today."

He stood up and pointed to the smoothie in Heather's hand.

Heather drank obediently.

"Shall I bring you your book, too?"

Heather nodded. She felt subdued. Deflated. And oh so tired. She'd just take a micro nap before reading. Kyle was right. She was only tired—still recovering from the surgery really. They'd walked all over Blair Atholl their first day there—saw the quaint post office, a museum that used to be a schoolhouse in 1823, and Blair Castle. They had been planning to go to Bruar Falls today. They were going to take a picnic.

"Thanks," Heather said, disappointed, accepting the novel he handed her. "I didn't sleep too well last night either. I thought after all our traveling and walking around, exploring, I would've slept hard, but—"

"It was the excitement of it all," Kyle said. He touched Heather's jaw and smiled.

She token-smiled and gently pulled away. "Plus, I'm not used to sleeping next to a man. I forgot about the one bed thing in bed-and-breakfasts. It wasn't going to matter with Jill. I guess we'll have to rebook in hotels from now on." She pulled the blankets up higher on her chest.

Kyle smiled with a twinkle. There was actually a twinkle. *Damn him.*

"Enjoy your book then," he said, and left the room.

AFTER WAKING FROM DISJOINTED AND AIRY DREAMS OF castles and a woman with blond hair, running, Heather wished to go for a walk. Kyle, of course, complied.

As they walked away from Atholl Inn, the gray afternoon greeted them with a nip and a gash. Heather and Kyle were wrapped in creamy wool scarves made in Scotland that were thoughtfully, and entrepreneurially, sold in the common room.

Clad in leather boots, sweaters, mittens and hats, Heather and Kyle walked toward the Bridge of Tilt and crossed over to the eastern part of the village. Gray sky met with soggy, foggy fields. They followed small roads, walking sedately and with child-like wonder at their new surroundings.

Heather wanted to see Scottish moors and a loch and cliffs. She also wanted to hear local music and see historical sites and learn more about Scottish culture.

Kyle thought that was a bit ambitious.

Heather thought Kyle was being overcautious.

Kyle thought Heather was being risky and not cautious at all.

"Let's not overdo it, Heather. Let's just take each day as it comes and see where it leads us. We have to be careful."

"I don't want to be careful!" Heather snapped. She bit off her thoughts and didn't speak them aloud, but they came whooshing through her brain like a wild wind.

This might very well be my last opportunity to travel. I want to see all I can before I have to go home … and what if I can't come back?

Somehow, Kyle knew what Heather had left unsaid.

He reached for and held Heather's hand. Heather allowed it, and they continued their walk.

They saw only a few people out and about. They both sniffed from the cold, and their breath puffed out in front of them. They simultaneously chuckled at the silliness of seeing the *breathpuffs* at the same time. Kyle squeezed Heather's hand, dropped it, and ran ahead with a shout and did a mittened cartwheel. Heather laughed again and when Kyle turned to look back, Heather waved heartily.

The crispness of the air stilled the ache in Heather's heart. She wasn't really in denial about her cancer, nor *too* scared, really. She was pretty confident that it could be eradicated with the follow-up round of chemotherapy. The whirlwind planning and the travel and the passport stamp had prevented her from thinking too much about her health.

Scotland was just as wet and gray and green as Veneta was. But there was something more. Excitement bloomed in her rib cage. Going on this walk today was her first opportunity to really soak up the essence of Scotland.

Well, at least the Scotland she'd seen so far, which, admittedly, had only been a couple days' worth. Still, she felt in her bones that no matter how much or how little she was exposed to it, she had found her right place in the world.

She laughed. In relief and in irony. Her grandparents had given everything they had in both energy, money, and stamina to get their family to America, and here she was—in Scotland—feeling a sense of home she hadn't ever felt before.

She shook her head. It was dreadfully cliche. And Heather hated nothing more than being a cliche.

She blew her nose with force and stuffed the handkerchief back in her pocket.

Kyle, up ahead, attempted a handstand, twisted, and fell on his butt.

Heather bent forward and laughed. She sniffed again, her depression lifting for the moment. Kyle got up and dusted himself off. He shouted back at Heather.

"I heard you laugh! Scoundrel!"

Heather waved again and then looked toward the sky. The sun wasn't visible through the thickness of gray, but its light permeated enough that when she closed her eyes and upturned her face, she thought she could still feel the warmth of it. Even a little.

This place would warm her.

She wondered if she could stay here. Not go back.

She looked at the village and the stones around her. The three houses in the distance left her with the peace and serenity of not having any neighbors at all.

Could she live here?

No. Her shoulders slumped.

Her mother.

She'd never leave her mother. Heather wasn't completely dense. She knew that part of Kathryn's insistence that Heather take over the farm was so that Kathryn would always have a home. A home to die in.

But what if I die first?

Heather shook herself. She wiggled in a little dance to slough off the negativity and wished suddenly for her banjo.

She would return to Veneta in less than three weeks. She would get the treatments she needed. And she would come back to this place.

She breathed in deeply and turned toward Kyle, who was approaching. He pseudo-punched her in the arm and they started back to the hotel.

29

Heather

"Dammit, Heather! You need to take it easy. You don't need to do everything on your list."

Heather's hands were shaking, and she leaned against the bathroom countertop in a moment of dizziness. They were in a new place, the next one on their itinerary. The city of Inverness.

"Let's just relax and enjoy the day," Kyle said. "We don't need to see another castle ruin. We can stay around here for the next three or four days."

She wondered at the logic of this. It was true. They *had* seen two ruins already. They *could* stay in. A long hot bath sounded delicious to her, truth be told. She just didn't want to waste any time. She could read and bathe

     Valerie Ihsan

in Oregon. There weren't castle ruins there.

Kyle slammed down his hairbrush and Heather flinched.

"If you don't take care of yourself, you'll end up dying here!" Kyle said.

Heather rolled her eyes.

He stormed out of their room for wherever. Probably across the lane to the neighborhood pub. Kyle didn't smoke cigarettes, but Heather got the sudden image of him lighting one up in a fury and stomping around in black boots.

Where'd that come from?

Since coming to Scotland, Heather had been having more and more vivid and elaborate dreams and she'd thought more than once about her mother and Flora. She wondered if there was any connection. Perhaps coming here, her ancestor's home, the home of her blood kin, was creating some sort of psychic connection to ... *Well that's just ludicrous.* Heather turned around and brushed her teeth with slow circles, partially holding herself up with the other hand.

She stopped mid-brush, spit, and inhaled as much oxygen as she could—feeling her heart thud inside her, promising animation. She was still alive. And she would stay alive.

Suddenly, she wished for her mom and the comfort of her bed. She wanted to get the medical procedures out of the way so she'd start feeling better. So she could come back here.

Kyle was right. Not about the dying part. That was

a bit premature. True, Heather had been preoccupied with her own death for days now. Probably she *would* die before she was ready, but then who was ever ready? She didn't feel like it would be too soon though. Even the doctor's suggestion of five years didn't seem right. *Couldn't* be right. Other people survived cancer. She'd be one of *them*. Kyle was being dramatic. She wasn't going to die on this vacation—not from cancer anyway. But he was right about overdoing it.

They didn't need to see every castle and cathedral, every loch and standing stone. When she stopped and thought about it, just being here was enough. And truthfully, her favorite moment of their time in Scotland so far was that walk they'd taken in Blair Atholl.

The air here was different. Whatever was in it matched up so perfectly and completely with her DNA, that when it permeated her pores, she felt more clean and real than she'd ever felt before. A sweep of embarrassed heat rushed across her face from the repeated cliche of it all.

When she'd read of people going to other countries and feeling *home*, she'd always rolled her eyes at the melodrama. But in truth, she'd been secretly jealous. She'd never felt altogether right for any place she wandered in. And now here she was. Feeling alive the very month she discovered her cancer. It was irony with a neon flashing "I."

But then maybe it wasn't this place after all. Maybe it was just being out of the United States. Maybe it was just being away from the farm. Maybe it was just being away from her mom.

Her face looked gray in the mirror, and the toothpaste

was making her feel sick to her stomach. Her hands were still shaking. She cupped water from the faucet to clean her mouth out and dried off her face with the hand towel next to the sink.

She contemplated the long walk to the bed. She could make it. She wasn't *that* tired. She just felt so achy. Maybe she was getting the flu again. She seemed to have a penchant for it. Heavy, slow steps took her back to bed where she fell asleep for the second time that day.

When she awoke around noon, Kyle was still gone.

The creamy walls accepted the mild sun and seemed to brighten, despite the dark day. The four-poster bed Heather lay in was delicious and decadent. The rest of the room was a hodgepodge of furniture that tried to look stately and failed. But the bed made up for it. It was certainly the focal point of the room.

The posters were a rich and glossy dark brown, with simple carvings. A thick down mattress cocooned her in luxurious comfort, complemented by the smoothest of percale sheets. A thin wool blanket and a down comforter on top made her sleep that of a queen.

The prints on the walls were not the sort she'd put up in her own home, but they looked perfect in this place. Cottagey. Floral. Old-fashioned. She liked them, and now that she thought of it, she did have a similar print of her grandmother's in her bedroom at home. It was of a woman in a long dress tending an English cottage flower garden. The colors were muted; impressionistic.

Thoughts of her mother neatly followed thinking of Granny's print.

Kyle was right. She needed to care for herself, so she could take care of her mom.

Who'd take care of Mama if I'm gone?

Who'd take care of the farm when her mom was too old?

Aren't parents supposed to die first? But then she felt like a shit for thinking it—practically wishing for her mother's death. She shivered in her gloomy thoughts.

I wonder what Mama's doing now.

She called her then, contrite.

"I'm not doing so well, Mama …Yes, I'm doing the herbs every day …Yes, I think I'm overdoing it. I just don't want to be sick, Mama." She started to cry. God, she *hated* it when she cried. She slammed her hand down on the bed.

"Come home, baby," Kathryn said.

Heather sniffed. "But changing the ticket will cost too much. I'll just stay. I'm going to take it easy from now on. I promise. Today, I'm just going to stay in bed and read."

"I already looked it up. It's four hundred dollars. If four hundred dollars will get you home so I can get you well again, I'm willing to pay it!" Kathryn said.

"No, Mom. That's ridiculous. Kyle says we should just stay around the hotel for the rest of the week and not do any sightseeing. I'll be uber-specific with my diet and take super good care of myself. And then we'll see. I'm sure this will pass." Her voice warbled.

"Sorry," Kyle said. He stepped closer to the bed. "Did I wake you?"

Heather stretched and blinked the sleep out of her eyes three or four times and cleared her throat.

"Yes. But that's okay." She pushed herself up and looked out the window to gauge the time of day. "What time is it?"

Kyle sat on the bed.

"It's 4:00 p.m. Are you all right? I'm sorry I stormed off like that." Kyle looked down at his hands.

Heather snorted.

"I slept almost the whole time. I didn't even know you were gone."

They looked at each other, then laughed.

"I can't believe I slept the whole day." She was still befuddled and looked around the room, as if it held the solution to her grogginess. "I called my mom though."

Kyle nodded. He ran his hands over his hair and combed it forward toward his face, like a tousled longer version of a Julius Caesar haircut.

"What did you do all day?" Heather said.

"Mostly I just walked and took lots of pictures. It didn't seem fair to do something without you. Wanna see the pictures?"

Kyle sat on the bed and scooted closer to Heather. He leaned back against the headboard and held his iPhone out, swiping through the camera roll with his finger, narrating here and there.

Heather was delighted with this impromptu bedtime story—even though she was just waking up. Kyle's body heat was enticing. Heather seemed so cold all the time now. Kyle smelled of crisp Scottish air—*what does Scottish air even smell like?*—and an afternoon pint from across the street, she guessed.

She had a sudden urge to lay her head on Kyle's shoulder but didn't.

What if he took it wrong?

Heather still felt groggy from her nap, her eyelids heavy.

"Am I boring you?" Kyle asked when Heather yawned.

"No," Heather smiled. She turned on her side toward Kyle and scooched down until her face lined up with his elbow. Now she could see the pictures better, and it was a more comfortable position. She was sort of snuggling, but not. Kyle didn't seem to react, so Heather relaxed into the storytelling.

Heather

Downstairs, the next morning, Heather and Kyle enjoyed the breakfast included with their lodging. Heather loved B&Bs. They were almost always cozy, cottagey affairs and they catered to the more romantic of furnishings, which was just perfect for Heather. That's what she liked. Her home was a little too prayer-flaggy, neo-hippie for Heather's taste. She liked the eclectic vintage feel of it, though, and her desk was beautiful. She liked old things, but beautiful-old, not rustic-old. Shabby chic was okay, if it wasn't too shabby.

The hardwood floors in the breakfast room were made warm with carpets in green and ivory. The lace cloths on the tables around the room were topped with glass to protect them.

Each table had fresh flowers, despite it being January. Perhaps there was a greenhouse the owner sourced from. Lovely mixed china graced each place setting. It was obvious the owner took pride in the presentation.

Kyle had brought down a smoothie for Heather. She was sick of them, but since she was feeling weak, she accepted it. She wanted to experience the good food the owners had promised on their website. Not this green thing. She took a sip from the plastic shaker cup, curled her lip and pouted.

"Give me that," Kyle sighed. He held his hand out.

He took the lid off and poured its contents into the stemmed water goblet on the table.

"If you have to drink it, when you so clearly do not want to, at least do it with style," Kyle said, and winked.

Heather dropped her chin and giggled. She felt warm in her face, and wondered if she was blushing. It was nice to be babied every once in a while.

All through breakfast, Kyle doted on Heather. Pouring her more water. Fetching her a cup of hot green tea. Going back upstairs to get her a sweater when she felt a little chilled, despite the fire crackling merrily across the room.

She ate small bites of her chevre and kale omelet and continued to sip at her green smoothie via the fancy glass. The glass did seem to make it more palatable. She smiled. *Kyle.* He'd been right. *Better to be stylish in my self-pity.* She giggled at herself.

"What is it?" Kyle asked.

Heather shook her head.

"Just laughing at myself. I'm happy."

Kyle's eyes softened. The maroon sweater he wore deepened the brown hue in his eyes, and the cuffs were long enough that they brushed his knuckles, hipster style. His hands were pale and his fingers long—a feature Heather envied for her banjo playing. Her own stubby fingers often looked fat in comparison, and it was harder to play the chords with shorter fingers. The banjo's fret board and neck were more narrow than a guitar's, and that was partly why she'd chosen the banjo to begin with.

"You look good today," Heather said. "I like the sweater. And, I've never said this before, but I really like your hair. *Tousled* suits you."

And now it was Kyle's turn to blush.

Alarm rushed from Heather's elbows to her temples. *Oops.*

She sat straighter in her chair. She picked up her napkin and dabbed her lips.

I can't fall in love with you again.

"I'm all of a sudden feeling a little dizzy," she said.

Kyle's face fell and he started to stand. Heather waved him off.

"No. Let me just catch my breath." Her heart pounded.

She wondered if Kyle could still love her. She hadn't really wanted to end their relationship last year, but she was too fucked up for the *real* thing. She wasn't good enough for him anyway. She couldn't saddle him with her complications. Once again, she felt the cancer diagnosis taunting her, shaming her.

"I think I'm done with breakfast. I feel like sitting in the common room and resting a little." She stood, and Kyle looked crestfallen.

"It's okay. I'm fine. I just want to rest for a bit. Take your time and enjoy your breakfast." She gestured to their table. "Come find me when you are done, and we'll decide what to do today." She smiled at him, trying to reassure.

She left, feeling like a shit. Using her weakness as an excuse to get out of the room was lame. She flopped into a wing-backed chair and closed her eyes. She didn't want to deal with this—her growing attachment to a man who was clearly out of her realm. And in the darkness of the room, another darkness drifted down from above and settled into her torso, trapped under her rib cage. It clung to her lungs and made breath difficult, strained. She would never have a man in her life. No one falls in love, and stays, with a person who has cancer.

Maybe the universe was trying to shake her up a bit. Maybe these were all learning lessons. She forced another breath and gripped the arms of the chair. She'd never felt like one of those "strong female characters" that her mom liked to watch in movies. She mostly did what she was told and seethed in silence, or settled, thinking it was all she could handle. Which was stupid. How would she ever get what she wanted in life, if she never actually *stated* what she wanted. Or tried new things.

What *did* she want?

She'd been trying to figure that out for forty years, but she was a little closer to knowing now. She began a list in her mind.

No farm. *That was a given.* She'd always known that, despite her mother telling her different.

She wanted a place of her own. One where she could make mistakes and not have her mother correcting them along the way.

She knew business management, having done that side of Herbal Junction for years. It wasn't her calling, but then whose job was, really?

What if she found a different job? What if she moved out? Could she do that? Could she take care of herself without her mother's help? *Once I get better from the chemotherapy, maybe.*

At forty years old, it was certainly time. Yes. She could. Her rib cage expanded, and she took a huge lungful of air. She would. Heather slapped the chair arm and opened her eyes. This cancer was a wake-up call. That's what it was.

Stop fucking around. That's what it was saying—this cancer with its sharp maw of pointy teeth.

Well, she would.

She'd stop fucking around. She still had time to live a life of passion. In evidence, her heart beat mighty and strong. Her new life would start with getting off the farm. She'd tell her mom that she was going to get a new job, maybe even start her *own* business. Some cute shop somewhere. She didn't even care what she sold. She just wanted to wear pretty dresses and have nice things around her. What was so wrong with that?

It seemed too late in life to be figuring out her career path though. She should've done it at eighteen, like everyone else. She felt hot and sweaty and tears welled up. Her euphoria suddenly squelched, she sniffed and wiped her eyes.

She couldn't leave the house without getting a new job first. She couldn't get a new job without dealing with the cancer first. It seemed she was stuck. Stuck on the farm again.

But no. She cleared her throat and sat forward on the edge of the chair.

This was just a checklist. One thing before the other.

First, get home and do the cancer treatments. Second, recover and start looking for new work. Then, tell her mother she was leaving farm life for good and move out.

Her momentum slowed again. *She's gonna freak.*

Heather wasn't completely heartless, but was it right that she had to give up on being happy just to make her *mother* happy? How was *that* the way things were supposed to go? It wasn't right. There had to be a compromise.

What if her mom hired a manager? Someone that did everything that Kathryn did. Then, she could retire but still live at the farm.

Heather leaned back in the chair and crossed her legs at the ankle. The manager wouldn't work though, would it? There wasn't enough money to hire anyone, and that was certain; Heather took care of the accounting.

Well. They'd just have to figure something else out. She didn't want her mother to lose her home, but she also didn't want to have any part of the farming business anymore. This was her wake up call. It was permission. No more farming.

And whatever else she decided, travel would be a big

part of her new life. Adventure and breeziness. No more being afraid.

Kyle walked into the darkened common room.

"Are you all right, then? Why are you sitting in the dark? Do you have a headache?"

Heather sighed.

She was wrong again.

The *first* thing she had to do was talk to Kyle. Her head pounded and she felt sick to her stomach. She wanted nothing more than to ignore it all and pretend that she wasn't falling for him again—*damn the four-poster bed!* How was she supposed to keep her distance when she woke in the night to him spooning her? It might ruin the rest of their vacation, but she had to nip this in the bud. She was wrong for him and had to make sure he knew it. Their quasi-flirty friendship had to be confronted.

"Let's…" Heather faltered. She stood and gripped her hands together. Did she want to walk outside with him and talk there? Was their room better?

She looked back and forth, seeking escape from the conversation she knew she needed to begin. Kyle stepped forward and cupped Heather's elbow.

"You look frantic. Are you okay?" he said.

Heather pulled away from his touch.

"I'm fine," she said. Too sharply. Heather winced at the sound coming from her mouth. She didn't want to *hurt* Kyle. Just discuss things. Figure things out. Control things. That stopped her. She wanted to control things? That was a first. And a last. She wasn't her mother. She never wanted to *control* Kyle.

"I'm sorry. I'm feeling a little weird. I'd love to talk. But I don't know whether I want to go outside and walk while we talk, or go back upstairs to our room."

A shade lowered in front of Kyle's eyes. She could see it. His eyes widened and he looked away.

"All right." He gestured to the stairs and walked ahead of Heather.

Heather followed, chastised. Was she making a huge mistake? If she could take charge of her life and move out of her mom's place, why couldn't she have a boyfriend, too? Maybe it would even make the rest of it *easier* to manage, with Kyle by her side.

Kyle closed the door. The room felt stuffy. They should've gone outside.

31

Kathryn

Heavy exhaustion pressed down on Kathryn's shoulders. Sorting clothes was not what she wanted to be doing right then. She walked away from the laundry and sank into the couch. Janet and Mica both snuggled against her legs. She wondered what Heather was doing right then. Ever since her last phone call, Kathryn had been more than worried.

Heather should be home. She needed Heather. And Heather needed her. They were a team. They'd always been.

Some people just weren't parent material, and that was true of Heather's biological father. When Kathryn told him of their pregnancy, he freaked and did the asshole thing for a few months. He'd wanted her to get an abortion, but—even though she was pro-choice—it wasn't the choice for her.

He'd moved to California shortly after she refused to terminate the pregnancy, "for a clean slate" he'd said. He sent money every couple of months until Heather was eighteen. He wasn't stingy about his responsibilities, he just had no desire to parent. When Heather was ten, and then again at sixteen, she'd reached out to make contact with him. She got polite responses and a picture or two, but he was never the one to initiate communication.

And then he died ten years ago.

Of cancer.

Shit. Kathryn skipped a breath. She'd never thought about health history from his side of the family. She had no way of contacting them anymore. She couldn't even remember his sister's name and didn't know if his parents were still alive.

It didn't matter now anyway. But the memory of his cancer-related death chilled her. The wind outside didn't help either. Empty lilac branches scraped against the living room window.

She moved to the fireplace and opened up the stove to poke the wood around a bit—exposing the coals—and added another chunk of oak. Oak burned slower, and the house stayed warmer longer. It was hard for her to tell the difference between the pine and oak sometimes, so she started putting them on different pallets on the side of the house. And when she brought stacks inside, she'd put the pine on one side of the woodstove, and the oak on the other.

The pine was great for getting a fire started, but it burned up too fast. Hot and fast. After the fire was good and strong, she'd switch to oak to slow it down. And that's when the heat would creep through the house and spread out like honey on a warm roll, fresh from the oven.

She found some hand-knit socks from her dresser and sat on the bed to put them on. They were thick and lumpy and didn't fit in any of her shoes, except her rain boots, but Heather had made them for her as a winter solstice present five years ago. Kathryn wore them around the house over the top of other socks, like slipper socks. Only without the non-skid details on the sole, which always reminded her of puffy paint. The kind that decorated sweatshirts in the '80s.

She missed Heather.

Why didn't I just go with her?

"I hate this cancer," Kathryn said aloud to the windowpanes. The wind sloshed the rain sideways onto the glass and pelted the uncut grass until it danced.

"And I hate that Heather's not here. And I hate that…" She swallowed. *I hate that Heather might die.* She refused to say it out loud. She was just working herself up. Heather was going to be fine. She just needed some chemotherapy, and then everything would go back to normal.

Already tired from the hate and the worry, she moved back to the couch and pulled a crocheted blanket over her lap. Hot tea sounded good, but she didn't want to get up and get it.

Who will take care of me when I'm old if Heather's gone?

Guilt swooped in. Disgusted with herself for the pity-party, she thought of her parents, now dead, and felt a different strain of guilt. Guilt for not doing. Not saying. Not visiting enough. Not *being* enough for them in their old age.

They'd lived in Springfield, a cheaper version of Eugene in many ways, in a condo with no yard and had had a home health aide who checked on them every day. Kathryn had visited them every Sunday morning, usually with Heather. Sometimes not. Most times not, she conceded. And never after Heather had graduated high school.

Heather had preferred to write them letters on pretty stationary.

She always did prefer to deal with unpleasant things from a distance and with pretty wrappers on them. She could deal with her grandparents getting old and smelling weird if she imagined them differently, and if she wrote on lavender-scented paper.

Heather had said it was more romantic that way and that everyone liked getting mail. If she visited, then eventually the visit would be over. But Granny could read a letter over and over if she wanted. It was a keepsake, really, Heather had said.

But Kathryn thought that Heather just didn't want to see her grandparents get old and die, so she'd created distance.

And perhaps that's what Scotland was right now. Her way of creating distance with lavender-scented paper.

Only this time it was with tartans and brogue. And the lochs.

Kathryn smiled. She did like the lochs she'd seen on her trips back with her parents.

And the clean air in the villages.

Kathryn closed her eyes and drifted into a hazy nap, with the woodstove keeping her warm and Janet curled in her lap. When she woke, she discovered that Mica had found a previously nonexistent spot on Kathryn's neck to sleep on, and she pushed him off. He *murphed* his reply and shook his ears with disgust, stalking off to a less populated area of the couch.

Kathryn cleared her throat and sat up, dislodging Janet as well, who took it far better. Janet yawned, stretched in a comical yogic combination of downward dog and upward dog, then wagged and sat, waiting to see what Kathryn would do next.

She chuckled and closed her eyes just for a moment more, capturing the echoes of the dream she was having before her bladder woke her up.

It was a Flora dream, but different. No movie this time. And only one visual. Old hands. And the warm scent of apple tea. Mostly, the dream left Kathryn with a secure and homey feeling. Of growing old and safe in her home.

Heather

AT THE TOP OF THE STAIRS, KYLE OPENED THE DOOR for Heather and they stepped into the room.

Heather's hands were sweaty and she wondered how in the world she was going to say what she needed to say in a way that wouldn't embarrass either one of them, or hurt Kyle's feelings, *and* would keep their friendship intact.

He closed the door and sat on the bed. He crossed his legs, tailor style.

Heather paced the room.

Finally, Kyle said, "What is it? What are you so worked up about?"

Heather looked out their window onto the River Ness.

Old High Church stood on its banks, on an ancient hill called St. Michael's Mount. Heather longed to see inside, but it was only open during the summer.

"You know, sometimes—on this trip—I think we act like an old married couple," Heather said. She turned and smiled sadly at Kyle. She turned back to the courage of the window, to the soft ripples of current in the river. "Maybe it's *because* of this trip. You open doors for me, we sleep in the same bed, we eat together."

"Well, we *are* traveling together. That's what travel companions do," Kyle said, and Heather thought she heard belligerence in his voice.

"Yes." Heather traced her finger along the window-pane. She sighed and turned to face him and lowered herself to the floor, crossing her legs as well. She began the only way she knew how.

"You are my very good friend, Kyle. We've shared some lovely things in the past, and some not so lovely things."

Kyle's face was a mask.

"But?" he said.

"No buts," Heather said. "I'll always love you, in my way. And I want to thank you so much for your help and attention since I found out I was sick."

"Of course, and I love you, too. *Friend,*" he added quickly, getting up.

Heather put up her hand, staying Kyle's approach. He sat back down, his face impenetrable.

It was silly; Heather knew him enough to know when the mask went on and why. If Kyle was trying to hide his feelings, the mask just highlighted them. And it highlighted what she was afraid of. If Kyle *did* still love her, then she had to confront her own feelings—which seemed to be butting in a lot these days. And she just didn't have the energy for that right now. Maybe that's what she should say.

She wiped her hands on her skirt, lowered her head into her palms, and covered her eyes. In her self-made darkness, she bluntly continued.

"I get the strong vibe that you care for me *like you used to*. Romantically." She looked up. "Is this true?"

Kyle hesitated, then nodded.

Heather's heart stopped, in the way that a heroine's did in nineteenth century love sonnets. Her eyes filled and she shook her head.

"I'm sorry!" he blurted out.

She had to get out of there. She couldn't catch her breath. He loved her. There wasn't enough air in the room. Placing a hand to her chest, she scrambled to her feet and headed for the door.

"No, wait!" Kyle said. He shot up and grabbed her arm. "Don't run away. Let's talk about this." He pulled Heather to the bed and they both sat down.

Heather wondered briefly about the intelligence of sitting on a bed with Kyle at that particular moment, but there weren't a lot of other seating options in their room.

Kyle tucked a lock of Heather's hair behind her ear and lifted her chin.

What to do, what to do, what to do?

How would she fix this? She couldn't let *him* love her. She would only hurt him. If she lived, she would always come with a lot of hard work and some not so fun times. Major depression was no joke. And if she didn't live…

"Kyle," she said. Tears fell. "*I'm* sorry."

"Why?"

"Because I need you. I've needed your help and assistance and your friendship and companionship. And I've seen what I thought was this growing love of yours, and I didn't say anything before. I'm sorry if that means I've used you." She wrapped her arms around herself. "You can't love me," she added.

Kyle chuckled and smiled like one would at a small child. "You can't tell me not to love you. It doesn't work that way."

"But I'm broken," she whispered and caught her breath.

Kyle gathered her into his arms, shushing her through her sudden sobs.

"I don't want to be sick," she said, snuffling into his sweater. "You can't love me, Kyle." She gripped him in a fierce hug. "What if I die?"

"Shh." He held her until she breathed normally and sat up of her own accord. He sighed then. Deep. Like he'd been holding his breath. Like he wanted to say something more.

But she didn't ask him. And he didn't offer.

Heather

Heather was getting weaker. She was so tired, with zero strength. They'd canceled the next leg of the trip, and now Kyle was phoning Mrs. McDoogle, the proprietor of Inverness Inn, from their room to coordinate a longer stay.

"She's just too weak to move on yet. Our flight is next Thursday, a week from now. Is there space for us to stay until Wednesday?" Kyle asked. He cocked the phone receiver out from his ear so Heather could hear Mrs. McDoogle.

"Bless you, child. Of course you can stay. January isn't a busy month for us, so there's room."

Heather could imagine her talking on the other line.

 Valerie Ihsan

She was a short woman with a square frame and curly gray hair that was always styled neatly whenever Heather and Kyle saw her downstairs.

"Will you need us to change rooms, Mrs. McDoogle?"

"No. There's no one due in after you."

"Actually, while we love the room we're in, and moving to a different one would be slightly inconvenient, I was wondering if you had a room on the ground floor. The stairs are a bit too much for Heather at this point. They tire her out an awful lot."

Heather laid her head back on the headboard. She was getting old before her time. Too tired to climb stairs. She hated herself for being that weak. It was lame, and embarrassing, and now alarming.

Maybe I should *go home early, and get in to see the doctor sooner. Yes, I will.*

She closed her eyes. She wanted to sleep and make it all go away. She had imagined her Scotland trip a lot different than this. She hadn't thought that she'd get sicker here. She'd wanted a tiny respite before having to deal with her chemotherapy.

She imagined the cancer cells multiplying and bulging into squishy tumorous monsters inside her body.

"No, luv. I'm sorry. We don't have any rooms for guests downstairs. It's just our living quarters off the back of the kitchen."

"All right. Thank you anyway, Mrs. McDoogle. We *do* like the room, and we have enjoyed our stay with you. We're glad to extend it," Kyle said.

He hung up.

Kyle puttered around the room and straightened their things into tidy piles. He set out Heather's pajamas and counted out the nighttime dose of herbs that Kathryn had sent with them. He filled a glass of water from the bathroom tap and brought it to Heather.

"Here."

Heather limply took the capsules.

Kyle held out his arm for Heather and she sat up. She slowly pulled her feet to the floor, and Kyle helped her stand.

Heather inhaled deeply and wobbled.

"Dizzy?" Kyle asked, concern darkening his face.

She nodded imperceptibly.

He held Heather's elbow and led her to the bathroom. She didn't know if she should feel grateful or irritated when Kyle put toothpaste on her toothbrush for her. Both, she conceded. But she snapped when Kyle offered to help her up from the toilet.

"I can do it myself!"

Kyle, without response, waited in the bedroom and got into his own pajamas. When Heather emerged from the bathroom, she didn't look at him. She hated her sudden dependency. She struggled with pulling her shirt over her head until Kyle stepped in to assist, but Heather drew the line at him taking off her pants.

She forced her fingers to exude strength that they didn't have and pushed the metal button through the hole of her jeans. She pushed herself up and shimmied out of them—down to her knees—one side of her underwear dragging down with them. She sat back down on the bed and heaved a sigh. She flicked her feet until the jeans fell off the rest of the way, crumpled on the floor.

Like me.

Worthless. Crumpled on the floor. Not able to even care for herself. Whenever she'd start to feel the cancer, or anxiety, whooshing in circles through her torso, fatigue always clamped down on it. Suppressing the energy out of it. Suppressing the energy out of everything. The low-grade fear was always there, though, like a headache.

Kyle handed her a pair of light blue satin pajamas. Heather stared at them and already felt the exhaustion of trying to put them on. She looked up at him then. And his face echoed the worry and fear that Heather felt.

"Would you help me?" Heather whispered. Her hands rested limply in her lap and tears dripped down her face.

Crumpled on the floor, worthless.

He, wisely or not, said nothing. He got Heather into her pajamas and into bed. He knelt next to her and smoothed her hair back and wiped the tears from her face.

"Let's call your mom tomorrow morning. We need to get you home," he whispered, and kissed her forehead.

IN THE MIDDLE OF THE NIGHT, HEATHER POKED KYLE TO wake him.

"Sorry to wake you," Heather chattered. "I feel really terrible, Kyle."

He felt Heather's forehead and audibly inhaled.

"You've got a fever, baby. Let me get you some Advil and another blanket." He rummaged around in the bathroom until he found what he was looking for.

"Four?" Heather said when she saw the rust-colored tablets in his palm.

"Yes. It's a high fever, and I want that temperature to come down fast."

They weren't traveling with a thermometer. Heather wondered briefly if Mrs. McDoogle had one they could use. Kyle must've had the same thought.

"It's only two in the morning. I'd hate to wake Mrs. McDoogle for a thermometer, and I don't think there's an all-night pharmacy around here to buy one. Let's just see if we can get it to come down." He took the water glass back from Heather and tucked her in. He pulled out an extra blanket from the wooden chest at the foot of the bed and brought it and Heather's knit cap to her.

"Do you want this?" he said.

Heather put it on. He covered her with the extra blanket and rubbed her arms and back through the covers, but Heather felt little warmth from it.

"Here you are, once again," Heather said through violent shivering. "Sitting by my bed."

"Whatever you need, I'll get," he said, matter-of-factly. He got up and—using the bathroom light to guide him—found a lone packet of Emergen-C from his backpack and added it to Heather's water glass.

"Here. Drink this all down, if you can."

Heather drank half. "It's so cold." She handed it back and tucked her arm under the blankets.

Kyle sat in the chair by the window and watched Heather.

Heather tossed and moaned and felt completely shitty.

Nothing like a high fever for muscle aches.

"I want to go home now." She whimpered like an abandoned dog in the rain.

"Yes. I'll pack up tomorrow and see about getting us a flight home. Just try and go back to sleep now."

Heather rolled over and tried to get comfortable. She rocked under the covers, trying to warm herself and disguise the fever pain. Sometimes moving helped for that.

Ten minutes later—still awake—she asked Kyle to read to her. She thought she heard a yawn, but he dutifully picked up the book that Heather had been reading two days ago and began on the bookmarked page.

"Leave the bookmark where it is," Heather interrupted. "In case I fall asleep, I want to know where I was. I don't know if I'll really listen to the story. I just want to hear your voice." Heather continued rocking.

After about twenty minutes, Heather felt Kyle approach and place an ice-cold hand on her forehead. Barely awake, she winced and pulled away.

"Still so hot," Kyle said, standing upright. He turned around in circles. "Do you want another Advil? Maybe there's some Tylenol in the first aid kit."

Heather didn't care.

"Do you want me to keep reading?" he said.

"I don't know." She'd stopped rocking, but her joints and bones and muscles hurt worse than ever. And here Kyle was putting his freaking freezing hands on her again.

"Stop. Your hands are so cold." She didn't even have the energy to move away this time. His touch felt like shards of icicles stabbing into her forehead.

He sat down in the chair again. Whenever Heather opened her eyes, she saw Kyle staring at the clock. She must've dozed because the next thing she experienced were those stabbing hands again. Only this time, she couldn't tell if he was actually there or not. She moved her head from side to side, looking for him.

Vibrations of sounds played around her, and she couldn't quite tell where her body ended and the sheets began.

Where was Kyle?

"Heather?"

She turned her head to where she thought he was, but no one was there.

"Heather? Can you hear me, baby?"

There he is.

She wanted to ask why he was so far away, but she must've fallen asleep again because she never got the words out.

34

Kathryn

WHEN THE PHONE RANG AT EIGHT ON A FRIDAY night, Kathryn ignored the ominous buzz on her scalp. It was quick. A blip. She wondered if she'd imagined it.

She hoped it was Heather calling to check in. Her scalp prickled again, and she was suddenly scared.

"Hello?" she said, her voice shaking.

"Hello, Ms. Gordon? This is Kyle. Heather's in the hospital."

Short and sweet.

Her heart thudded to her feet. Her hands suddenly ice.

"What happened?"

"She woke in the middle of the night with a fever. I gave her Advil and monitored her temperature as best I could without a thermometer, checking her every twenty or thirty minutes. It never went down. I mean…I couldn't tell."

Kathryn shook from cold, or fear, or—she didn't know. She wrapped an arm around herself and shifted from foot to foot.

"At 3:00 a.m. I called an ambulance. Heather wasn't responding to me." Kyle's breath heaved. "She looked right through me. She couldn't see me."

Kathryn's scalp tingled again.

"It was…*chilling*," Kyle said, and Kathryn knew what he meant. Felt that same chill.

Neither of them spoke then, but Kathryn could hear his breath rise and fall, fast, staccato, matching her own. Kyle cleared his throat.

"Anyway. She's in the hospital now. She's on fluids, and they've managed to bring her fever down enough that she's cognizant and a little more comfortable."

Something niggled in the back of Kathryn's mind. An idle curiosity, surely, but something made her ask.

"How high was her fever when she got to the hospital?"

Kyle didn't answer at first and dread filled Kathryn.

"In the ambulance, she had a febrile seizure."

Kathryn's eyed widened and dried out in the kitchen's dark air. She held her breath.

"*Jay-sus.*"

"Yeah. The paramedic said her fever was 41.1 degrees Celsius."

Kathryn couldn't remember how to convert that to Fahrenheit. She started to ask, but Kyle beat her to it.

"That's 105 degrees Fahrenheit, Ms. Gordon."

"*Jay-sus*" Kathryn said again. *Just like last time.* She put her hand to her forehead. "I'm…let me…." She stumbled on what she should say—should do. And then it hit her.

Of course!

"I'm coming," she blurted out. "I'll figure it out. I'll be there as soon as I can. Tell her I'm coming." Kathryn started to hang up the phone, but stopped and returned the receiver to her mouth.

"*Thank you* for calling, Kyle." And then she hung up.

After pacing around the house and talking to herself for ten minutes, she forced herself to sit down and take four slow deep breaths, even though every part of her screamed to hurry up.

Logic.

Heather said logic solved everything. Kathryn squeezed her eyes shut. First things first. The animals.

She called Tonya.

Of course she would help, Tonya had said. She'd come over in the morning.

"Just leave a key under the front mat," Tonya said.

Tonya would feed all the animals and stay at the farm with Bailey for as long as Kathryn was gone. And she'd communicate with any farmhand that Kathryn engaged for help.

"And call my cell phone anytime, day or night," Tonya said.

With that done, Kathryn frantically started packing a suitcase. Janet circled under her feet and continuously jumped from the bed to the floor and back again, following Kathryn everywhere.

The airline!

She stopped packing and went to the computer to look up flights to Inverness. Thankfully, the closest airport to where Heather and Kyle were happened to be in the same town. She thanked God that she'd made that extensive itinerary with hospital information for them.

It would take her two and a half hours to drive to Portland. *Drat!* What about leaving from the Eugene airport? It was considerably more expensive to do that because it meant changing planes more than once, but this was an emergency.

She cross-checked between Portland and Eugene and discovered that if she flew out of Eugene, she'd be traveling for *three days* just to get to Heather. Panic stabbed at her temples and she banshee-yelled into the living room, terrifying poor Janet. Mica bolted from the room.

"This is impossible!" Kathryn poked her crone finger at the computer monitor. Rage coursed through her veins and fueled her amygdala. She would get to Heather before it was too late.

Kathryn could leave Portland *tomorrow*, early afternoon, and she'd still get there a day earlier than if she left today. She purchased the outrageously priced tickets and almost swooned when she thought of what would've happened if she'd never originally said yes to going with Heather to Scotland. Kathryn wouldn't have had her passport, as she did now.

She wanted to throw together a carry-on bag and leave right then for Portland, but that wouldn't do anything. She chewed her lip, thinking.

She didn't want to wait for her luggage on the other side, so she packed her most essential things in a backpack, along with a water bottle and snacks for the flight.

She sat on the edge of the couch, her heart racing. What would she do for the next twelve hours? She doubted she'd get any sleep. Mica ventured back into the room and edged toward Kathryn. The warmth and texture of his fur released her from the strangling hold of fear for a moment, and she melted into the couch, pulling Mica onto her lap. He deigned to be petted and soon the buzzing in her ears was replaced by his purring.

The next day, she smothered Janet with kisses, made sure the cat and dog both had water, put her key under the mat, and left without looking back.

What good is the farm if Heather's not there?

SINCE KATHRYN HADN'T ARRANGED FOR ANY LODGING, she had a taxi take her directly to the hospital. That was the only reason she was there anyway. She could probably just stay in the hospital with Heather, on a cot in her room.

The taxi approached the tan brick towers of the Raigmore Hospital and pulled up to the main doors. Kathryn used her credit card to pay because she hadn't changed her dollars into pounds yet. She grabbed her overly stuffed backpack and climbed out of the car.

"Thank you," she called out behind her.

"I'm here to see my daughter," she told the volunteer with gray hair at the front desk. She'd called Kyle as soon as the airplane landed to get the room number, but he hadn't answered. "What room is she in, please? Her name is Heather Gordon."

"It's only 11:20 a.m., ma'am. Visiting hours aren't until 2:30 p.m.," he said.

Kathryn felt nauseated. The inside walls of her skull pounded to the bass of her heartbeat. She hadn't been able to stomach her airline breakfast. Nerves.

"Look. I'm her mother. I just flew in from the United States to see her. I got word she was ill enough to land her here," she gestured to the desk, her voice rising, "and so I've come. It took thirteen hours to get here. I need a shower and real food, but mostly, *I need to see my daughter.*"

Silence.

A sticky film of embarrassment coated her pores. She knew that honey drew more flies than vinegar so she started over.

"I'm sorry," she said to the belligerent jaw behind the welcome desk. If he was her ticket upstairs, she needed to make amends. And quick.

"Is there any way to see her now? I don't even know if she's critical, or anything. Can we ask someone else if it would be all right? I'm sorry. I'm really nervous."

He checked the computer terminal on the desk. "I'll send you to the seventh floor, ma'am. You can plead your case to the nurse on duty. The elevators are just through there." He crossed his arms and leaned back in his chair.

In the elevator, her hands began sweating. Her heart rate accelerated. What would Heather look like? It had only been two weeks since she'd seen her, but she didn't know what this cancer was doing to her. And was it the cancer that sent her to the hospital this time? Was the fever from something completely unrelated? It had to be. Cancer didn't give you fevers. Tumors weren't pathogens.

She went through her same speech with the nurse on duty, but with considerably more humility, and was pointed in the right direction. Thankful, Kathryn heaved a sigh and found the door she was looking for. She paused in front of it, suddenly afraid to go in.

She knocked, opened the door, and poked her head in. Kyle lifted his head from where he was resting in a chair. He motioned her in and stood up. His hair stuck up on one side and his clothes were wrinkled.

Kathryn walked in and looked over to the napping form in the bed. Her baby. Her grown baby. She was wearing the customary hospital johnny gown, her lank hair smudged against the pillowcase. Heather's already fair skin was driven even paler by her illness and the fluorescent lighting.

Kyle greeted Kathryn with a quiet hug. He took her backpack and tucked it beside the window bench. They both walked to Heather's bedside, one on either side of her. Kyle gently touched Heather's upper leg, and Kathryn clutched her purse handles. Heather opened her eyes and took them both in.

"Mama," Heather said with a croak. She reached her arms out and Kathryn dropped her purse and held her daughter's hands. She breathed a sigh of relief.

"It's all right now, darling. I'm here." Kathryn's eyes darted to Kyle, embarrassed. It was what she used to say when Heather was little and had woken from nightmares.

I'm here. Kathryn's shoulders tightened in resolve. *This time* the nightmare was ongoing though. She gripped Heather's hands tighter.

"I'm here now, so you just rest easy. Though I'm sure Kyle's been taking good care of you."

Heather smiled at Kyle. There was an ease and a tenderness between them now, Kathryn noted, and she was glad that Heather hadn't been alone. *What if she'd been mad enough at me to go off to Scotland by herself?* What if Kyle couldn't have gone with her? Kathryn shuddered to think of Heather dying from her fever, all alone in a strange land.

"I'm glad you're here, Mama."

"Me, too, Ms. Gordon," Kyle added. "Would you like something from the dining room or coffee bar? I can get it while you two visit."

Kathryn's stomach had been aflutter for so many hours that food hadn't been a great idea, but now that she was starting to settle down, perhaps it would do her good.

"Yes, dear. That would be kind of you. I'll take a sandwich of some sort. Egg salad perhaps? Or ham and cheese. And some juice, I think."

Kyle nodded, grabbed his wallet and left.

Kathryn turned back to Heather.

"Let me just get a chair." She wanted to sit as close to Heather as possible. She never wanted to be parted again.

And then she corrected herself.

She sat down and held Heather's hand loosely, sighing through a smile. Of course they would be parted. If not at her death or Heather's, then at trips like this one. Or even—Heather was still young—what if she married? It wasn't too late for her. Kathryn promised herself it wasn't too late. She kept a smile affixed to her face despite the blinked-back tears.

"Do you have everything you need?" She didn't see Heather's laptop. "Are you feeling up to reading? Do you want your laptop? Is it still at the inn?"

"Honestly, I haven't felt up for much. I seem to be sleeping mostly. I don't know if that's good, or normal."

"Perhaps you're just recuperating from your infection. When you sleep, you repair," Kathryn said.

"That's what I thought." Heather closed her eyes. "How was your flight?" She opened her eyes again. "I really do appreciate you coming all this way and spending the money to do it. I'm sorry."

"My dear! Of course I would come. *Always.*" They both fought the tears and voice anomalies that come from trying to keep one's voice steady. There had been too many tears already. Kathryn leaned back in her chair.

"Well, then. And what does the doctor say?"

Heather's face paled even more.

"It's just a nasty bladder infection, but…I start chemotherapy in two days," she said.

"What?" Kathryn bolted upright.

"Kyle told them I'd been diagnosed with ovarian cancer back in the States and that I hadn't yet begun treatment. They did another scan, saw a swollen pelvic lymph node and did a needle biopsy. The cancer's back. Not a lot, but since the cancer cells are in the lymph node now, it can spread easily, so I need the chemo now. Quickly.

But only if my blood work comes back okay. If I still have the infection, I can't start the chemo yet."

Kathryn's vision seemed to tunnel.

"Well." Alarm fluttered in her chest. She pressed her lips together. "I'm glad I came then."

"Me, too," Heather said. Her eyes spoke of fear. "I check out today but will be coming back here for my treatments."

Kathryn looked around the room, wishing that she'd thought to bring her knitting from home. Frankly, she was surprised she remembered her toothbrush, but at least she could've bought one of those. Yarn and needles were a little harder to come by. Maybe she'd ask one of the nurses or the innkeeper where Kyle and Heather were staying. She had a feeling she was going to be sitting and waiting a lot on this trip. It would be nice to keep her hands busy.

35

Kathryn

WHILE THEY WAITED FOR KYLE TO RETURN WITH the food, Kathryn heard news both desperately happy and desperately sad. And it scared her. Mostly because she didn't know what to do or say with Heather's confession.

Still groggy from her nap, Heather whispered her secret.

"He loves me, Mama."

Kathryn waited.

Heather gasped. "I love him, too." Her eyes widened, glassy and red, and she shook her head. "But he can't know."

Kathryn frowned. "Why not, dear? It's lovely to love someone who loves you back." Her heart yawned wide in hope for her girl. She'd always liked Kyle. He was a good boy. He would treat Heather well.

"You could be happy with him, Heather. Is this still about your depression medication?"

"No."

"What then?" Kathryn said.

"I have *cancer*. I know we're taking care of it, but what if—"

Kathryn squeezed Heather's hand, stalling her into silence.

"He's here because he wants to be. He knows about your condition. If Kyle has told you he loves you, then he doesn't care about that. Just accept the love he's offering. It's a gift from him to you."

Kathryn hoped she hadn't sounded too soapbox-y. The words, and the feelings behind them, were genuine, but sometimes the way she spoke to Heather could be mistaken for lecture. She kissed Heather's hand and softened her voice back to the whisper that the low light in the room called for.

"It's a gift," she repeated.

Heather closed her eyes. Kathryn gently withdrew and sat on the window bench, still wishing for her knitting. Farmers were never idle, and her forced stillness was a small torture.

"But what if he's just feeling sorry for me?" Heather asked suddenly.

She thought Heather had been asleep. Kathryn cleared her throat, then chuckled.

"So what?" Kathryn said. "*I'm* feeling sorry for you.

I'm feeling sorry for *me*," she admitted. "Even if he's feeling sorry for himself, *and* you, that doesn't negate the love he feels."

Silence filled the room again. Kathryn leaned back against the wall and rested until Kyle joined them.

WHEN GIVEN THE CHOICE TO STAY ANOTHER NIGHT OR check out of the hospital that same day at 4:30 p.m., Heather said she vastly preferred to go back to the inn. And when they arrived, Kyle introduced Kathryn to Mrs. McDoogle, who was beside herself—fluttering and starting a pot of tea.

"Actually, Mrs. McDoogle," Kyle said, "after being subjected to the hospital food for so long, I think a green smoothie would do Heather a world of good."

"Oh, brilliant, Kyle!" Kathryn said. Gratitude welled up through her body and out her eyes. She sniffed. "You blessed man," she said. "You're so right. We need to get Heather back in tune with Mother Earth. *And* get her outside!"

"First things first. May I help you in the kitchen?" he asked Mrs. McDoogle. They walked off together.

"I wonder if Mrs. McDoogle knows what a green smoothie is," Heather said and smiled. "It's not normal Scottish fare, is it?"

Kathryn giggled.

"Do you want to settle down here for a bit? I bet you're tired of sitting in a bed. Or are you looking for some privacy upstairs?" Kathryn asked.

Heather debated.

"Down here, I think," she said, eying the couch.

"Grand," Kathryn said.

Heather chuckled. "You seem to be slipping into the local vernacular, Mama. And your Scottish brogue is stronger here."

"I suppose that's true." Kathryn stopped fussing around Heather, realizing it would start irritating her in a minute. Kathryn sat down at the other end of the couch.

After Kyle brought Heather the smoothie, he decided to go on a run. He said that being cooped up in the hospital had made him a bit stir-crazy.

"You're looking a little worn out now, dear. Do you want to go upstairs and rest?" Kathryn said.

"Not yet. Let me finish this first." Heather sipped at her smoothie and sagged into the couch.

"It's really boring being laid up," Heather said. "I wish I had the energy to sightsee and traverse the wild Highlands and eat in the local pubs." She held up her glass. "Not drink fucking green smoothies."

Kathryn *tsked* but didn't criticize. She was just glad to be in the same room with Heather.

"Although, if I'm honest, this green smoothie is pretty heavenly after Jell-O and mashed potatoes made from a box."

Kathryn smiled.

"My favorite was the Lipton *cup-o-broth*," Heather said.

Kathryn laughed at the twinkle in Heather's smile.

Kathryn

KATHRYN WENT ON A WALK. SHE FELT INVIGORATED by the mild rain and nippy breeze skating through the Highlands of Inverness. She'd borrowed an umbrella from Mrs. McDoogle and followed her directions to a shop where Kathryn bought yarn and needles. Afterward, she wandered the streets until she got too cold.

She stepped into a public house and bought a bowl of Cullen skink. She remembered the fishy leek-and-potato chowder from her childhood. Her mother always made it in the chilling wet winters, when the potatoes were at their mashable best.

She unpacked her purchases from the yarn shop and started a hat for Heather. She'd chosen the softest of wool-blend fibers—designed for infants. No scratchiness at all. This hat would be for when Heather lost her long red locks. She knew Heather's pride would falter at that. Heather loved her long hair. It was beautiful and romantic and soft. Like Heather. Like this hat would be.

Kathryn cast off one hundred stitches in the round.

So far Kathryn hadn't felt a "coming home" sensation. She thought she might, since the rest of her family had lived here. And, even though she'd been there for only a couple of days, there had been no Flora dreams yet. Which was really weird. She thought Flora would be even more prominent here.

Kathryn's fingers wove through the yarn and grasped the size four needles. They moved seamlessly, dipping the needle into the first stitch, then wrapping the yarn around, over and over, needles clicking quietly.

The bartender brought over a cup of tea and her soup.

"And how are you today, missus?"

Kathryn lowered her knitting and smiled up at the jovial beer-bellied man.

"Oh, you know. I'm doing pretty well." She blew on her tea. "I'm just over from the States, visiting."

"Well, that's grand," piped the bartender. "What are your plans while you're here?"

Kathryn thought. She didn't really have any. She'd just come to see Heather. That was it. But now it seemed she was to stay a little longer than expected.

She frowned.

The bartender stepped away.

"Well then. I'll leave you to it, missus. Enjoy your soup."

"I'm sorry!" She faltered. "I…" She laughed. "It was an unexpected question, that's all."

The bartender looked perplexed. Of course the question wasn't unexpected. What else would someone in the tourism industry ask a tourist on vacation? It was quite logical actually.

"Well, you see." She set her teacup down and straightened the silverware on the table. "I don't actually know what to do." She looked at the bartender. "I'm here to see my daughter. She came here ahead of me on her own vacation, and got sick. I came to see her and help out if I can. But I don't know how long I'm staying, or, really, what to do while I'm here." She shook her head. "I can't just sit by her bed and wait. It would drive us both crazy."

The bartender looked distinctly uncomfortable. He alternated his weight on each foot, back and forth, and looked toward the kitchen, as if trying to conjure a problem that needed urgent assistance.

Poor man. He was just making polite conversation. He didn't really want to know any of this.

"Thank you for the tea." She raised the cup in salute and looked down at the table, dismissing him. It might have been her imagination, but he seemed relieved that the awkward exchange was over.

Strangely, Kathryn wasn't quite sure that *she* was though. She hadn't thought about her next steps—she'd been so intent on just getting here—and the bartender's question had shuffled the deck of possibilities. She wondered what hand would play out.

Her fingers itched for the knitting project, but she

ate her soup instead and bustled off for the inn and Mrs. McDoogle. On the way back to the inn, she had second thoughts about approaching her. She didn't want to burden a stranger with unwanted requests for advice. Mrs. McDoogle didn't know them or their situation. But there could be no harm in asking about lodging.

Mrs. McDoogle was on the telephone when Kathryn walked in. Kathryn raised the damp umbrella to catch Mrs. McDoogle's eye and placed it by the door where she could see it. She lingered in the lobby area of the house, which was really just the living room, and waited for her to get off the phone.

"Hello there, Ms. Gordon!" Mrs. McDoogle called out. "How was your walk? Not too wet, I hope."

Kathryn turned the corner and met with the happy lady. The warmth of her smile and her cheerfulness buoyed Kathryn's spirits.

"I wanted to talk with you about lodging options around here."

Mrs. McDoogle gestured to the eating area.

"I was just about to sit down with a cuppa. Would you like to join me?"

Enchanted, Kathryn said yes, even though she'd just had one.

She nibbled on the biscuits Mrs. McDoogle brought out with the tea and began her inquiries.

"You know of our situation," she said.

Mrs. McDoogle cluck-clucked and shook her head. "It's a sad thing, Ms. Gordon, to see your own child so sick."

"She's doing better." Kathryn suddenly wanted to defend Heather. She put her cookie down and dusted off her hands. "Kyle and Heather have already stayed past their original check out dates—"

Mrs. McDoogle put up her hand. "Now now, Mrs. Gordon. They are welcome to stay as long as they want to. We have the space right now."

"Yes. Well. The cost … " She smiled apologetically. "But never mind that right now. What I wanted to talk to you about was something else entirely." Kathryn's heart quickened, an idea forming on the spot.

"It looks like Heather needs to do her treatment here in Scotland, rather than at home in Oregon. I'd—of course—want to stay with her." The glorious plan arose in her torso and spilled out in excited spurts.

"I don't know yet how long her chemotherapy treatments will take, or if there will be other treatments she'll need to do after that, but I wondered about renting a small cottage for me and her to stay in while she goes back and forth to the hospital."

Mrs. McDoogle crossed her ample arms and leaned back in her chair. Her fingers tapped her elbows.

"Let me check around," she said. "In the meantime, you might check Craigslist on the Internet for any rental listings. But I do hope that you'll consider staying here, Mrs. Gordon. I don't know if the rooms upstairs would be suitable for Heather, but if it's the cost you're worried about, we can work out a deal for a long-term stay."

"Thank you. That is very kind of you." Kathryn was grateful. She had briefly imagined a sunny cottage with flowers in the back, but realistically, having the sponsorship of a local helping them was tempting. And it was winter anyway. There were no flowers.

37

Kathryn

THE NEXT MORNING, KATHRYN HAD BREAKFAST IN the dining room downstairs and used Mrs. McDoogle's computer to look up the directions to the part of town where her parents used to live.

She borrowed the umbrella again and called for a taxi to pick her up. She paid the driver with the pound notes that she'd exchanged with Mrs. McDoogle that morning, and stepped out of the cab onto the sidewalk of Old Mill Road.

This wasn't here in the '40s.

Kathryn blinked and turned to survey the street. Each house had a long front yard neatly encased by a short stone fence. The houses were all two-story stucco, yet each seemed to maintain its own individual charm. The driveways were all cobblestone or brick. If she sold her entire farm, maybe it would buy one of these homes.

Kathryn slung her purse over her shoulder and held onto Mrs. McDoogle's long black umbrella for later. It wasn't raining just then, but the sky was gray and the chilly air hinted at woodsmoke. She looked up the road, silent except for the cars passing at the larger cross street. She turned and looked down the other way.

She didn't quite know where to go, or really what she was doing there. The addresses were different now, and she wasn't sure where the old house might have been.

Suddenly it didn't matter. Kathryn sighed. She started walking and soon realized that the old paths her brothers and sisters once trod on as children weren't even accessible. All paved over. All built over. There was nothing here that called to her. Nothing that said, "This is where you came from."

The land maybe. Kathryn was a land gal after all. But it was hard to imagine what the earth looked like seventy years earlier. Quite different from now. She didn't need to be here; she needed to be in the country.

That is where she would find her Scotland. If she had one. *That* is where she'd find Flora again. Confusion and muddled worries blocked her breathing and befuddled her thoughts.

Scotland isn't my home. Why am I looking for it here?

A dark yawning space opened in her center and tickled the back of her neck. What *was* she doing here? Once Heather was well, they would go back to their real home. Scotland wasn't hers just because it had been her mother's. Kathryn had chosen Oregon. Veneta held her roots. She was planted *there*. Inverness was…a side trip.

Kathryn walked around the suburban block, looking for hidden wild spaces, and took delight in the little bits of green she could find. Well-trimmed grass never looked so out of place to her. In her mind, she'd always imagined the *wilds* of Scotland. These manicured yards didn't mesh with the stories her parents told her, and left a slight jarring sensation deep in her brain, behind the ear canal—like a particularly dissonant piece of music played too loudly.

She stopped and frowned. This was a dumb idea. *Where would she get a cab out here?*

There was nothing for it. She oriented herself toward where she thought a busier street would be and started walking again. She'd ask the next cab driver to take her to a natural park, some place she could take a nice long stroll and fill up on her quota of earth beneath her feet.

38

Kathryn

Kathryn woke the next morning in her own room at the inn, across the hall from Kyle and Heather's. She told herself that she didn't have any opinion about Kyle and Heather sharing a bed. On the one hand, she was grateful for his help and wished for a normal relationship for Heather. But on the other hand, that scary sadness poked at her when she thought of Heather living elsewhere.

Kathryn never *really* thought she'd have to live alone. Heather had always needed her so much. And Heather had never made a lot of noise about wanting to move out, which suited Kathryn just fine.

The soft cotton pillowcase rubbed against her cheek

as she shifted to a supine position. The room was still dark from a wintry, sluggish sun that wouldn't quite come out yet. She padded to the window and opened the curtains, looking across the rooftops to the horizon. There it was, the sun barely peeking out—clouds obscuring its brilliance.

She pulled a wool sweater on and returned to the window and opened it a crack. Cold air rushed in and the muscles around Kathryn's neck and shoulders tightened up. She breathed in the freshness, filling her lungs with the Scottish morn. She blinked the sleep from her eyes. The bracing air brought more than a chattering of teeth. She shivered. Kathryn grinned with her eyes closed, and the first of the morning's birds called out.

Heather was right to come all along.

She'll get better here.

Kathryn breathed in the promises of the dawn and felt a relaxation pour over her that she hadn't experienced since they'd first got the cancer news.

Heather was going to be all right.

Downstairs in the breakfast room, Kathryn found Kyle sitting at the window, looking out.

"Where's Heather?" Kathryn said.

He turned, his eyes red and swollen. He held a balled-up napkin in his hand. Kathryn stepped forward, her heart in her throat.

Kyle shook his head. "She's in the shower," he choked out, crying anew. He quickly wiped his face and turned back to the window.

Kathryn sat at a nearby table and tidied the already

organized silverware. She placed her napkin on her lap and let Kyle compose himself. *The poor man.* Kathryn hadn't thought much about Kyle's feelings. And now she knew of his and Heather's mutual love.

Kyle must've been going through the same—*well, some of the same*—feelings and worries and fears that Kathryn had until this morning. And Heather. Heather must be scared. She *knew* she was. Chemotherapy was up next.

She walked over to Kyle and put her hand on his shoulder, hoping it wouldn't embarrass him. She never knew how to act around this younger generation of men. She would never have comforted her *father* like this. It would've been shameful to him to be crying in the first place.

"I'm sorry, Kyle. I didn't think about how hard this was for you, too."

He reached up and put a hand on top of Kathryn's. He nodded, holding his breath until another sob forced its way out.

Poor dear. He looks so unhappy.

"I'm sorry," he said. He coughed and wiped his face.

Kathryn sat down next to him and pulled him into a hug. She patted his back until Mrs. McDoogle poked her head out of the swinging kitchen door. Kyle pulled back and blew his nose. He stood up, paced around, smoothed his clothes, and cleared his throat, clearly not wanting to make a public scene.

Kathryn shook her head apologetically to Mrs. McDoogle, who scooted back to the kitchen to give them space.

"You don't have to be strong for Heather," Kathryn

said. "It's all right to cry." Something else she never would've told her father.

Kyle returned to the window vigil, his shoulders rigid. Kathryn wondered if he was holding his breath again. Shortly, his shoulders lowered and his back softened. He blew his nose again and turned around to face Kathryn.

"Are you hungry?" he said.

"Heather will be fine. The Scottish air will do her good. Chemotherapy will shrink those tiny cancer cells to nothing and we'll all go home."

She'd seen it. She'd smelled it on the air. Heather was right to come here. This is where she would heal.

"I just had coffee. I wasn't very hungry." Kyle busied himself at the table like Kathryn had done, straightening the dishes, refilling his almost full water glass, and moving his napkin to the left.

"Maybe I'll get some air," he said. "Go for a quick walk."

Kathryn heard footsteps coming down the stairs.

"I'll be back in a jiff." He scurried out.

Kathryn blinked at the closed door.

Heather emerged fluffing her wet hair.

"Oh hi, Mom. Where's Kyle?"

"He went for some fresh air, dear." Kathryn stood up and held out her arms for a hug. "You look wonderful!" She smiled. Heather really did look healthier today.

Mrs. McDoogle popped out from the kitchen again to survey the situation. Evidently she found it safe to approach and began listing her specials off. Heather sat down and asked for green tea.

39

Heather

THE DAY ARRIVED FOR HEATHER'S FIRST CHEMO-therapy treatment. She'd had to wait a couple of extra days for her infection to pass and for her blood levels to be high enough to support the infusions she was about to start. Her mother called for a taxi and the three of them piled in. Kyle held Heather's hand. Strangely embarrassed at her mother seeing, she pulled away but touched Kyle's arm and smiled at him.

Kyle and her mom had gone with her to a class the week before with one of the chemo nurses. They were told what to expect during Heather's treatments. Heather had felt mildly reassured by the information, but it didn't stop her heart from racing now.

        Valerie Ihsan

She touched the chest port site below her clavicle. It was sore. Two days ago, she'd undergone outpatient surgery to have it inserted. The Demerol made her more comfortable and it wasn't too bad of a procedure, all in all. She feared the worst was to come.

Her heart continued to race and she forced her breath to slow. In her nose, out her nose. Belly rise, belly fall. Heather fought the rising helplessness and panic. Her life would be radically different from now on. No more avoiding it. *In through the nose, and out. Belly rise, belly fall.*

She was to receive an intensive treatment of drugs every week for three weeks, and then a week of rest before subsequent cycles. There would be six in all. Then more tests.

Her mom and Heather had talked about it. They'd stay and do the first cycle here in Scotland, and go home during the resting period to finish the remaining five cycles in Oregon.

It would take four hours of her sitting in a chair hooked up to an IV drip. They all brought books to read, and Heather brought her laptop and a DVD to watch with her headphones.

While she was glad that Kyle and her mom would be there, it also worried her. She wouldn't be alone, but what if Kyle saw her puking all over everything? If she was going to be sick, she'd rather not have anyone see that. But the nurse had said there'd be anti-nausea medication. Perhaps she'd be lucky and not have that side effect. There would be plenty of others though. *In through the nose; out.*

The three of them walked into the clinic adjacent

to Raigmore Hospital, and Heather checked in. Kyle and Kathryn pulled out their books and started reading. Heather waited with her hand on her stomach, *already* nauseated.

Since she'd had all the blood tests when she came in for the port surgery, they didn't have to wait too long before they were led into the infusion room.

As it was her first time, the staff had reserved a chair right by the nurses' station so they could keep an eye on her—to make sure she didn't have a reaction to the medication.

"There's so many bags," Heather said. It was daunting. First the pre-meds: Benadryl, Ativan, anti-nausea medications, steroids. And *then* the chemo drugs: Taxol and Carboplatin. She'd never remember all these names.

Kathryn tucked a blanket around Heather's lap and went back to her book.

After a while, Heather started feeling lightheaded. Was that normal or was something wrong? *Am I having a reaction?*

"Mom, call the nurse over," Heather said. "I feel weird."

The port site was sore and she was exhausted from the relaxation drugs they gave her, and she did feel a little sick, but she didn't know if that was from the adrenaline, stress, and steroids—or the Taxol and Carboplatin. The nurse said all that she was feeling was normal. Heather sat back and closed her eyes.

After returning to the inn, Heather felt recovered enough from her nausea that she asked for a smoothie, but that turned out to not be the best idea.

"I can't finish this." Heather sat up suddenly, the frightful knowledge that she was going to throw up rising swiftly to her throat. She wasn't going to make it to the bathroom. Shame blanketed her senses, and she brought her hands up to cover her mouth.

There was a sudden flurry of activity, and Kyle brought her upstairs and sat with her, while her mother stayed behind and cleaned up. Heather's stomach rolled and her brain sloshed and swung around in her head.

Whenever she'd start to salivate, she knew she needed the stainless steel basin that Mrs. McDoogle had brought up. She reached down to the floor to pick it up just in time. Her hands and armpits—even her hair—were sweaty, and she shivered in disgust. She wiped her mouth and handed the bowl to Kyle.

She closed her eyes so she wouldn't have to see any disgust mirrored in him. Embarrassment flashed hot in her chest and ears. She rolled over and silently begged for sleep, her skin burning like ice.

Heather

"LOOK WHAT I'VE GOT FOR YOU, MY SWEET," KATHRYN said, waking Heather. It was midmorning. Kathryn went to the window and opened the curtains. She placed a narrow planter tray in the windowsill. Three tiny green plants merrily reached out for the winter sun through the glass. Heather didn't know what kind they were, maybe evergreen seedlings. They looked vaguely like pine trees.

"You seem cheery this morning," Heather croaked out. "Where's Kyle?"

"He's downstairs. Breakfast is over, but Mrs. McDoogle has given us free rein in the kitchen to make you whatever you need." Kathryn folded up the bag that had previously held the planter. "What do you think? Can you stomach a smoothie right now?"

Heather grimaced. She was so sick of smoothies. *Sick.* What an understatement. If she didn't feel so wretched, she might've laughed at the irony.

"You need something. And if you can swallow a few sips of it, you can also take another anti-nausea pill."

Heather nodded the best she could without moving. "Can I…"

Kathryn leaned in close.

"Yes?" she asked.

"Hash browns. A little bit," Heather said.

Kathryn smiled.

When her mom left the room, Heather curled back up and prayed for sleep again. Fried foods were supposedly bad for the nausea, but she had a craving. *So there.*

All she wanted now was sleep. To sleep this whole part away. After today and one more treatment next week, her body could rest from the poison for a while.

They had to leave Scotland then. There was so little time left to look around before they flew home. Heather shifted on the bed and sighed, still exhausted. She couldn't imagine traveling right now. She felt like shit.

Eighteen weeks of this.

They'd rented a wheelchair because the chemo drugs had caused almost immediate neuropathy in her feet. Walking was awkward—her balance was affected—and it felt like her feet were perpetually in a state of "falling asleep."

But, with her mom's ever-present enthusiasm leading

the charge, the three of them took in the sites around Inverness. Heather carried on as best she could—until her fatigue wiped her out completely. It didn't help that, despite her exhaustion, she suffered from insomnia a third of the time. As the old saying went, she couldn't win for losing.

Blackness curled around her irises.

Her oncologist here suggested a short walk every day before one of her meals to stimulate appetite, and they usually combined it with the morning's sightseeing. Her mom insisted on taking her to some natural setting every day and helped her walk in the dirt or sod, saying that the earth would heal her.

Which could be rubbish.

But since Heather didn't have the energy to argue, or debate the scientific side of it, she followed along. And she was grateful for the outside excursions. It broke the monotony and the self-pity she easily found herself swimming in. She hated feeling sorry for herself.

Here she was in a beautiful place, with a man she seemed to be falling in love with all over again—against her better judgment—and her loving mother. She was getting the care she needed to survive her deadly disease, and she had the incredible belief from her mother that she could beat this and that they were in the very best place for her to heal.

Which begged the question, why didn't they just stay in Scotland to finish the whole thing? Money, of course. The National Health Service didn't cover non-Scottish residents, so Heather's care wasn't free. The hospital bills might be cheaper in Scotland, but the cost of lodging wasn't. And she knew her mom was paying someone to work the farm while they were gone.

Having use of the kitchen was a plus, making the cost of food not too much more than what it would be at home.

Home.

She did crave her own bed, her own quilt. She wanted Janet curled up next to her in bed. She wanted to linger over her banjo.

It *was* fun here though. If fun was the right word. Sometimes she wondered if she'd ever have fun again. Ever be happy again. But maybe she wouldn't make it anyway. She inhaled deeply and closed her eyes with the effort it took to draw oxygen into her lungs.

It's just the chemo poison talking.

She recognized depression. It was coming back full steam. She'd ask the doctor about her antidepressant dosage when she saw him today. She didn't like her new cynicism. Every day it seemed worse.

She rolled back over and inched her way into a seated position. She needed to pee and wondered if she could make it to the bathroom okay by herself. She wiggled her toes and stinging, sharp needles shot up to her shin. She sighed. *Better get it over with.*

She sat on the edge of the bed, testing whether she was too nauseated or dizzy to move safely. It was all right, so she put weight on her feet. She steadied herself on the bed posters, wincing from the pins and needles, and slowly made her way across the room.

After relieving herself—flushing the toilet twice as instructed by the nurses—she washed her hands twice. Once after using the toilet, and once after cleaning the toilet seat with the Clorox wipes her mom had picked up at the grocer's.

Apparently the drugs that flushed out of her were still quite toxic for anyone coming in contact with them, so they all had to wash things twice and wear double latex gloves for cleaning any bodily fluids. Heather understood the precautions, but it still made her feel unclean somehow, and embarrassed.

She washed her face and brushed her teeth and hair. She applied deodorant, too, then wobbled back to the bedroom.

She straightened the bedding a bit but chose to sit in a chair instead of the bed. Her body ached from lying down so much—though her joints and muscles could be hurting from the poison that dripped through the IV every week, too. She didn't know where her pain was coming from. She just knew it was there.

One perk to this will be a medical marijuana card back home.

Earlier in 2010, Oregon had passed a law that allowed medical cannabis to be sold from dispensaries with a doctor's prescription—though it had been technically legal back in 1998. She would definitely qualify for a medical card now, and she could openly smoke in front of her mom.

Heather smirked. She was sure her mom, an old hippie who looked forward to the Oregon Country Fair each year, had had many opportunities to smoke pot over the years. She probably already knew that Heather smoked. Heck, maybe her mom regularly did, too, and they'd been unnecessarily hiding it from each other all this time.

She guffawed, then wished she hadn't. Pain jarred in her head.

After Heather's tiny breakfast, the three of them took a cab toward Brodie Castle on the coast. Unfortunately, it wouldn't be as leisurely of a tour as they would've liked. They would need to return to Inverness in time for a 2:00 p.m. appointment. Another blood test and more chemo.

It was raining and cold and Heather couldn't seem to get warm, no matter how many layers she'd put on. Her fingers even felt a little numb. She rubbed and squeezed at them through her mittens.

They arrived and the cabbie took the wheelchair out of the trunk and set it up for Heather. Kathryn paid the driver, and Kyle wheeled Heather up to the front door of the castle.

After twenty minutes of viewing the architecture, the paintings, and the French furniture, Heather decided she didn't really want to be there after all. It was fascinating, of course, and a place she'd wanted to see, but today she couldn't seem to get into it and felt drawn instead to go back to the standing stones at Clava Cairns. Maybe tomorrow. They'd have to go home to Oregon soon, and there was still so much she wanted to see and experience.

She willed the chair to turn around and take her someplace outside, away from musty interiors and stale rooms. But of course it didn't. It wouldn't, unless she said something, and that would take too much work. And both Kyle and Kathryn had seemed interested in coming here. Heather forced her attention back to the interior of the castle and its plastered ceilings.

"I'd like to save some time to be outside before I go to the treatment. Can we do that?" Heather asked them.

She thought she saw mild disappointment flit across her mom's face. Kyle, though, seemed game for anything Heather wanted.

"Maybe I could take you around the grounds, and then your mom could stay here a little longer," he offered.

Kathryn shrugged, distracted by the Japanese artifact in front of them.

Impatience pinballed around Heather's shoulders and into her temples. She didn't want to be stuck inside *sitting*. She'd be *sitting* for the next four hours eating poison for fuck's sake.

She gritted her teeth and grasped the arms of the chair.

"Whatever," she spat out.

Kathryn

Kathryn missed being able to go out to the garden and pick whatever food she wanted. She asked Mrs. McDoogle if there was a farmers' market in town anywhere.

"Not this late in the year," Mrs. McDoogle said.

"There's a year-round one near where I live. I have my own farm back home, and whenever I get bored from my own selection, I go to the market and bring home something tasty," Kathryn said.

"A farm! Well that's something." Mrs. McDoogle nodded approvingly, or so Kathryn thought.

They were sitting in Mrs. McDoogle's kitchen, leaning over a small table together, gossiping in the old way, a cup of tea in hand.

"Where do you get your produce, Mrs. McDoogle? For the guests, I mean. You always have the yummiest dishes. They must be local. Shipped in food just doesn't taste like that."

Mrs. McDoogle preened and smiled and fluttered.

"They're my mum's recipes. Most of them anyway. Good and honest home-cooked food. And you might as well call me Helen, dear." She got up and set the kettle to boil again.

"Actually, I get the food from old Thom McVay down in Reelig. He sells to me off-season. Says it might go to waste otherwise. There's not enough produce to sell at a stand, but too much for his family, now that his son moved to Edinburgh."

"I'd love to put my feet on some farmland. I'm missing it." She wiggled her toes inside her shoes. She wondered if the farmer would mind if she came along next time Helen went.

KATHRYN SAT IN A CHAIR NEXT TO HEATHER IN THE infusion room. It was Kyle's turn to sightsee, and the Inverness Museum and Art Gallery was on his itinerary that afternoon. Kathryn was just finishing up Heather's hat. She'd tried it out on herself a couple of times to test the sizing, but her head was bigger than Heather's. Now that Heather was plugged into her drip, Kathryn used the opportunity to get the final measurements knitted into the alpaca hat.

Heather read her book. Then napped for twenty minutes. Then asked for her laptop. Then a glass of water. She often opted for napping as much as she could because it took the edge off the nausea, she said.

After the treatments, Heather went to bed for a couple of hours before dinner. She would read a great deal while resting, too.

Kathryn had often wanted to take Reading Vacations. She always had more books to read than she knew what to do with. Her needles clicked to a stop.

I probably won't have enough years left in me to read all the books I have at home that I haven't read yet.

The only time in her life where she'd done anything remotely close to a Reading Vacation was caring for Tonya after emergency gall bladder surgery. She wondered how Tonya was doing with the farm right now. She committed to calling her before Heather's appointment the next day, to accommodate the eight-hour time difference. It was already too late to call today.

"There!" Kathryn said. She held up the newly finished hat to Heather, who was watching a video on her laptop.

Heather smiled. "It looks lovely, Mama."

"Let me do one more thing, and then we'll try it on you." Kathryn hid the remaining yarn strands into the existing stitches. She stretched and blocked it to the shape she wanted and stood up.

"There," she said again, placing it over Heather's head.

"Mmm. It's warm." Heather closed her eyes.

Kathryn

THE NEXT MORNING, AFTER BREAKFAST, HELEN AND Kathryn went to Thom McVay's place to pick up some produce for the inn. Kathryn was itching to get back on farmland and talk to a fellow farmer. Kyle stayed with Heather. They were going to take a walk around the neighborhood to get some fresh air, and Heather would wear her new wool cap. The chemotherapy hadn't taken all of her hair yet, but large chunks of it were gone. Perhaps Heather was right to not shave it off. With the cap on, it wasn't immediately obvious that her remaining shanks were half gone and lackluster.

Kathryn assumed it was Heather's vanity that kept her from cutting it all off and from wearing turbans and

                    Valerie Ihsan

scarves instead. That's what she'd do in Heather's situation, but then she didn't actually know that. She had no right to make assumptions or judgments. What Heather wanted right now was what Kathryn was trying very hard to get her.

Helen drove a van. A green Chevy Astro. She placed a couple of wooden crates in the back to bring home the food.

They drove out of town and talked up a storm about each other's families, why Kathryn's had left Scotland all those years ago, and what she missed in Oregon right now.

Soon enough, they approached a long gravel driveway, longer than hers back home. Helen slowed the van and crept along until they reached a white stucco farmhouse. A man with an outrageous shock of thick white hair stepped out the door.

"Greetings!" he called out to Helen.

She approached the house with Kathryn following. Kathryn was suddenly shy to talk to this man, but then felt so at home on his small family farm, that she was soon herself.

"Thommy McVay!" Helen yelled back. "I've brought you a visitor."

"I see that. Come in, come in!"

Thom offered tea and introduced his wife. They briefly chit-chatted, and then Thom, Helen, and Kathryn all went outside with the wooden crates and harvested what Helen wanted. Thom and Helen settled on a price, and Kathryn was issued a standing invitation to drop by anytime she was in the neighborhood.

She left with ideas percolating.

"Why?" Heather said. "Do you think I'm so sick that flying home would kill me?" Alarm and bitterness laced her tone. She burst into tears. Kyle handed her a box of tissues.

"No! That's not it at all. Heather, you were right. I should've come here much sooner. I should've gone with you from the get-go, at least given you my blessing. It's wonderful here. I love it. That's the truth." Kathryn surprised herself.

"Your mom thinks we should rent a house and stay in Scotland while you rest between chemo rounds and then stay for your second cycle," Kyle said. "We can leave when you are strong enough to travel again."

"And…" Kathryn's eyes shone from the inside out. She could feel Flora finally there, in the back of her mind, in the realm behind the veil, cheering her on.

"And?" Heather said.

"And, if we feel like staying after that. Well…" Kathryn shrugged her shoulders.

Heather's eyes looked like they were stuck open. Staring. Permanently.

"I don't understand. What about Herbal Junction? What about our home? You've made it clear that you want to live out your days there, and that you want me to take on the farming business—"

"Which you don't want to do," Kathryn interrupted.

"Yes, but." Heather stopped, perhaps realizing the ramifications of her mother, at last, giving her the okay she'd wanted for the past twelve years.

Kathryn laughed, glee glowing and multiplying in

her cells. *Yes.* This felt right. This is what she could give her daughter.

"I met a farmer yesterday. I'd love to take you to his farm. It's beautiful. You can tell he loves the land. Would you like that? I can't imagine even you wouldn't get a little homesick for walking through some loved farmland."

Heather nodded, eyes still wide.

Kathryn laughed again.

Kyle looked back and forth between them.

Heather

Dread filled Heather's lungs. Her ribs hurt, her arms hurt, even her hair follicles hurt. It hurt to breathe. It hurt to lift up her head, and every time the cab bounced over a dip in the road, her head would smack the chair and her brain would slosh around, hitting the side of her skull.

They were on their way back to the inn from another treatment.

Heather hated the treatments.

The drugs that dripped into her veins burned like an iron poker fresh from a fire, stabbing through her subcutaneous layers and flowing everywhere her blood flowed.

The nausea was pretty bad, too, but she'd been pre-

Valerie Ihsan

scribed Sativex, a cannabis-based medicine that made it manageable. It all seemed like part of who she was now.

She remembered an old acquaintance she had who, when pregnant, had what some would call crippling morning sickness. It had lasted all day, every day, for her entire pregnancy. Others would understandably use that as a crutch and feel sorry for themselves—stay home all day—but not that woman. She had continued on with her life doing whatever she was doing. If she was on the phone with someone and felt the need to puke, she'd just excuse herself and be back on the phone in less than a minute, as if nothing had happened.

Heather wasn't really likening herself to that woman from her past. Indeed, she was feeling pretty shitty about life right now, could get a medal for feeling sorry for herself. But the nausea was manageable simply because it really was part of who she was now.

Meet Heather. She pukes.

The cab jounced around. Her mother had been checking into the possibility of getting a hospital shuttle to ride to the outpatient clinic every day, but so far nothing had turned up. Apparently Raigmore didn't have one of those. But it would be a terrific business idea.

How would that be different than paying a cab, though?

Her mom reached for her hand, but Heather pulled away and leaned against the door. Heather's window was down as far as the other passengers could stand it in the dark January evening. The cab driver was only willing because he wisely admitted that opening the window to prevent Heather from barfing on his upholstery was far better than "freezing his *baws* off."

He was a pretty funny guy, actually. Heather would've laughed if she hadn't wanted to sink through a hole in the earth and drain all her poison into the soil.

She made a mental note to ask for him as their driver again. If she spoke now though, words wouldn't be what came out. She inhaled the cold fresh air blowing in her face and then looked around for his name, usually located on the back of the seat in front of them. There it was. *Charlie.* Charlie Stewart.

The bumping and jostling was not merciful today.

Please, oh please, don't let me barf in his cab.

She swallowed and breathed in sharply through her nose, saliva production increasing. *Shit.*

She reached for her mom.

"Please stop the car!" Kathryn barked at the driver. *Charlie.*

He mumbled an expletive and began the trek across the three-lane highway.

Heather fought the rising—*everything.* Rising panic, rising embarrassment, rising poison fighting to get out of her body. She choked and gagged, her hands over her mouth.

Next to her, Kathryn frantically looked through her purse for a napkin. Too late. Heather vomited into her hands. It exploded out the sides and smeared on her cheeks. Tears of shame combined with the mess. Heather looked into the rearview mirror. Charlie shook his head and swore again.

"I'm so sorry," Heather choked out.

"It's quite all right, dear," Kathryn said. She roughly shrugged out of her coat and handed it to Heather.

Not understanding, Heather looked at her mother's kind eyes.

"I can clean the coat. Use it." She helped Heather wipe off her hands and face. Her jeans were beyond helping but they wiped up what they could.

The smell, of course, was terrible. Heather wiped her nose with her sleeve, cleanliness not mattering anymore. And besides, her hands were disgusting.

She wished they were home. She didn't even care which one. Just one with a bed. And a place to hide from her severe humiliation. She began to cry and leaned her head on the cold window.

"Never mind. We've cleaned the best we can for now," Kathryn told Charlie. "Let's just get home, and then I'll help you clean up the cab."

Charlie shook his head and clamped his jaw down. They made eye contact in the mirror. His shoulders dropped away from his ears and he sighed.

"It's all right. It happens. You weren't the first, and you certainly won't be the last." He smiled, kindly.

She didn't know if he was telling the truth, but it was nice of him to say it anyway. She wiped her eyes and everyone cracked their windows.

When they arrived at the inn, Kyle helped Heather upstairs, and Kathryn went directly to the kitchen for the cleaning supplies.

Charlie was probably grateful for the extra assistance.

Heather stripped out of her clothes, and Kyle ran a bath.

"Make it a shower. I just want to rinse off and get into bed. It'll be easier to clean with the wipes afterward, too."

"I'll do that," he said.

Heather nodded, miserable. She hated that everyone around her had to take care of her. And not in a let-me-get-you-a-glass-of-water way. It was cleaning up puke and sanitizing the bathroom twelve times a day. It was demoralizing. Sometimes she got angry, other times she just cried. Everything seemed so hopeless and difficult, even though she knew it was only a short-term problem. That's what she kept telling herself.

"Don't forget to use gloves," she sobbed.

"Baby." Kyle gently held her.

Heather sagged into him, feeling dizzy. She couldn't imagine what this was doing to Kyle. She felt so wretched she couldn't even think about the hopeless love that surged under her rumpled skin, trying to get out and tell him. *Fuck.* She did love him. What a shitty time to know for certain. Her head tingled.

"I need to sit." She balanced on the edge of the tub and suddenly wished for a spa day. Someone to wash her hair for her. A manicure, a foot rub.

Shaking, she used the wall to stand. She just needed to rinse off and use soap in a few places. She'd wash her hair tomorrow.

She reached up to tie it in a knot away from her face, and the crunchy smell assaulted her. She burst into tears again. She'd have to wash it. But she was just so tired.

Kyle opened the shower curtain and silently steadied her as Heather climbed in. And then he followed.

Fully clothed.

"What?" Heather started.

He said nothing. Only shook his head and tilted Heather's hair back into the shower stream. Heather laughed and cried and held on to Kyle as he lathered and rinsed her body.

Out of the shower, Kyle dripped all over the floor while he dried off Heather.

"Do you want to brush your teeth?" he asked.

"Yes," Heather said.

"Can you do it by yourself?"

Heather, slightly revived, chuckled. "Yes." What would she ever do without Kyle? Her eyes filled once again, but she turned to hide them. These tears were harder to explain. They weren't feeling-sorry-for-herself tears, or humiliation tears. They were more like so-much-love-for-a-human-being tears. But how could Kyle love her with the cancer, *and the puke?*

Kyle stripped off his wet clothes and threw them in the tub while Heather brushed, then walked Heather to bed.

She cried then, and he spooned around her—Heather's heart breaking open even more.

Kathryn

AFTER THAT TERRIBLE TAXI RIDE, KATHRYN HAD told Kyle and Heather she was going to take it easy and sleep in the next day, that they should do whatever they wanted without her tagging along.

Kathryn made her bed and got dressed but couldn't seem to face going down to breakfast. She didn't want to see Heather just then. She was generally confident about Heather's recovery, but this morning she felt exhausted from cheering Heather on. Exhausted from putting on a brave front. It was hard to not give in to the "what ifs" that crept up several times a week.

Indeed.

What if?

Kathryn sat down abruptly on the end of the bed, a rush of heat and fear flooding her face. She pulled her socked feet off the floor, hugged herself, and rocked on the bed, surprising sobs cascading out of her. She grabbed a pillow to muffle the sounds.

Fairly certain Heather and Kyle were already downstairs, Kathryn still wanted the privacy to emote, express, and scream into her pillow. She didn't want any of these negative emotions to stay inside. She had to get them out.

What if she still had some lingering doubt trapped behind her sternum, say, and it ballooned into disbelief and Heather died. It would be her fault then. Emotions have power. Beliefs have power. If Kathryn believed that Heather would die after all this, then Heather would believe it, and then it would happen. It would be Kathryn's fault.

Kathryn rocked and sobbed, occasionally pulling the pillow away to take gulping breaths before going back to it.

She cried for forty minutes.

And then she slept for twenty.

No longer exhausted, but certainly drained and starving, she shakily made her way down to the kitchen. Breakfast was over by then, but Kathryn found Helen in the kitchen doing dishes.

"What's happened to you?" Helen said when she saw Kathryn's face.

Kathryn shook her head, afraid if she spoke too soon, she would fall apart again. And while she was enjoying her new friendship with Helen, it wasn't ripe enough for vulnerability and tears of that kind of magnitude.

Helen dried her hands on her apron and approached Kathryn.

Kathryn blew out a breath and clenched her hands into fists. She would *not* cry in front of this woman. She cleared her throat and took a step back.

"I just need some tea and a little something to eat. I'm sorry I missed breakfast. I had a little bit of a rough morning." Her voice broke at the end, and she quickly turned and looked out the small window next to the little eating table that Helen ate at. The same table she and Helen gossiped and giggled at days before.

Hoping she hadn't offended Helen, or behaved too rudely, Kathryn paced the kitchen and forced idle chit-chat while Helen started a kettle for tea. When she felt a little more in control of her emotions—at least the ones she displayed for others—Kathryn offered to get herself some toast and jam.

Helen remained quiet and went back to her dish washing. After Kathryn prepared her tea and toast, she guiltily scooted into the guests' dining area. When she finished her small breakfast, she'd go back and apologize. She just had to compose herself a bit more.

45

Kathryn

"Are you wanting to stay just while she's in chemotherapy? Or longer?" Helen looked strangely suspicious.

Kathryn squirmed.

"I don't know. And that's the truth. I know we'll be staying as long as Heather needs treatment here." Kathryn gulped and looked down at the dining room table. Her usual bravado—nay, her *belief* that Heather would get well—seemed full of holes today.

"Sometimes," Kathryn said, "I don't think she'll be strong enough to travel for a long time yet." *What if she never is?*

Helen leaned across the table and put her hand on Kathryn's upper arm.

"You mustn't think that way. Keep up your positive thinking. It helps. It really does."

Kathryn nodded. She leaned back in her chair.

"Anyway," Kathryn said. "Since we won't know how long we need the rental, we need to find a place that won't require a lease. What do you suggest?"

Helen thought. She pursed her lips then nodded to herself.

"You could probably check the holiday lettings," Helen said.

"Yes. You're right. Vacation homes might work." A thought occurred to her though. "But if we run into a space where the owners have it already reserved down the line, we'll come back and stay with you for those few days."

Kathryn smiled, hoping she didn't sound patronizing. She just wanted to have more privacy for her grief and stress and for helping Heather get well. And the stairs were just too hard for Heather. They needed to find a different place that could accommodate their current needs. She didn't want Helen taking offense though.

Helen huffed good-naturedly.

"Well! You do what you have to do for your family. We all do. But please stay in touch. You're always welcome here."

THREE DAYS LATER, KATHRYN SIGNED A "VACATION" RENTAL agreement and picked up the keys from a woman in her midforties with beautiful prematurely silver hair and brown laughing eyes.

The *chalet*—as she already thought of it—was brown

with white trim, located in Reelig, seven kilometers from Inverness. As she approached in Helen's van, she saw that the side yard had a short wooden fence without paint. Ferns lined the fence and the wooded beauty surrounding the small house was balm to Kathryn's soul.

She pulled past the ferns and into a driveway of sorts, small gravel crunching in the tires. A picnic table stationed next to the front door looked promising for warmer days, but not now. It was currently wet from that morning's rain.

Kathryn wrapped her sweater closer around herself and headed to the door, made of glass. It was flanked by a three-foot-tall potted plant that surprisingly still held quite a few green leaves. She scanned her mental Rolodex of plant varieties and couldn't find one that matched. Some sort of evergreen, no doubt. If she didn't know any better, she'd say it looked like a miniature rhododendron.

Inside, the combined living room/dining room was cute and quaint—which was code for small, but in a charming way. It was certainly bigger than what they had now.

The beauty of renting a vacation home was that it was already furnished. Kathryn looked around the kitchen, taking in the electric kettle plugged in next to the micro-wave, and the gas range. There was, strangely, a washing machine below the dish drainer, and only one small sink. The blond wood cabinets were lighter than she liked, but the tile floor was new, and everything was well equipped. There was even a French press for coffee.

The living room to her left was painted a deep wine red. The furniture was rattan with bedspreads for covers. Rather than put off by it, she was oddly comforted.

It's homey.

She looked out the living room window and melted into the greenery. There were tons of trees, then a big field past them, and stretching off in the distance were snow-capped mountains. Okay, they might've been hills, but they were still amazing to look at.

Kathryn put down her purse and went in search of the bedrooms.

There were two. A yellow one with two twin beds, and a bone-colored room with a queen-sized bed. They both had plenty of windows. While she preferred the bigger bed, and thought that sharing a room with Kyle would be a little awkward, she also thought that Heather might appreciate the privacy of having her own room. Sometimes, when you're sick, you just want to be left alone. And Kyle probably wouldn't stay with them for long. She'd seen him working on his laptop; he must have clients to get back to. It amazed her that folks could get satisfaction from building something digitally and not with their hands. Give her dirt anytime; she could never be a web designer.

A quick stroll outside—not even three minutes away— were walking trails and signs of quiet wildlife within the "Fairy Glen," as the website called it. Kathryn stopped on the path and listened to the rustle of the wind through tree needles. The breeze nipped at her shoulders and she wished she'd brought her warmer coat from the inn. She thought her woolen sweater would've been enough, but out here in the woods, it was chillier.

Kathryn wrapped her arms around herself and walked back to the van.

Heather

I N   T H E   N E W   H O U S E ,   H E A T H E R   L A Y   O N   T H E   B I G   B E D
in her room. They'd moved over that day—the first day
of her resting period. Next up: one week without chemo
treatments.

Kyle and her mother had done the bag lifting, but
she'd helped with some of the packing, and it had worn
her out.

It was early evening now, just after dinner. They'd had
grilled chicken breasts with pesto and broccoli and had
shared a big cucumber, kale, and apple smoothie in the
wine glasses stocked in the kitchen cupboards.

Heather had been tired after the excitement of the
move and had gone to bed early.

　　　　Valerie Ihsan

"I'm here to tuck you in," Kyle said, knocking on and opening the door simultaneously.

Heather smiled and sank into the uber-comfy bed. It was much better than the inn's bed.

Perhaps these folks used memory foam.

Kyle climbed onto the bed and lay down on top of the covers, Heather underneath them. They faced each other. He touched her lip once and sighed.

Heather looked into Kyle and saw his love and hope and quiet devastation. She couldn't be imagining it, and her heart hurt to see it. Hurt to not pull him closer and make his cares and worries vanish with a wish.

His tousled hair looked as cute as ever, and Heather wished fervently for even that much of her own hair to be left. The chemo had taken the last of her hair two days ago. She now lived in the alpaca cap that her mom had made her. She was even wearing it now, in bed.

"Thank you," she whispered.

"For what?" Kyle smiled lazily and blinked slow, like a cat.

"For being you. For helping me so much—"

"Hush." Kyle scooted closer. He smelled of herbal shampoo and chocolate milk.

"I'm stronger when I'm with you," she said.

He winked and kissed her forehead. They both closed their eyes and rested in comfortable silence.

Heather chuckled through her nose, softly. Just a puff of breath.

"What?" Kyle smiled.

"It'll be weird not having you in bed with me now."

He raised his eyebrows lasciviously and snuggled up closer to her until they were thigh to thigh.

She giggled and flapped her hand at his chest.

His grip softened and he scooted his face so close to hers that she could feel his breath on her chin. Heather watched his lips. They were full and he worried them back and forth in such a tiny way that Heather wondered if she would've noticed if he hadn't been so close.

"Besides. Helping you isn't even an option," he murmured. "I don't even decide to do it. It just happens." He paused, visibly struggling. "I want to be with you for as long as I can. For as long as you'll let me."

Heather's breath caught on the inhale. He stared into her soul, boldly but still tenderly.

"I love you, Heather. Always. No matter what happens." He put his arms around her. "I always have."

He touched his lips to hers and warmth rushed down to her toes. Her tears of relief and sadness and compassion and fear dripped across the side of her nose and he laughed, drying them off.

She sniffed. "But…." If she died before saying "I love you," then he would get over her quicker. She hid her face from his, buried into his chest.

"How can you love me like this?" She heard her own voice, both hollow and muffled at the same time. He couldn't be saying the truth. No one could love her. She was, like the saying goes, damaged goods.

She wanted to believe him but didn't, so she did the only thing she could in such an awkward situation. She changed the subject. Better to let him out gracefully in case he was just saying it to make her feel better.

"What about Eugene?" she said. "What about work? This trip is already longer and more expensive than you anticipated. Don't you need to get back?"

Heather's heart pounded. She knew that what she was saying out loud was logical. She couldn't—*didn't*—expect Kyle to stay with her but, in reality, her heart wished it.

She wouldn't be alone. She had her mother there. But it was different. Kyle was support in a different way. And maybe he *was* telling the truth and had been for weeks. And if that was true—she gulped—she wanted the same thing as him. To have as much time together as possible.

In case.

"Work, shmerk." Kyle winked. "I've already called and talked to my boss. It's cool. He's agreed to hold my position open until further notice. The web team is picking up the slack. I just need to keep in touch regularly and let my boss know what's going on here."

"He means, let him know if I die, or if we're going home," Heather said.

"Shut up," he said gently. "You just *feel* like you're dying because of the chemo. Just wait. You'll feel so much better in a few days. Promise."

Heather reached out of the covers and touched Kyle's sexy hair.

"I like your eyebrows," she whispered.

He smiled with one corner of his mouth. Placing one finger under her chin, he tilted her face up and slowly and deliberately devoured her lips.

She touched his collarbone and his earlobe and inhaled his scent, offering him the tip of her tongue.

This is about to get complicated.

47

Kathryn

Kathryn finally worked out the public transportation system, which was basically nothing where they now lived, but if she could get herself to the bus stop near Reelig, then she could travel to Inverness without too much trouble—just forty-five minutes and five pounds.

She'd called the old farmer who Helen bought her food from and asked if she could meet with him at the local pub. His tone of voice told her that he thought it was a mighty weird request, but he acquiesced with gallantry.

She got off at the Inverness bus stop and walked in the chilly morning air to The Castle Tavern. The bartender recognized her.

"So you're still here then! How is your daughter?"

Kathryn smiled.

"She's hanging in there. She's taking a break from her treatment right now, and we're staying in Reelig. I'm meeting a farmer friend I just met last week. Thought I'd see if he had any work for me. I own a farm back home in the States."

She ordered Cullen skink again and treated herself to the house ale.

Thom McVay entered then, and she waved from her booth. She got up when he approached and shook his hand.

"Thank you for meeting with me."

They sat and the bartender took his order—a coffee and a chicken burger. Looking at the bartender's white, always clean, bar apron, Kathryn realized she didn't know his name.

"Finnegan," he said when she asked.

"Thank you, Finnegan. I hope to see more of you during my stay," Kathryn said.

"Thanks, Finn," Thom said. Finnegan left.

"I know it must be a strange request to meet me here, but I wanted to chat with you about work."

"Work?"

"I need some."

"Ah." He played with the napkin on the table. "I don't want to be rude, Ms. Gordon, but I'll cut straight to the chase."

Kathryn held her breath.

"I don't have any work for you, if that's what you're asking," he said.

Kathryn fought a sense of desperation. Yes, the medical costs were considerably less here, but they were still astronomically high. If she took out a mortgage on her home, it would catch them up to date, but how long would the money last? And with what money would she pay the rent on their new place *now*? Kyle's financial contribution helped—rent and food would thankfully cost less—but they were still running dangerously low of funds. They'd racked up the credit cards on the extra food and lodging they hadn't counted on.

"Thank you for your honesty, Thom. As you know, I run a successful farm back home. I'm good at what I do, and I love the land." She wished her soup was there so she could warm her hands on the bowl. "I know it's off season, but—as a farmer—I know that a farmer's work is never done. There's *always* something to do. If you don't have work for me—" She looked into his weathered brown eyes, crinkly around the edges from squinting. "—do you know anyone who does?"

She leaned back in the booth and put her hands in her lap so he wouldn't see them balling into fists. She needed work, and he was her only lead.

Finn brought the beer and coffee out, along with her soup.

"Your sandwich will be along shortly, Thom."

He nodded. "Thanks, Finn."

They both took sips of their respective beverages and averted their eyes from each other.

She took a spoonful of the soup and let the tastiness and warmth soothe her. She put down her spoon and allowed the bowl's hot temperature to seep into her bony fingers. She would wait until Thom's sandwich came before eating anymore.

They both sighed together, then chuckled at their timing.

"Look, Ms. Gordon. It *is* true that a farmer's work is never done, but you also know that during the off season, a farmer doesn't make any money." He shook his head. "Of course I have work for you, but not the money to pay you."

She shifted her hands to a new place on the bowl and hoped her soup would still be hot when his sandwich arrived. Maybe she would take one more spoonful. She did, and it was delicious. Suddenly starving, she continued to eat.

"Do you mind?" she asked, gesturing to her bowl. He waved dismissively.

A thought was percolating, but she waited for it to simmer a little longer. She'd wait until he was eating to talk any further. She could see Finn moving around in the kitchen off the bar.

They sat companionably, Kathryn quietly eating her soup and Thom sipping his black coffee. The sandwich came, and Kathryn ordered another bowl of soup.

"It was very delicious. My compliments to the chef," she said to Finnegan, knowing that it was probably him.

Finnegan beamed. "I'll be sure to tell him."

Kathryn giggled to herself. She was pretty sure she saw a little jauntiness to his walk back to the kitchen.

Thom bit into his sandwich and washed it down with

the water that Finn had brought out for them earlier. Kathryn smiled and launched in.

"Thom. As I said before, I run a modest herb farm back home, and it does nicely *all year round.*" She looked at him meaningfully. He finished his bite and looked at her, expectantly.

"I have a proposition for you—an idea."

"I'm listening." He sat back and crossed his arms.

He had a strange look on his face. A combination of irritation and curiosity, as if he wanted to know what she was going to say but knew he wouldn't like it. Kathryn began anyway.

"During the off season, our farm still makes products from our herbs that we sell to repeat customers. We also give tours of our land to schools and organize a fairly large gathering after harvest in the fall for our community. It's kind of a last chance to buy fresh from the farm for the year. We do it up big—a band plays, we serve pressed cider, make snacks for everyone. And we sell our products." She took a sip of her beer.

Thom relented the crossing of his arms and took a bite of his sandwich.

"I know that what we grow is different, and that it's wintertime now, but what would you say to me coming on as a consulting farmhand? I know I could come up with a few things you could do at your farm to increase your revenue."

He finished his bite and wiped his mouth.

"I just told you, I don't have the money to pay you. I'm sure your ideas are good, and frankly, I'd love to hear them." He shrugged. "But I can't pay you."

Kathryn leaned back, defeat pressing her into the booth.

She sighed and nodded, spent. Her beer didn't look that appetizing anymore, nor did the second bowl of soup.

"Thank you, Thom. I do appreciate your candor, and your thoughtfulness. If you hear of anything, let me know." She gathered her coat and purse and slid out of the booth, leaving several pound notes on the table for her lunch.

Thom scrambled to stand up and shook her hand.

"I'm sorry I couldn't do more for you." He paused, struggling. He looked like he wanted to say something but didn't.

Kathryn forced a smile. "Well, maybe I could still come out and look over the farm with you and talk about a few of the things I do back home." She set her purse on the edge of the table and put her coat on. "No charge, of course."

"That would be grand," he said as she walked toward the door.

She looked back, her hand resting on the door. She forced her smile again. "Thanks again. I'll be in touch about the visit. And give my regards to your wife. Bye now."

She walked out the door, feeling dejected but still proud. She'd done her best and failed.

How am I gonna pay next month's rent, let alone the food until then?

48

Kathryn

THE NEXT DAY THE CHALET'S PHONE RANG. SHE wondered if the call would be for them, or if it would be a wrong number.

It was Helen.

"I got the owner's number off the Internet, from the house website. I called them and they gave it to me."

Oh dear. I hope they don't continue to do that. She didn't want everyone to know how to get in touch, only those she wanted to be in touch with. It hadn't occurred to Kathryn to give the number to Helen. Honestly, she thought Helen was probably sick of them and glad they'd moved on. But she was happy Helen found them; it was good to hear a friendly voice this morning.

Kyle and Heather were out for a frosty nature walk. Kathryn had been sitting inside, staying warm, but feeling sorry for herself.

"The reason I called is, this morning I went out to Thommy's place to get my produce, and he said he wanted to talk to you again. Wanted to invite you and the young ones over for dinner with him and his wife, Margie. He didn't have a way to contact you. Thought maybe I'd see you and could give you the message. And so I have."

Kathryn could hear the smile in Helen's voice.

The next evening, Kyle, Heather, and Kathryn drove to Thom and Margie's place for dinner. Earlier that day, Kathryn had taken the bus back to the inn and borrowed Helen's van. She had tried to give Helen money for gas but Helen turned it down, so Kathryn went to the petrol station and filled it up for her anyway.

It was kind enough for Helen to loan her the van, she wasn't going to let her pay for the gas, too.

Thom and Margie invited them in with open arms. Kathryn had been nervous, feeling awkward from the lunch meeting two days earlier, but her reception was far different in the comfort of Thom's own home. Kathryn decided to let go and enjoy herself. Whatever embarrassment and foolishness on her part that had happened before wasn't on the table now. She'd been invited to dinner as a friendly gesture, and that was how she was taking it tonight. Dinner with friends.

Thom took all the coats and gloves, Heather opting to keep her hat on. Kathryn smiled. She was glad she'd thought to knit it right away. Heather was never without it now. Margie fluttered around Heather, brought her and Kyle warm things to drink, and mother-henned them even more than Helen had done. Kathryn saw that they basked in her warmth, and Thom and Kathryn were able to carry on an interesting conversation about his crops. Kathryn could talk Farm all night.

Later in the evening, after a tour of the home and a scrumptious dinner and dessert, Kathryn told the McVays about Heather's treatments and about struggling to pay for the medical bills. She explained that in the States there was no socialized medical care and, as self-employed farmers, they didn't have medical insurance either.

Both of the elderly hosts gasped, and Margie put her hand on her ample bosom.

Kathryn hadn't meant to dampen the evening or close it with a muffled thud—perhaps Scots didn't talk about money as openly as North Americans. She'd just felt comfortable sharing the information, and it *was* her reality now. She was only speaking truth.

"This is why I felt like I could be a great asset to you. I know farms, I love farms, and I miss my own." She smiled with genuine warmth at her new friends. "But don't worry about us. We're currently exploring options. Right now, we like it here. Heather's treatments will continue in another week or so, and I'll continue to look for work," Kathryn said.

The McVays looked at each other. Somehow this seemed like a good time to exit. She stood and thanked them for the invitation. They all gathered their coats and things and Thom and Margie walked them to the door.

"You're welcome anytime," they said as Kathryn, Heather, and Kyle left.

EARLY THE NEXT MORNING, KATHRYN DROVE THE VAN back to Helen's and stayed for breakfast. Kyle and Heather had opted to stay behind and sleep in, and to take another walk in the woods and do some reading. She knew Heather yearned for her banjo, and Kathryn had suggested that they try and find some live music to watch, or find a music store where they could play around on a new instrument. The idea had made Heather sit up straight and smile.

After breakfast, Kathryn talked to Helen about an employment agency. Helen didn't know if Kathryn could find work through regular channels like that, since she was not a British citizen. Kathryn wondered about work visas then.

What if I can't get a job at all?

It frankly hadn't occurred to her that she wouldn't be able to work. She knew she wasn't a "catch" for many employers due to her age—who hires a sixty-four-year-old with no skills other than farming?—but she thought she'd probably find *something*.

It was time to do an Internet search on work visas in Scotland. They simply wouldn't be able to stay in Scotland if none of them could work.

She thanked Helen and walked toward the bus station. Waiting there with her new umbrella in hand in case of rain, she missed Herbal Junction Farm like a stab to her solar plexus. She gasped and her eyes prickled. She missed her dog, Janet. She missed her fluffy chickens running around like toddlers, their wings uplifted behind them like superhero capes. She missed the Angora rabbits and missed plucking their fiber for spinning. She missed harvesting the herbs and drying them. She missed talking to her faithful customers and to the brand-new ones. She missed her Country Fair booth.

Her heart hurt, and the rest of her held the unmistakable signs of an impending anxiety attack—instant sweatiness and shallow breathing.

What if Heather doesn't make it somehow?

Kathryn's arms dropped to her sides, and she stared at a discarded Pepsi cup at the curb. Traffic noises blurred in her brain and created just enough white noise to envelope her in a haze of nothingness. Cars drove by, pedestrians looked at her, and the rain began to fall. But Kathryn didn't see or feel any of it.

The number sixteen bus pulled up, and the other people waiting with Kathryn jostled passed her to get on the bus. The driver called out and she blinked, her eyes swollen and scratchy. There simply weren't enough tears to lubricate them anymore. Maybe she'd lost her ability to cry.

Numb, she climbed on the bus, one heavy step after the other. She sat. She rode for thirty minutes before getting off and walked half a mile to Reelig Glen and on to the chalet.

Coming out of her stupor—a Wintry Walk in nature does wonders—she realized that some sort of extra transportation would be necessary. A half-mile walk wasn't much, but Heather certainly couldn't be expected to make the trek. Her treatments would be starting again soon, and daily cab rides would be around fifteen pounds—twenty dollars—each way. Not sustainable *at all.* But renting a car would be expensive, too.

Kathryn sighed. Her feet crunched on the gravel near her door, and she looked at the cozy chalet that she was starting to grow fond of. But it wasn't Herbal Junction. Homesick all over again, she carried her depression into the house, conscious of not letting Heather see it. She didn't want to talk to either Heather or Kyle, so she went directly in her room, waving to them in the living room on the way, a fake smile plastered to her face.

She didn't even know if they could stay for Heather's chemo treatments. They were running out of money that fast. She sat on the edge of her bed and scrubbed at her face with her palms. Circulation and alertness returned. She massaged her scalp and took off her shoes and coat and curled up in her bed, clothes on.

She closed her eyes and wished the world away. She couldn't make any decisions right now. There wasn't anything to decide anyway; they didn't have any choices really.

She needed to call Tonya. Maybe Tonya could think for her.

49

Kathryn

When she woke from her nap, she went to the bathroom, and then poured herself a glass of water. Heather and Kyle were playing cards at the dining room table. Heather was smiling and the two were laughing.

It was bittersweet. Why was everything tinged with smiles *and* tears, hope and despair existing at the same time? It didn't even make sense.

She filled her water glass again and got her cell phone out. She checked the signal outside, but there wasn't one.

Of course.

She needed to call Tonya to find out how the farm was doing, how Janet and the cat were doing, and if the rabbits were getting enough exercise. And, she needed to mortgage the farm. She had decided the night before while everyone else slept.

Kathryn gulped and fought back tears. So much for her "retirement." Subsisting on their farm income was hard enough, and now there would be a mortgage payment.

She shoved her cell phone into her pocket.

She needed to call her best friend. It was the only way to avoid mental breakdowns. That's how it worked for her. But, she didn't want Heather to hear her talking to Tonya. There were things Kathryn wanted to figure out before she discussed them appropriately with Heather. She didn't want Heather to feel any more stress than she was already dealing with. Stress could turn the tables. Heather seemed to be holding up well; she was feeling stronger. It might've been recuperation from chemo though.

Kathryn paced in the back of the chalet, eying the mountains in the distance, as if they held the answer. *Flora.* Kathryn gulped. Heather had told Kyle about Flora, and Kathryn hadn't heard from her since.

Heartbroken, Kathryn had hoped Flora would show up for her in Scotland, thinking that maybe the connection would be stronger in the land of Flora's birth and in the place she died. But nothing yet.

In the past, Kathryn had never tried to connect to Flora in any other way than through dreams. She just waited until they came, and if they didn't, Kathryn would sometimes say a little prayer to Whomever, asking that Flora come to her in a dream. Dreaming was the only way they'd ever communicated. And it really wasn't a *conversa-*

tion because Kathryn had never spoken back. She'd only ever received the messages.

Sure, Kathryn had said a thank you to the ethers when she woke from her dreams, but it suddenly didn't seem as if she had really made any effort at their "relationship." Kathryn frowned. Could Flora's feelings be hurt?

Well.

What better place to change that than in Scotland, in the woods? A small crack of lightness opened in her dark world, and Kathryn walked into the trees surrounding the chalet.

She walked a mile or so along a trail until she found a nurse log that she could rest on without disturbing too much of the foliage. She briefly wondered if there was poison oak in these woods, or the equivalent, and nestled herself on the ground with her back to the log. The ground was cold beneath her trousers but not unpleasant. Yet. It would probably seep in the longer she sat there. But that was okay. It was for a good cause.

Kathryn closed her eyes and rested her arms and head on top of her bent knees. This would kill her lower back and tailbone eventually, but for now she ignored her sacrum and any coldness she felt, and let her mind drift.

The wind whispered through the pine needles, and sometimes a gust would crack through the bare branches of the deciduous trees mixed in with the evergreens. She listened for birds or any kind of wildlife that would cement her in the here and now and connect her to the natural world. It was so easy to be pulled away from that with airplanes, cars, and hospitals, and IVs.

Insects crawled on the log, and she had a sudden wish to lay among the ferns and decompose in the forest with everything else. To peacefully become part of the life cycle and feed the next generation of forest-y plants and insects and larvae.

She breathed deeply and the coldness crystallized in her nostrils. Her hands were cold without her mittens, so she pulled them inside her coat sleeves.

Flora. My dear ancestor. I've loved our connection. I feel special and honored that you've singled me out—chosen me to communicate with. Thank you. In all these years, I don't think I've shared how much gratitude I have for you, your help in my business and in my personal life. I'm sorry about that. And I'm sorry—Kathryn's throat squeezed—*about Heather. I'm sure she didn't mean any harm.*

She paused when a sudden thought intruded.

The broccoli! Kathryn laughed, her eyes still closed. Today Kathryn pretended Flora was right in front of her, in this forest. She imagined Flora sitting across from her and the nurse log, listening.

I'm at a crossroads, of sorts, in my life, she told Flora. *Some pretty bad shit is happening around me.* She frowned. *And I need assistance. I don't know which way to turn. Which way to lean. I don't know how to deal with what's in front of me.*

The wind whipped up and swirled her hair. Usually she kept it in one long braid down her back; it was better for working on the farm. But since starting her vacation, Kathryn had taken to pinning her hair at her temples, leaving the back long and unbound. It was warmer on her neck, too. It seemed the wind sprites were taking great pleasure in mussing up the freed hair and dancing it around her shoulders and into her eyes.

She smoothed it back with her hands and tied it in a temporary knot. It still fluffed up and tickled her face. She had the sudden urge to laugh, and a giggle bubbled up from her chest. She threw back her head and gave a mighty chuckle.

Perhaps Flora could hear her and sent the wind to tickle her face and share her laughter. Flora was happy.

Kathryn smiled, happy to have her back.

"I love you," Kathryn said aloud, impulsively. The trees towered majestically above her, and the gray sky made the contrast to the winter branches that much more artistic. She couldn't see the moody mountains from where she sat, but just knowing the ancient cragginess was there was enough to soothe her. Nature settled Kathryn, brought her firmly into who she was. Allowed her to be fully Her. It calmed her panic. Always. And calm was what she needed these days.

Dealing with cancer sucks. Kathryn frowned. Her muscles were always tight and painful now, and she'd never known such stress in her life. She needed this peace in the forest, away from the cancer, away from Heather.

Metallic nausea burbled in Kathryn's stomach. What kind of mother thinks dealing with her child's *cancer* is too exhausting and so takes a time-out in the woods? As if the cancer's bad for *me*. Poor Heather. It was more terrible for her, of course. Kathryn felt a stab of guilt and swallowed back the stickiness in her throat.

She breathed the intimate oxygen of the woods until she felt grounded again. She focused on the contact her body made with the earth and shifted to a more comfortable position. She allowed the natural world to cradle her in peace once again, just for a little while longer, and she returned her attention to Flora.

She closed her eyes again and pictured Flora's red hair braided around her head. She imagined Flora wearing a simple wine-colored dress topped with a white apron. She saw her tucking booted feet under her dress and sitting on the forest floor with Kathryn again.

What do I do, Flora?

Kathryn didn't really expect an answer. Still, she looked at the mental image behind her closed lids, and Flora smiled sweetly. There were no words back from Flora. Only a sense of love and happiness.

Kathryn had no problem taking that from her.

Thank you. Thank you for your love, Flora. I'm so grateful for you.

She breathed deeply and opened her eyes, the lush green around her a balm to her senses. Kathryn stood and tested her hips and knees for stability, some parts feeling marginally numb from sitting so long on the ground. She brushed off the dirt and made her way back to the chalet. No wiser. No decisions made. No life made easier by spirits from beyond.

Kathryn laughed. But then again, maybe something had changed. She definitely felt better from her time in the woods with Flora, and Kathryn loved the idea that they'd just had a visit. She promised herself she'd go back every day to that same spot and have that nature-Flora-alone time. She deserved and needed that self-care. Staying alert and rested was hard right now. This would help.

When she walked in the chalet, Heather looked up from her book.

"Mr. McVay called while you were outside. I couldn't find you, so I said you'd call back. I took down his number in case you didn't already have it," Heather said.

"Oh." Kathryn felt momentarily lost. Reentry into the mundane from the spiritualism of Nature was always unnerving to her. "Okay. I will in a little bit."

Kyle was in the kitchen, plotting their next meal, she supposed. He smiled at her as Kathryn hung up her coat. The peace of the forest followed Kathryn for the rest of the afternoon, and when "the kids" planned a walk to the creek before it got too dark, Kathryn thought of calling Tonya on the house phone.

But the call would probably last longer than they would be out, and she didn't want Heather to walk in on Kathryn crying into the phone. Plus, what time was it in Veneta anyway?

Kathryn looked at her watch and calculated the eight-hour time difference. If it was almost four in the afternoon there, it was midnight for Tonya. Way too late. She'd have to call her in the morning in order to catch up. She could always e-mail her, but she wanted to hear Tonya's voice and have a conversation.

She put it out of her mind again. Too late today. Maybe she'd call first thing in the morning before Heather got up. Kathryn counted on fingers again. She'd have to get up before six if she wanted to catch Tonya before she left her house to pick up Bailey from Veneta Elementary.

And then there was Thom's phone call she needed to return. He wasn't a stranger anymore. She'd been to his house twice now, but Kathryn's skin crawled thinking of having to interact with even a very nice and friendly person right now. She wanted to hold on to the magical peace she'd felt earlier in the afternoon. She pulled that contentment around herself, like a peace burrito. She'd call him tomorrow, after talking to Tonya.

Her peace burrito sagged a little then, feeling guilty for ignoring a nice family that had invited them to dinner just the night before. But what could they possibly want to say the very next day? She frowned and took her book to the couch, hoping to escape into the story she was reading.

When the other two returned, they all ate a simple dinner and watched a DVD, then went to bed early.

Tomorrow. She'd call him tomorrow, she thought as she pulled the covers up around her. He *was* a nice man. She'd call him tomorrow.

50

Kathryn

KATHRYN HUNG UP WITH TONYA. SHE HEARD Heather moving around in her room and wondered if she needed any help. Kathryn didn't know what was too much when offering help.

Would she feel discouraged and helpless if I offered too much?

But then perhaps she was too proud to ask for the help she needed. Kathryn opted for a sneaky in-between version.

She tapped quietly on Heather's bedroom door and then cracked it open.

"Are you up?"

"Yes," Heather murmured.

Kathryn opened the door wider. Heather was sitting on the edge of the bed in her nightgown, a dresser drawer open in front of her.

"I was just wondering what to wear today."

"Are you wanting breakfast now, or do you want to wait? Kyle's not up yet."

"I'm not too hungry yet. Maybe I'll have a smoothie and a piece of toast in thirty or forty minutes."

"Okay. Need any help?"

"No. I think I'm fine." Heather hesitated. "Maybe you could just leave the door cracked open so I can call out to you if I change my mind."

Kathryn smiled. "Of course."

Kathryn puttered in the kitchen, heating up more water for a second mug of tea, and looked through the dwindling produce, herbs, and tinctures for Heather's smoothies.

The phone call to Tonya didn't put her mind at ease nearly as much as it did for Tonya, though she had managed to discuss giving her power of attorney for dealing with the mortgage details while Kathryn was still out of the country.

She sat on the little sofa in the living room and pulled Heather's computer onto her lap. They didn't have Internet at the chalet—she'd have to go to an Inverness coffee shop for that—but she could at least pen the e-mail she would send to Jack, as she had promised Tonya, about the extra farm duties that were accumulating. If the e-mail stared back at her every time she opened the laptop, she'd have a better chance at remembering to send it. She hoped

Heather wouldn't see it before Kathryn could send it.

After writing the e-mail, and drinking her cup of tea, Kathryn made Heather's smoothie. Kyle, now up, opted for coffee and toast with cheese. Kathryn ate a piece of cheese, too.

"Well," Kathryn said, standing up. "I suppose I should call back Thom now. I wonder what he wants so soon after having us over. Did we leave anything behind?"

"I don't think so. Plus, wouldn't he have just said so when he called the first time?" Heather said.

"True."

Kathryn settled into a comfortable position back on the sofa and dialed the number.

It rang four times before anyone answered.

"Margie? Hi, this is Kathryn Gordon. I'm returning Thom's call from yesterday. How are you?"

"Kathryn, dear! How lovely to hear from you."

Flattered, Kathryn smiled to herself.

"I had a grand time at dinner, Margie. Thank you again."

"You are *quite* welcome, dear. Now. Thom and I have spent a lot of time talking about you and your situation. We have an idea that might suit you. But if it doesn't, don't you worry. We'll help in other ways if we can. But let me pass the phone to Thom, and I'll let him tell you about it."

Kathryn's heart pounded. Did he change his mind? Was he going to offer her a job? She opened her eyes wide at Heather and Kyle. They waited impatiently to hear her report. She shook her head and waved her hand at them to carry on with what they were doing.

Thom got on the phone. She heard him clear his throat.

"Kathryn? How are you today?"

"Fine. Thanks for dinner the other night."

"Of course. Now. The reason I called was, as Margie told you, we were touched by your circumstances. We've thought a lot about it, and we'd like for you to accept an offer of lodging from us. Now, it's a small place, and there will need to be a little bit of work done on it to make it more comfortable for you, but, well, there it is. If you'd like to come and see it, I'd be happy to come and pick you all up."

"*Mom!*" Heather whispered. "You're turning red. What's going on?" Heather looked almost angry.

Kathryn realized she'd stopped breathing for a second and inhaled. Her face was hot, and she blinked her eyes to stem the tears that threatened.

"I—I don't know what to say, Thom. Such a generous and thoughtful offer. I, um. Yes," gulped Kathryn. "Yes. I think it would be a good idea for us to pay you another visit."

"Wonderful! What time is good for you?"

"As you know, Heather is between treatments, so anytime is good for us."

"How about today? At..." Kathryn imagined him looking at his watch. "...two o'clock?"

"Yes, that's fine, Thom. Thank you. See you then."

Kathryn hung up and burst into tears.

Heather and Kyle rushed to her, Heather next to her on the couch and Kyle kneeling before her on the other side.

"What is it?" he asked.

"It's wonderful, really. Just unexpected. It might be the answer to our money problems." She wiped her face with her sleeve. "You know how I get around compassionate people." She laughed at herself and Heather rubbed Kathryn's knee.

Kathryn sat back and Kyle crossed his legs. Heather and Kyle looked expectantly at Kathryn, waiting for enlightenment.

"Thom and his wife might have a place for us to live, rent-free."

Heather raised her eyebrows.

"Wow," Kyle said.

"He's picking us up this afternoon at two to show us what he has. He says it'll need some work to get it comfortable, but *think*." Kathryn rocked forward and bounced on the couch, her tears gone. "If we had a place to live without the housing costs, we'd have enough money to stay here for the rest of your treatments without having to risk the germ factory of the plane."

"Well, let's see the place, first," Heather said. Her eyes narrowed.

Heather

THEY DECIDED TO BRING HEATHER'S WHEELCHAIR, just in case she got too tired from the outing. None of them knew what to expect.

Thom arrived five minutes before 2:00 p.m. in his extended cab pickup truck. He put the wheelchair in the bed of the truck and helped Heather climb into the backseat, and Kyle followed. Kathryn sat up front with Thom.

"Off we go!" he said, merrily.

"I'd be lying if I said I'm not curious about today's adventure," Kathryn said.

He chuckled. "Well. You just wait and see. It might not do for you at all. In which case, we'll just have to put our thinking caps back on. You see, when you were asking for a job before, I couldn't see how I could help if I didn't have the money to pay you, *but* if I could pay you in room and board and throw some food in, well that could work, couldn't it?"

Kathryn agreed that, yes, it certainly could work. Thom was all smiles, and while Heather had certainly thought him a friendly man from the dinner party the night before last, she saw now that he was also kind and genuinely wanted to help them out. This wasn't a casual handout. This was inviting someone—*many* someones—to live with him. She put her head on Kyle's shoulder and reached for his hand. It was warm, and she breathed in his spice. Her shoulders relaxed.

It was a sobering thought, actually. She didn't know Thom. She didn't think she could live with a stranger, but then there were lots of things she didn't think she could handle but was managing some way or another. She sighed and closed her eyes. Kyle put his arm around her and kissed the top of her head. She was weary today. She couldn't imagine starting another round of treatment while feeling this depleted, let alone while moving again *and* losing their privacy.

When they arrived, they first went into the McVay's house. Heather sat down right away at the dining room table. Kyle sought her eyes. His lips were set with concern. Heather assured him that she was all right, just tired. She wanted to look at the room but shooed them off, asking them to look at it first and report back.

"If you think it'll work for us, then I'll go and see it. I just need to rest here first," Heather said to Kathryn.

"I'll stay with you," Kyle said.

Margie stepped forward.

"*I'll* stay. You go and look at the room."

He thanked her, kissed Heather's fingertips, and joined Thom and Kathryn.

Margie prepared tea and a plate of scones while she and Heather chatted about Scotland and waited for the others. When her mother returned, Heather identified her expression right off. A kind of fervor. The wheels were turning. Kyle looked thoughtful but was frowning. They sat down next to Heather at the table.

"It's small. But it'll work," Kathryn said. "There's some clean up to do, and we'll need to add furnishings. If you're up for sharing a room three ways, I'm up for making it work. I'll see what I can get done before your treatment starts up again."

"Well then. I best go see it. How far of a walk is it?"

"Mmm. Let's bring the chair. It's not too far, but the ground's uneven, and if you're feeling fatigued today, you should treat yourself to the wheelchair." Kathryn pushed back and stood up, picking up a scone off the platter. She smiled at Margie.

Heather liked her mother's "treat yourself" perspective. Instead of whining that she wasn't strong enough to do something, she would now "treat" herself to the use of the chair. It made it all the more regal, much like drinking her smoothies out of wine glasses. She looked at her loved ones by her side and thanked the universe for bringing them together during these hard days. It made them bearable.

Her mom pushed her about one hundred yards from the house to a somewhat crusty-looking barn. It was definitely *weathered*, that was for sure. Thom pushed aside the rolling barn door and they all went inside.

"It was wired for electricity some years back when my son moved to the city, so I could get a milking machine; William did all the milking before that. Now there's only two cows. That's enough for us. It got to be too much work for me by myself. I sold the rest. Now I just milk the last two by hand," Thom said.

He flipped on the meager lighting, and Heather could see that since most of the stalls no longer housed cows, they were used for storage for the rest of the farm. She was familiar with what farm storage looked like. This didn't bode well. Heather set her lips together and tried to keep an open mind.

There were six stalls in all, straw everywhere, and the pungent reminder that cows lived there, too.

This was ridiculous. Heather turned around in her chair and looked up at Kathryn. *Really?* She beamed the thought at her mom, hoping some mother-child-ESP thing would allow the communication through. She couldn't live next to cow shit. Just the thought of it was making her nauseated. She nestled her nose into her sleeve and tried breathing through her mouth.

Kathryn struggled with the wheelchair over a squishy part of the ground.

"I can lay a piece of plywood down for later to make it easier," Thom said.

Heather closed her eyes. She just wanted to go. Surely

things weren't so bad that she and her aging mother had to live in a *barn*.

"Here we are," Kathryn said.

Heather opened her eyes. They'd reached an office of sorts that had also become farm storage—a complicated collection of items that neither belonged in the house nor in the fields. They weren't tools, or office supplies—just *things* that farms accumulate and don't belong anywhere. It was a purgatory for semi-useless items that hadn't yet found their purpose.

Kind of like me.

The "office" was roughly the size of a double-car garage. There was a desk, but it was heavy with piles of said useless items. A resin shelving unit held cans of paint, the heads to various garden tools, extension cords, and one red plastic gas can.

The floor was cement and there was only one small window. It reminded Heather of a porthole. The room did seem to be insulated; the walls were finished. A Farmer's Almanac calendar from 2006 hung, ironic and crooked, on the wall behind the desk, jaunty with age.

Heather tried to look at it with optimism and a home decorator's eye, but both were hard to do with disgust coursing through her veins. She hated her own bitterness, and figured it probably wasn't good for her health to dwell in the negativity, but *come on*, it was pretty hard to shake, given the circumstances.

She eyed the room again. Kyle kept looking at her but she didn't engage. Even if they gutted the whole thing, maybe leaving the desk to use as a table, how could they possibly fit two or three beds, a dresser or two, and a couch?

Chairs would be nice. The sarcasm crept in.

Even with only the dorm-room basics, she couldn't see how they could possibly live there, especially with Kyle still with them. Maybe this would secure his decision to leave. Heather gripped the arms of the wheelchair. She wished she had the strength to stand up and run and run and run. Run far away. Run back to Reelig. Run to a warm tropical beach. Run home to Veneta.

Heather's head sweated underneath the wool cap even though it was cold in the barn. Her skin felt crawly, and she wanted a bath more than anything right now. She looked over at her mom and Thom talking in low voices. Margie had come out with them, and she was puttering around the desk, attempting to organize the impossible. Her mother's face was merry and her cheeks were pink from the cold. She was gesturing around the room and giggling.

She really was so beautiful.

All her hard work raising me; all her hard work caring for me. She must be heartbroken.

Heather straightened her shoulders and sat up taller in the chair. She was being a negative ass again. She couldn't give much to lightening her mama's load. She had no money to extend; they'd already maxed out her credit card. She had no strength to contribute to work or keeping house. She had no energy to even be a good companion right now. But she could give her mother this concrete corner that she seemed to like.

She looked at Kyle, who understood that Heather wanted to get up. He set the brake and moved the footrests out of the way, then extended his arm to Heather once she had pushed herself up to standing. She walked slowly to her mother, whose back was to her. Thom saw her and lifted his chin. Kathryn turned around.

Heather looked into her mother's eyes and nodded. She wanted to bawl and be held in Kathryn's arms but remained stoic instead. She didn't want to cry in front of the strangers who were now weird family-hybrid landlords. She held her breath when Kathryn grabbed her hand.

"It'll be great. You'll see," Kathryn said. She looked relieved and excited at the same time.

Heather did cry a little then but masked it with nervous laughter and averted eyes. Even though it wasn't what she wanted by any stretch of the imagination—hers or anyone else's—she was determined to give this gift, such as it was, to her mother.

Heather

Heather rallied the next day. She took all her supplements and downed the smoothie without so much as a cringe. She felt empowered in the knowledge that she was actually contributing to the outcome of her health. If she stayed positive, if she emotionally contributed to the "cause," making it easier on Kyle and her mama, and if she rested for whole days in between sightseeing days, rather than for only the couple of hours she wanted, then she could feel herself healing.

She could beat this cancer. She was killing it already, and while sometimes she felt like she was fading fast, if she kept her perspective, she could see that it was just the effects of the chemotherapy. And if resting was the best thing for her right now, then she would rest with a vengeance.

Heather smiled at the discrepancy between the words *rest* and *vengeance.*

Since she was feeling stronger today, she wanted to go out and do something. See something. Maybe she and Kyle could go somewhere. Take a lover's outing—because she'd fully succumbed. He loved her, and she loved him, and it was stupid to waste time. It was improbable and risky and messy, but neither of them seemed to want to address that. They just slipped into the way it had been before, a year ago.

He'd been "tucking her in" at night at the chalet, which led to kissing—and more on the nights she felt stronger—but no sex yet. It was awkward with her mom there, and now that they were all going to be sharing a room, sex would be impossible. *Why didn't we share the chalet room to begin with?*

Heather looked around the chalet's little living room-kitchen combo. She delighted in the wilderness outside and the mountainous backdrop. She'd miss it.

The farm would at least afford them some nature, an improvement over the inn they had stayed at, but nothing would beat the bagpipe melody she heard internally whenever she looked at the ocean from Chanonry Point, just north of Inverness. She wanted to go back there. They'd seen it when they first arrived at Inverness and began staying at Helen's inn.

That's where she wanted to go today. Her mom was probably at the farm working on the room already. She hadn't seen Chanonry Point yet. Would she prefer to see it, or stay and work? She knew that her mom wanted to get enough done on the Barn Room to be livable by the time Heather started up with the chemo again next week—if she needed it. They only had five days left before her next scan. Usually a patient would go through a couple rounds of treatment before scanning. It took time for tumors to shrink. But since hers were removed, she'd pleaded to do a scan early—hoping against hope that she wouldn't have to do another chemo round.

Heather's heart fluttered and raced. She pressed her hand to it and a familiar rush of panic told her it would be too late if she waited to go to Chanonry Point. She didn't have time to wait around. What if she didn't get better?

Kyle walked in as Heather visibly shook herself. He looked at her funny.

"Just shaking off the negativity," she said.

He kissed her forehead, and she breathed in his smell from that space between his neck and his collar. Her heart was happy today, despite the fear of what the scan would show.

Kyle headed for the corner shelf near the sink and started making himself a cup of coffee with the French press.

"I was thinking we could go back to Chanonry Point for the day," Heather said, walking up behind him, sliding her hand across his back. "I'm feeling rested and pretty strong. I'd like to go. It would only take a few hours."

He stopped his mission for caffeinated sustenance and turned around.

"Oh. I said I'd help your mom at the farm today," he said. He gave a puppy dog look requesting pardon.

A hot wave of irritation surged to her cheekbones and settled in her chest. So much for a happy heart. She took a breath, reminding herself she'd just committed to emotionally supporting the "cause"—whatever it happened to be at that moment.

Could she go by herself? She could've before. She *delighted* in her alone time before. But it probably wouldn't be safe if she went by herself now. She felt strong there in the kitchen at nine o'clock in the morning, but she knew all too well how her body could ambush and betray her at anytime.

She paced a little in the kitchen, and Kyle went back to the French press. She fought back sudden tears and panic again. She stuffed her feet in boots, put on her coat, and clomped out the door—forced to go slower than her dignity allowed. She hated how quick to tears she was lately. It was so *babyish*. She stood facing out at the gravel road that led back into the little village of Reelig where the bus stop was. She folded her arms and set her jaw.

"Fine," she said aloud. She'd see if someone else could take her. If her mom and Kyle wanted to waste their time cleaning out a shit hole *barn* bedroom, she'd let them. *She* was going to Canonry Point. But who could she ask? Helen? Margie? Not her favorite choices, but she didn't know anyone else here.

The screen door slammed behind her, and Kyle joined her at the edge of the lawn, coffee mug in hand. Heather breathed in the brewed steam and her taste buds craved an Americano from Starbucks. She hadn't had one since her diagnosis. They'd all been so careful to make sure Heather consumed nothing but the healthiest and wholeest of organic foods. Her mom said that there had been cases of people's cancer clearing up completely with only a change in their diets. Heather didn't think she believed that, but who was she to turn her nose up at any chance she had at recovery.

"Let's plan it for tomorrow. Let's go on over to the farm, and I'll work with your mom. You can rest for another day and then you'll be even more prepared for a good time at Chanonry Point," he said.

Heather didn't answer. She was still pouting and she knew it. But she had the perfect *right* to pout. To be angry and frustrated. She had *fucking cancer*. She went back inside, headed straight for her room, and closed the door.

She sat on the bed, then got up and paced the room. She took off her coat and sat down again.

Helpless and hopeless. Dejected.

All she wanted was to go to fucking Chanonry Point.

Kyle tapped on the door.

"Come on, Heather. We need to get the room finished before your treatments start."

"You said that already!" she called out through the door.

After a beat or two, he spoke again.

"I'll be ready to go in fifteen minutes."

Heather heard him walk away.

She flopped back on the bed. She was being a shit. And Kyle was witnessing it. She twisted her lips together and bit at the tiny shreds of skin.

Heather knew that her mother was doing the best she could. Heather knew that they were out of money and that Thom and Margie were doing them a huge favor by allowing them to live in their home, for while the three of them would be sleeping in the *barn*, they still had to go inside to use the bathroom and the kitchen. It wasn't ideal for anyone, and here she was making a big stink out of everything. She knew she was being childish but couldn't, somehow, stop herself.

A derisive snort escaped from her nose. *How many times this morning have I had to remind myself to be* helpful *right now? That it's all I can offer. Yes, it's shitty that I have cancer. And it's shitty that I might not make it. But maybe I will, and I don't have to be an ass to those people trying to help me.*

Heather didn't like people helping her. She wanted to be able to do things for herself. But since that wasn't possible—*right now*, she reminded herself—she collected a few things to keep her occupied at the McVay's, picked up her coat, and went to sit on the couch and wait for Kyle.

She had to endure the continued humiliation of using the wheelchair to get to the bus stop with him and then escaped into her book on the couch under Margie's nurturing care.

It could be worse.

53

Heather

THE NEXT DAY, THEY SPENT A GLORIOUS DAY AT THE ocean, and Heather took so many pictures, she filled up her SD card. She felt warm and content in the van on the way home. Kathryn wanted to get the Barn Room emptied and cleaned by the end of the day, leaving the weekend to shop for some essentials. Monday would be Results Day. And they were all nervous about it. Heather got sweaty just thinking about it.

Once at the chalet again, Kathryn treated Heather with a rare honey-sweetened herbal tea. While Heather rested with strict instructions to call *whenever* she needed help for *anything*, Kyle and her mom left for the farm a few miles away to maniacally haul stuff out and sweep for a couple hours. Heather was happy with *both* her honey and alone time. *Bliss!*

They returned with measurements and a sketch of the room. Then they began talking about what they thought could fit in it, as far as furniture went.

"First, I was thinking of a couple of big rugs to cover the cement. It would be great to find a bunk bed we could share—I'll be on top—" Kathryn started.

Heather laughed.

"That's crazy," Heather said. She shook her head, imagining her sixty-four-year-old mother climbing to the top bunk.

"It'll save floorspace, and Kyle has graciously offered to sleep on a cot or a nice air mattress. We can tilt it up out of the way during the day, and remake it at night, like a hide-a-bed," Kathryn said.

"Sounds like you've got it all worked out," Heather said. She felt excluded from the planning.

"It's not all worked out," Kyle said, sounding irritated. "We're discussing it with you to get your input."

Heather looked at the sketch.

"What's that?" she asked. She pointed to a penciled circle in the corner of the paper.

"A plant," said her mom. "We need to bring some nature in here if we're to stand it, especially since there's barely even one window."

Heather looked up sharply at Kathryn. That was the first ungenerous thing she'd said about the room. Perhaps her mom wasn't idealistic and overly optimistic. Perhaps she *knew* that living in a cement box in a barn was ridiculous but also knew there weren't many other options left to them. Perhaps she was only trying to make the best of their situation.

"I've started a shopping list. It's probably more than we can afford, but I'd like to share it with you, and we can maybe brainstorm ways to do without some things on the list."

Heather nodded.

"Let's sit at the table and look it over," Heather suggested. "Should I make us all some tea?" She was determined to not be a bitch and to be supportive as best she could.

"I can do that," Kyle said.

Heather smiled her gratitude and settled herself at the dining room table. She pulled her un-dyed wool sweater sleeves over her hands, leaving just fingertips out, and adjusted her scrunchy socks over gray leggings.

Kathryn showed her the list.

"I thought if we did bunk beds and an air mattress, with some rugs and a few plants, it would start feeling like a bedroom. We need a place to store our clothes, but our suitcases might have to do for that. We can hope that the luggage will fit under the bottom bunk.

"And Kyle thought of having a full-length mirror," Kathryn said.

"Mirrors make spaces look bigger," he called over. "We can get one pretty cheap."

"We could use the desk in there as a table if we needed to," Heather said, trying to contribute.

"Yes, that's a thought," Kathryn said. She crossed table

off the list. "And with that saved money, maybe we can get you a more comfortable chair to sit in."

"A couch would suit us all better," Heather said.

Kathryn nodded. "I just want you to have something nice."

Heather smiled at her mama. "Let's get linens first."

Heather

"Here are the results." The oncologist pushed the images across his desk toward the three of them. They looked at the scans and then back to the doctor.

"What does it show?" Heather asked. She held her breath and looked to the oncologist for signs of the answer before he said anything aloud. What she saw on his face filled her stomach with stones.

"There is a pea-sized tumor on the left lobe of your liver, Heather." His tone held no emotion, but it wasn't without kindness.

Heather inhaled deeply and her face crumpled into a grimace. She curled in her chair and sobbed aloud, emotional heat shimmering off of her skin, evaporating any hope she once held. Now that the cancer was moving, she'd *have* to continue chemo, and maybe that wouldn't even work.

Kathryn stayed in her chair, her hand resting on Heather's shoulder until Kyle gathered Heather awkwardly in his arms, half twisted in her seat. When Heather had cried herself out, Kathryn retrieved tissues for Heather to blow her nose.

"Thank you," she whispered.

And that was that.

Metastasized cancer.

Depressed, they all stayed another night at the chalet and took a walk in the woods one more time before heading to Heather's chemo treatment. Kyle stayed with her at Raigmore because Kathryn said she wanted to get a few last minute things settled at the new place before Heather came home and return the chalet's keys to the property management office.

Heather pulled out her book, careful not to jostle the IV in her left arm.

Here again.

Maybe another round of chemo would shrink the tumor in her liver to nothingness. But she doubted it.

55

Kathryn

Helen had found them for her. Kathryn had gone to Helen and explained what she was looking for, and Helen knew right away who to call and where to direct her.

Kathryn approached the bungalow on Culduthel Road and rang the bell.

"Hello. You must be Kathryn," the woman at the door said. "Helen said you'd be by today. Come on in. The kittens are over here." The woman was probably in her early thirties, and Kathryn could see the evidence of small children in the hallway, in the living room, and on the back patio.

"The children are napping, so let's be quiet." She

smiled at Kathryn. She had a short pixie haircut and wore leggings under a cotton sweater, a turtleneck underneath. She led Kathryn into a bedroom closet. The bed had been hastily made, covers pulled up but not tucked in. A drowsy cat slept in a circle on the duvet cover, and four kittens romped around the room in various places.

Kathryn was delighted to see they were calico. She loved calico cats. She scooped up one of the kitties and peered into its face. It meowed with indignation and struggled.

Too rambunctious.

She put it down and it scampered off. She looked at the remaining three. One was sleeping as close to the windowsill as possible. One was stalking dust motes. And the last one was clawing at the bed linens, trying to get to its mother, who was enjoying her solitude. Kathryn chuckled. She plucked it up and set the kitten on the bed. It scurried over and dive-bombed the mama, snuggling into her belly. She could practically hear the mama cat sigh as she rolled back to accommodate her offspring.

She wandered over to the kitten sleeping near the window. He, or she, seemed so comfortable, it was a pity to disturb it. Its markings were dark and contrasting. Whites, blacks, browns, and those delightful splotches of orange. She extended a finger and traced it lightly along the kitty's furry spine. It *murphed* and lifted its head, blinking. She held her finger in front of its marbled pink and black nose. The little nose quivered in its sniffing, and then the kitten pushed its whole face against Kathryn's hand. She scratched under its chin and she swore it smiled at her, content.

"This is the one," Kathryn said to the woman behind her. She was now lying across the bed, petting the mama kitty.

"That's a female. We've taken to calling her Muffin, but of course you can call her anything and she'd take to it."

Kathryn lifted the sleeping beauty and cradled her in her arms. She'd let Heather do the naming.

"How long since she's been weaned?" Kathryn asked.

"Four weeks. We give the kittens Kitten Chow with a little bit of water mixed in to make it softer. They scarf it up."

"Litter box trained?"

"Yep. Though, from what Helen told me, you might just let her roam around the barn and farm. She'll be ecstatic," the woman said.

"True. That would be nice for her, though I'm really hoping to provide a companion for my daughter who's going through chemotherapy right now. I'd love a lap kitty for her," Kathryn said.

"Well, kittens are notable rapscallions. But she does seem to be the more gentle of the lot. And thanks for helping us thin out the litter." The woman smiled.

Kathryn drove her borrowed car—Margie's this time—to the pet store and she and the Cuddly Calico Kitty acquired a cat carrier, a soft blanket, a bag of food, a litter box, litter, cat treats, a collar with a bell, and a feather on a string. She also had plans for little balls of aluminum foil.

Satisfied with her purchases, she put the blanket and the kitty in the carrier in the car and headed for the hospital. She'd probably get some flack for bringing the kitten into the facility, but she'd just operate under the assumption that if it was good for morale, it was okay with the department head. She'd read about therapy dogs before. How was this any different?

At the hospital, Kathryn cooed at the kitten through the carrier and fed her a treat through the bars. She looked a mite stressed and refused the treat. She wondered at the advisability of introducing the stressed kitty to a possibly nauseated and equally distraught Heather. She couldn't drop the kitten at the Barn Room without them. It would be terrified. What if she carried the kitten in by hand? The carrier would call too much attention to her anyway.

She opened the carrier and scooped out the baby. It struggled a little but Kathryn held her to her chest and pet her gently until she calmed down. She gathered her purse with one hand, made sure she had the keys, and pocketed a couple of treats in her coat. She tucked her scarf around the kitty for warmth and carefully climbed out of the car. She was terrified the kitten would jump away and run off—which would surely be a death sentence.

When Kathryn walked into the shared treatment room, Kyle was setting up a DVD for Heather to watch on her laptop with headphones, and Heather looked like she was aching for a distraction. Maybe this would be an all right time to introduce the new member of their family.

"How are you feeling, Heather? Doing all right?"

Heather shrugged.

"A little nauseous."

"I've done something rather impulsive, and I hope it was the right decision," Kathryn began.

Kyle and Heather turned their attention to Kathryn immediately and expectantly.

She looked around her and waited until no hospital staff was looking. She sat down close to Heather and pulled back her scarf to reveal the sleeping snuggle bug.

"Oh," Heather breathed. She smiled up at her mother.

Kathryn settled the kitten into Heather's lap, along with her scarf. She wanted the familiar scent to be with the kitten.

"What will you name her?" she asked Heather.

With only a moment's pause, Heather said, "Sophia."

Kathryn laughed.

"That was fast," she said.

"But look at her. She's totally a Sophia, don't you think?"

"Absolutely," Kyle and Kathryn said.

Heather stroked Sophia, who stood and stretched and curled up again in Heather's lap, not scared at all.

"She's precious, Mama. Thank you." Heather beamed, the nausea seemingly forgotten.

Fifteen minutes later, Kathryn snuck the kitten back outside and waited in the car for them.

At their new home—which Heather had dubbed, unimaginatively, the Barn Room—the kitten scampered and sniffed and explored while Heather napped. After introducing the location of the litter box and the food and water bowls to Sophia and playing Aluminum Ball

Chase with her for ten minutes, Kathryn showed her where she would sleep. She brought her to Heather's bed—the bottom bunk—and let her pad around on top of Heather, watchful that it wasn't disturbing Heather too much. Pretty soon, the worn-out Sophia curled up beside Heather's sleeping form, and that was where Heather found her upon waking.

Kathryn

Now that Kathryn had finished cleaning out and decorating the Barn Room, she was itching to help out on Thom's farm. She went in search of him the next morning, hoping to discuss his expectations—if he had any.

He was fixing a downed fence section but still stopped and leaned back for a moment to address her.

"Why don't we sit in the dining room and have a spot of tea around ten. I often take a break around then," he suggested.

"Sounds perfect."

At ten, Kathryn was at the table with a tablet and pen, ready to be helpful. Margie served tea and sat down with them.

"What were you thinking you wanted in exchange for the Barn Room? I realize you hadn't originally entertained the notion of having three extra adults living with you." Kathryn laughed and the McVays smiled.

"I want to make sure that you don't feel taken advantage of in any way," Kathryn said.

They shook their heads.

"We wanted to do it, dear," Margie said. She reached across the table and covered Kathryn's hand with her own.

"Thank you," Kathryn said. "But, again, I think it is only fair to work for our room and board." She deliberately pulled the tablet closer to herself, ready to start taking notes the minute Thom said anything.

He rubbed his forehead.

"Well," he said. "Right now I'm working on cleaning and oiling the equipment and tending to some electrical work in the greenhouse. You could always just help with the regular chores; that would make my days shorter." He grinned.

"Of course. What are they?" she said, pen poised at the ready.

"I can show you the chores today, but what I'm most interested in is hearing what you have to say about my productivity. Is there anything you do on your farm that you would recommend I do here? That sort of thing," Thom said.

Kathryn smiled. *Right up my alley.*

"That sounds quite fun, actually," she said.

"You could come along now if you've got some clothes you don't mind getting dirty," he said.

"That's my whole wardrobe," she said.

The McVays chuckled knowingly.

Kathryn let Heather and Kyle know what she was doing and, bringing her tablet, met old Thom at his back door.

The winter's green moss contrasted brilliantly against the stone fencing around the yard, and a bare tree near the house rattled in the wind. The scent of mud and fresh air calmed her mind like nothing else ever could.

Besides the two cows, Thom didn't have any animals on the farm except an aging miniature Severe macaw named Lughie that belonged to Margie and had been a pet for the last twenty years. Lughie lived in the living room in a magnificent cage that took up almost a quarter of the room, but he went anywhere Margie did.

If she was folding laundry in the laundry room, the bird was there, too, talking and bobbing on a perch that she had installed in there. He loved Margie and only tolerated Thom when he arrived at his cage with food. Lughie also, begrudgingly, allowed Thom to move him to various perches around the house, though he often used his beak a tad too frequently on Thom's fingers for the old farmer's comfort.

Kathryn wouldn't have to milk the cows, but she wanted to learn so that Thom would have a backup, in case he were to wake up sick one morning, for instance. He pondered that.

"You can watch me this afternoon. I milk at five in the morning and five in the evening," he said.

"After milking the cows in the morning, I muck out

their stable pens and check the pasture for their grazing patterns. They might need to be moved to a different pasture in order to let the grass regrow. I reseed often so they always have fresh grass to eat. During the summer when the grass is dead, and whenever it snows in the winter, I have to feed them hay in the barn."

He walked to his truck, which was parked near the barn today.

"We'll drive to the other side of the farm." He turned on the heater and cleared off the front seat for Kathryn. As they drove down the dirt lane to the fields on the left of the house, Thom listed off his bounty.

"I grow lettuce, arugula, kale, spinach, beets, radishes, corn, carrots, tomatoes, onions, and garlic. Pretty much your standard salad garden, just on a large scale, and with a few extras. I also have a field devoted to the hay I feed the cows when they need it."

After an hour of extensively touring the farm and hearing about his current systems, and how profitable they were, and taking five pages of notes, Kathryn parted ways with Thom.

"I'll meet you at the barn for the milking at five o'clock then," he said.

Kathryn waved and went back to her room. She nibbled on some cheese that she had in the mini fridge they'd installed for such snacking and for the occasional beverage that wasn't tea or water. She read through her notes and meditated on if, and then how, she would implement any changes in how Thom ran his farm.

She started a new list, behind the notes, of ideas for

increasing revenue. Scottish climate was fairly similar to the Pacific Northwest, so the growing seasons were roughly the same. Thom and Kathryn had different clientele because of their different products, but she was still certain there were things she could suggest.

Kathryn scribbled notes until it was time to take Heather in for her treatment. They borrowed Margie's car again, who said they could always use it for that purpose. Margie rarely used the car in the afternoons anyway, preferring to get her errands done in the mornings.

Kathryn helped with the evening milking every night that week. She'd been nervous about it the first couple times, but after ten or fifteen minutes of pulling and squeezing, and knowing how much the cows appreciated the escape of aching pressure on their udders, she softened into the experience and offered to take over that evening chore from there on out. Thom agreed but came out to see how she was "coming along" three or four times the next week. He always stood back and watched his cow, rather than her technique. If the cow was uncomfortable, then Kathryn was doing it wrong.

That first week, she had followed Thom around and helped him do the morning chores. Kathryn could see that Thom was enjoying the camaraderie of working alongside someone, and it certainly endeared Margie to her to see him getting the chores done faster, and with less effort.

"He's been far less achy these past two weeks, Kathryn. I'm so glad you've come to stay with us," Margie said one day while Kathryn was checking the greenhouse. There was still some kale growing in that warmer greenhouse air.

Kathryn beamed.

"I'm just glad we're all working together as a team. It makes living together so much more enjoyable. I love my job," Kathryn winked. "Kyle is keeping Heather company and helping with her care. Sophia, the kitten, is settling in—it's such a joy to see her curled up on Heather's lap. I got her so Heather would feel more comforted in the wheelchair.

"She seems to be needing it a lot this round of chemo. The chemo's taking more out of her than last time," Kathryn said.

Margie shook her head and looked down, apparently at a loss for consoling words.

No matter. Life was life. It was what it was. And while there was a load of stress, and she'd signed what she needed to sign to mortgage her farm—which devastated her—and she still didn't know what would happen with Heather, at least they were together now. That's all that mattered in the moment.

Kathryn felt more grounded with the job. Without work, she'd started micromanaging Heather and Kyle, and that was no fun for anyone.

Margie went back inside to start a boiled dinner for later that evening. Heather didn't eat much after chemo—usually sticking to a smoothie, a piece of bread, or a couple of broccoli florets—but somehow her spare hunger seeped into Kyle and Kathryn, and they were famished after the appointments. Kathryn was convinced it was because of the stress of the clinic and watching

Heather go through that whole process. Many calories were burned up in that stress. Thus, the hunger.

Kathryn stuck her fingers into the earth around the kale and then examined her fingertips. They were dirty enough that Kathryn decided the kale didn't need another watering today. She could harvest some of it, but it wouldn't go to seed if she didn't. Plus, it was so much tastier if it was picked right when you needed it. She left it alone.

Exiting the greenhouse, Kathryn closed it up tight and stood for a moment, looking at the surrounding fields rolling away almost as far as she could see. She breathed the cold air deeply into her lungs. The cold pricked at her cheekbones and stung her fingertips. She smiled. Yes, stress had formed knots in her neck and shoulders, and her lower back was aching from the nightly milkings—she must remember to engage her stomach muscles while she milked—but she couldn't help feeling the gift of healing from the land.

She just wished that Heather could feel that healing, too.

Maybe she'd wheel her out a little before her treatment this afternoon. She'd wrap her up tight and tuck a wool blanket—plus the kitty—onto her lap. She'd be warm enough and the nippy air would clear her lungs out and bring color to her face again.

Kathryn walked the perimeter of the hay field. The hay was short now but still had a hint of the fresh-cut smell that she so loved. Another benefit of living in a barn. She laughed to herself, but the chuckles quickly stifled into pity. The frosty nippiness of the new year had not brought good tidings, or hope for the future.

But Kathryn resolutely set her shoulders back again, *certain* that good thoughts and the power of positive thinking would direct Heather's healing. There was no room for fear. She quickly squashed it down, like punching risen bread dough.

57

Heather

KYLE STAYED WITH HEATHER WHILE KATHRYN DID the farm chores. Heather was bored and pensive and the Barn Room felt like a prison.

"I wish I had my banjo," she said.

Kyle nodded. He paced the floor and then erupted in spontaneous calisthenics—further intensifying the caged-in itchiness creeping up Heather's spine, vertebra by vertebra, like spider legs.

She rolled over, her back to Kyle and his energy. For while she wanted to race over the peat bogs outside and smell the frozen farm air, her body forbid it and she curled up instead, knees up and arms crossed. Feeling restless was exhausting. Watching Kyle would put her in a coma.

Heather looked at the wall. She was a burden to her mother, when it was Heather who was supposed to be caring for Kathryn. She'd *always* been a burden to her mom, from raising Heather as a single mother, to employing her when her depression prevented another job, to caring for her while she sickened from cancer.

And poor Kyle. What a wretched disappointment she must be to him.

Kyle approached the bed.

"May I?" he said, climbing on without waiting for permission.

She tensed. What good does her love do him now? She'd missed her chance. It was too late. Familiar moisture pooled into the corner of her eye, and she turned her face into the pillow.

"Hey," he whispered, his hand on her shoulder. He tucked his knees under the back of her thighs, spooning.

She resisted out of habit and then melted into his strength. Her mother was right. Kyle's love was a gift. If she was going to die—and on good days she still wouldn't allow that as a possibility—she could at least fully offer her love in return.

"I love you," she said, hopelessness warring in her breast.

Kyle hugged her from behind and she let him. Was her love for him real? Or was it only obligation and gratitude?

Kyle bent his lips down to her cheek.

Feeling all the world like a charlatan, a freak, an evil bitch, and a scared mouse of a girl, Heather took Kyle's hand in hers and kissed it. Her body shook and she clasped his hand to her sternum.

"What can I possibly give you but pain?" she said, and the lump in her throat burned cold, sending tentacles of pain to strangle her heart.

"Heather," he crooned. "Don't say that."

She pulled out of his backwards embrace and faced him. "No, I'm serious," she said, swiping at her wet face. "What do you want from me?"

Kyle sat up, his mouth hanging open.

She thought she could see the ghost of what he wanted to say, but wouldn't, lingering in the breath behind his teeth.

He clamped his jaw shut and backed off the bed, folding his arms over his chest.

"What do *you* want, Heather?" Kyle said. His voice was low and heavy with the sound of accusation.

"To not have *cancer*," she spit out. Steel nails stabbed at her temples and her hands began to sweat.

He shook his head. She watched him silently put his shoes on and leave the room. His slow underwater movements spoke for him. *I'm right here. Standing before you. Isn't that enough? Why won't you let me love you?*

Heather could tell herself it was because she was trying to protect him. But wasn't she actually judging him? Wasn't she deciding that he couldn't be an honest person because if the tables were turned, she wouldn't love him, if *he* were dying?

Heather looked at the closed door and swallowed down the dryness of fear and the taste of self-loathing.

Kathryn

GETTING UP THAT MORNING HAD BEEN HARD. SHE briskly walked the perimeter of the hay field behind the barn, pumping her arms, trying to kick the crawling, restless feeling advancing down her spine. Her night had been full of nightmarish memories. And not her own memories. *Flora's* memories. She knew they had been memories, and not messages, because they were all dark. Shadowy. Not tinged with the golden light of her usual dreams.

She'd seen the memory before, too—the only one Flora had ever sent. The one of Flora dying. Kathryn remembered the tears and the strange screaming at the end—and her husband, terribly alone, heartbroken, his fear crashing through the underbrush. She imagined him

          Valerie Ihsan

dirty, unwashed, crazy in his grief, digging Flora's grave and burying her next to all their children. And she saw him digging his own grave next to Flora's, crawling into it, lying in it. Napping in it. Eating his bannocks in it. And slowly growing madder and madder until he opted to never leave Flora's side—lying in his own grave, eyes open, staring at the crying sky.

Kathryn stopped at the corner of the hay field, just twenty-five yards from the barn. She sank to her knees on the hard frost of earth and sobbed, panic and pain settling in her hips.

"I'm sorry," she cried out to the man she never knew. She didn't know if he'd died that way, but she knew that fear, the kind tinged with madness. She'd felt it anytime she thought of Heather dying. And before that, anytime Heather turned her nose up at the farm inheritance. And anytime she thought of herself dying alone as Flora's husband had, after Flora.

She cried for Flora, who she only knew through dreams. She knew they would've been dear friends if they'd known each other in real time. On this plane of existence.

"I'm sorry," she said again. So sorry that Flora had felt that helplessness—had needed to sentence her other half to a death *crushing* in its loneliness.

Kathryn heard crunchy footsteps hurrying to her.

"What's wrong? You okay?" Thom asked.

Startled out of Flora's memories, she stuttered.

"Um. Yes." She wiped her face. "I mean, no. I mean…" she shook her head. "My daughter's going to die!"

Kathryn broke out into a fresh round of sobs.

That was what the dream last night was for.

The old farmer gruffly patted her shoulder and tried smoothing her arm but then stopped. Kathryn smothered her sobs with both hands. Horror seeped into every cell and her whole body perspired with clammy coldness.

There had been golden light last night, too.

Memories were gray, dreams were golden. The golden light burned through Flora's shadowy memories just before the screaming started.

"Come. Come. Let's get you inside to the missus. She'll get you a nice cuppa. It'll give you strength. I'm so sorry, Kathryn."

Her daughter was dying.

And she would be left alone.

Flora said so.

59

Kathryn

THE NEXT NEWS FROM THE ONCOLOGIST WAS BOTH startling and, somehow, not surprising. The liver tumor wasn't shrinking anymore, and because the chemotherapy was affecting her immune system so dramatically, Heather now had a respiratory illness that was dangerously weakening her. At least pneumonia had been ruled out. She was coughing, but the x-rays only showed a few marks that could be considered fluid.

Heather's hands and feet were numb and tingly all the time now, and she needed help buttoning anything she wore.

The three of them, with the oncologist's agreement, decided to stop Round Three of chemotherapy prematurely. She needed to recover from the respiratory illness before she could do any more anyway. Worse yet was that when she *could* start it up again, she'd have to redo the third round. This week hadn't counted.

All that suffering for nothing.

Kathryn encouraged Kyle to take a walk so that she could talk to Heather.

She helped Heather to the bathroom and back to bed. She'd measured out the last of the tincture from home last week; today she could only administer the cough medicine and a pain pill.

"Do you want anything else?" she asked Heather. She smoothed Heather's brow and lifted Sophia closer to Heather's arm so she could pet her. The coughing intensified when she lay down completely, so Kathryn propped up some pillows and made her as comfortable as possible. Heather breathed better after a few minutes, and Sophia purred in her deep rumbly kitten way. Kathryn sat cross-legged on the floor near Heather's bed.

"I was taking a walk a couple days ago, after some chores, and I started thinking of the oddest thing," Kathryn said. She stroked Sophia in Heather's lap. "Flora. Do you remember me talking about a dream where she showed me how she died?"

Heather shook her head.

"I was so upset when I found out. I said I had the flu and stayed in bed for two days."

"That I remember," Heather said. "I had to get up at six in the morning to feed the animals while you were sick." Another round of coughing sent Heather sinking into the pillows again. She moaned.

Kathryn rubbed Heather's knuckles.

"She died of some fever. The whole family did. All the children went first. Then her." Kathryn took a deep breath. "And then her husband last. He died all alone." She squeezed Heather's fingers. "And now," Kathryn chuckled humorlessly, "after all these years, I think what I did was transfer that onto me."

Heather opened her eyes and looked at Kathryn with a question in them.

Kathryn rubbed her daughter's knee through the blankets and smiled sadly.

"*I* was afraid of dying alone. Like Flora's husband did. *That's* why I've been such a bitch to you all these years. *I* wanted the security of living on my own land, with my daughter by my side. That's why I wanted you to take over the farm, Heather." Kathryn teared up. "I'm sorry I didn't hear your wishes and dreams. I'm sorry I didn't bless them when there was still time." She put her head down on Heather's lap, old regrets flowing out onto the blanket. The kitten, disturbed and haughty, moved over, but only just slightly. Heather petted Kathryn instead.

"Well," Heather said slowly and evenly, "you did it now."

Kathryn raised her head and the kitten dove back to the warm spot.

"It doesn't do me much good at this point," Heather continued, trying for a wry smile, "except for knowing you felt it and that you came and told me." She held Kathryn's face in her hands. "Thank you."

Kathryn grabbed at Heather's hands.

"Know that, for what it's worth, I won't leave you. You won't be alone whenever it is that you do go." Kathryn squeezed at Heather's hands and Heather squeezed back.

60

Heather

THE HILLS AROUND THEM OOZED ANCIENT, AND Heather could feel it seeping into her pores. Her mother's feet made soft chufling noises in the field behind the barn. Despite her fears and fatigue, Heather still felt alive here. Her eyes were open wide. No more delusions. If she had to die, she would die. People all around her died. Everyone died. And lots of people died before they wanted to. She was no different.

There had been a strange warming in the hills the past four days, so it wasn't cold enough to frost her tears to her cheeks. She smeared them off with her mittens instead and sniffed. She pulled a mitten off and fished around in her pockets for a handkerchief. She didn't want to cry anymore. Not now. Crying felt too close to defeat.

While she had battled severe depression for years, this place had originally taken it out of her. At first, she had secretly wished, and then illogically *believed* that staying in Scotland would cure her after the hysterectomy. They *all* thought she would go into remission after that.

Her face burned with unshed rage and sorrow and pure unadulterated guilt. Was it her fault she was dying? Her fault that she was leaving her mother behind?

And Kyle!

If she had stayed in Oregon and started treatment right away, would it have made any difference? She blubbered and sobbed and coughed. Her chest burned and her throat felt raw. She'd found love too late, turned her back on it when it was first offered. She'd wasted so much time not loving Kyle when she really *did* love him. *Poor Kyle.* She sobbed silently now, regret and shame spilling over into her collar, even coming out of her nose, her handkerchief useless now. She would gladly accept all the sorrow if Kyle didn't have to suffer. She'd ruined his life again. She *knew* she wasn't good for him. All she ever did was bring him pain. If only she hadn't broken it off last year. She could have at least given him that year.

Her beautiful man.

I'm sorry I loved you, Kyle.

She blew her nose into the wet handkerchief and took in the stone fences and shorn fields. So many things left undone. She hadn't traveled as much as she'd wanted. She'd never found her dream job, and she'd never made it off the farm—though she couldn't imagine ever wanting to leave it now.

"I'm ready to lie down again, Mama." Heather called out, coughing again.

Kathryn hurried from around the barn and pushed the wheelchair back toward the Barn Room.

Kathryn

SHE NEVER KNEW WHAT GOT THEM LAUGHING, BUT joy was with them two weeks later when they all sat at the table playing cards. Sophia, never far away, batted aluminum foil balls at their feet and then scurried and scampered and tumbled out from under the table. Perhaps that was what started it. Sophia's goofy furriness. Her big eyes and the tufts of white fur that grew from the tips of her ears, like a cross between a lynx and an old man.

They laughed until they had no breath.

Until they had tears streaming down their cheeks.

Until their sides hurt.

Until Heather started coughing again.

The respiratory infection had finally cleared up but,

at any rate, Kathryn got up from the table and started preparing more hot water.

Heather was back on those magical herbs. Kathryn had sought out all the health food stores she could find and rounded up as many supplements as possible to replenish her supplies. They'd opted out of the chemo.

"No more," Heather had said. "I just barely start to feel a tad normal, and then the poison comes back. If I'm to die, let me do so without the nausea and illnesses. Let me just go at home—" she'd gestured to the Barn Room with a shrug, "—without the hustle and bustle of the clinic and treatments and my hair falling out again."

She'd raised her hand then and wiggled her fingers and made a fist.

"Look! I can feel my fingers." She put her arm back down. "No more chemotherapy. It's not working anyway." Her eyes pierced into Kathryn's.

The latest scan showed the tumor's increase of four centimeters. It was growing fast.

The herbs made her feel better and she was back to drinking smoothies in wine glasses and trying to make Kyle and Kathryn laugh.

Love was, indeed, all there was.

Despite the wretched despair of knowing that she would outlive her daughter, Kathryn put on a brave face and just loved as hard as she could. It was all she could do. And it was what *Heather* was doing, so she must've wanted it that way.

Heather

Lying in a haze of pain reducers for the ache in her diseased liver, Heather still luxuriated in the feel of Sophia's fluffy baby fur. She stroked it as long as Sophia tolerated it. She vibrated *with* Sophia when she purred. Except for the frequent coughing fits—she just couldn't kick the cough—and the fairly certain knowledge that she would die at the end of this, she was able to reside in a state of complacency that almost resembled peace. She made music in her head, melodies she played on her banjo back on her Oregonian farmstead, and she most resolutely did not think of anything bad anymore. There wasn't time for it.

She didn't miss the Veneta farm. But then maybe she wouldn't.

　　　　Valerie Ihsan

She *would* miss this kitty by her side. Heather stroked and petted and swam her fingertips in Sophia's softness.

She would miss her mother. And Jill.

And she would miss Kyle. Her heart quivered and she gasped at its *heartpain.* She immediately turned her thoughts and treacherous heart away and listened to her mind music again.

She'd miss her banjo, too.

She sighed in her bottom bunk.

If she stuffed the sadness down, she might be able to enjoy the last days or months with Kyle and her mom, in her great ancestral home.

She'd asked her mom to buy her a woolen blanket in their tartan, and she already had it in use, draped across her bed. She would bring it with her in the wheelchair, and anywhere she sat in the Main House, or in the Barn Room. She had it now, around her shoulders.

Her hair had started growing back. It was still red but much darker and more wiry. Also curly. Kyle couldn't stop touching it.

"You look so good with short hair. Who would've known?" he said.

In the past, she'd not-so-secretly coveted those short spritely locks on other women, but had always been too vain to cut her long hair. She and Kyle had laughed until they cried the day before, that she finally had that pixie hair cut, whether she wanted one or not.

She wished she had her banjo now. She would've liked to have plucked a few more tunes on it. She wished that Jill was there with her guitar, playing for her right now.

"Mama?" she called. "Could you find some bluegrass for me on my laptop and play it?"

"Sure," Kathryn said. Sophia crawled onto Heather's abdomen, stood on tiny kitten toes and kneaded Heather's belly, and then fell into delicious kitty stupor and went to sleep again. Heather practically swooned.

She couldn't understand it. They had Mica and Janet back at home. She didn't love either of them as much as she loved this little furball though. Her calico baby. Sophia was an angel. *Her* angel. Bringer of peace and reconciliation.

Heather blinked.

Could she really have reconciled with dying, if she was still this sad?

There didn't seem to be any point to wishing things were different, or lamenting that she had more time to get things done—bucket lists to cross off, dreams to fulfill. She'd lived her life—such as it was in length—and she was grateful for the time she'd had. Plus, she knew that once she did die, she wouldn't care about any of it anyway. She imagined herself floating away above the clouds.

Kyle looked up from his book then and Heather smiled drowsily at him from the bed. How could she be so in love, so sad, and so…relaxed about dying? The feelings seemed to go back and forth—these waves of denial, anger, sadness, and peace. But perhaps that was just the way of things.

She petted Sophia again and again and then dozed to Gillian Welch playing the banjo.

When Heather woke, Kathryn had a surprise for her.

Margie's car was already packed and ready to go, and so were Kyle and Kathryn. They were going on a mini trip that afternoon to Granny and Grandpa's old stomping grounds.

Kathryn drove them past where their street used to be, and then on to the Old Town streets. Kyle and Kathryn bundled up Heather in the wheelchair and walked up and down all the side streets off Church Street. Heather laughed with them, and they all tried to put away their thoughts for the day and just enjoy the outing. It was difficult though, and more than once Heather saw Kyle passionately looking in the other direction, or her mother swiping at a tear.

Heather sighed. It was hard to keep the spirits up when you knew you'd be leaving forever. She didn't feel like she could talk to Kyle or her mother about it either. It was too sad for them. But today Heather mostly tried to look at death as another adventure she'd be going on. She didn't know exactly what to expect, of course, but she didn't believe that her consciousness would just blip out, cease to exist. She would continue on in a different form, in a different realm.

Like Flora.

Heather wondered why Flora had never come to visit her. Why only her mother?

Then, a voice inside her said, "You didn't want me."

Heather sensed it rather than heard it. Maybe it was her imagination. Or maybe the veils were thinning for her since she was closer to death than before. Maybe Flora did say something. Maybe she didn't.

I wonder when I'll die.

The shops on Church Street were exquisite. Old and full of stories and charm. Heather imagined what it must have been like without electricity, paved streets, or cars.

She closed her eyes and felt the crisp air cut across her face. She heard music inside herself again. Pipes and organs. Harps and flutes. Music filled her up and she was happy. If she could take music with her anywhere she went, she would be content. She hoped that the music would follow her to the other realm.

The chair stopped. And then so did the music.

Heather opened her eyes.

"Picture time," Kathryn called out.

At first Heather wanted to get out of the chair for the photos, but a surge of dizziness prevented her. The anemia that had plagued her since her chemotherapy treatments also caused great fatigue. Sometimes she wept from how tired she felt.

But not today. Today she felt loved and cared for.

They took a photo of Heather and her mom for Kathryn's special photo box, and one of Heather and Kyle in the same place. Heather held both their hands and squeezed hard, saying good-bye right there. Just in case.

They began walking again, Kathryn pushing Heather, tears on their faces.

"Let's go find some music," Heather said.

Kathryn

KATHRYN HAD ANOTHER FLORA DREAM THAT NIGHT. Mixed images of Flora bringing flowers to Heather. Of planting the purple heather of the Highlands in the windowsill next to Heather's bed. Of reading to her. Of bringing her chamomile and peppermint tea, with marshmallow root, for her nausea.

Kathryn woke in the top bunk, so pleased to have heard from Flora. She laughed when she recalled the final scene of her dream. A cannabis plant and a lighter.

So pot it is.

She wondered why Flora hadn't sent this miracle drug to her in a dream before.

And then she realized that Heather must be entering

a very painful phase. A sudden stone of panic sat on her chest. She gathered her breath, sending it to the back of her throat, inhaling as far as her lungs permitted, and then more and more. She took little sips of air, stretching her lungs and her rib cage. The knot of panic began to dissolve; she exhaled with a quiet "ha" sound at the back of her throat. Yoga breath. She did it four more times.

Oxygen flowed to her brain and her body tingled with aliveness. Then she momentarily felt guilt for that very feeling of life. She would gladly die instead of Heather. Kathryn continued with her deep breathing and blinked back early morning tears. The rest of the room was still sleeping. With only the one square window, the room was swathed in darkness and there was no telling what time it actually was.

Now that she was fully awake, she had to use the bathroom. The trek to the Main House sounded terrible, but then so did lying there having to urinate. She threw back the covers and descended the bunk ladder. It hurt her feet and never in a million years would she have offered to take the top bunk, if not for their current situation. There was no way Heather could make it.

Kathryn blinked.

But Kyle could.

Ha!

She'd never thought of it until then. She shook her head in the dark. She must be getting better at this asking for help thing. It was slow-going though. Why did she always make things harder for herself? She'd talk to him about switching beds today.

She slipped her feet in boots and wrapped a new robe around herself. She pulled on her hat and grabbed her cell phone to check the time. 5:25 a.m.

Pleased that she'd gotten a full night's sleep, she headed toward the Main House, passing a sleepy Thom in the milking pen on her way. When she returned to the Barn Room with teeth and hair brushed, and hands and face washed, she quietly set some water to boil on the hot plate that sat on top of the mini fridge.

She dressed in warm, comfortable clothes and put her boots back on, then took her tea outside. There were only so many hours one could spend inside a cement box without losing a part of one's soul. The barn was chilly, but the cows' steamy breath warmed her hand when she touched their noses in Good Morning Gratitude. She raised her mug in silent salute to Thom. He nodded back and laid his head on the cow's side while he filled his bucket with what would later turn into buttermilk biscuits and pancakes, and then later still, yogurt.

The sun was still asleep and would be for another hour or so, judging by the shade of gray around her. She paced in the darkness just outside the barn, filling her insides with hot liquid.

Pot, huh?

Where would she get that around here? It wasn't exactly something she could ask Thom and Margie, or even Helen, for. She'd call the oncologist's office when it opened. Or maybe she'd call the hospice number they were given when they opted out of chemotherapy the last time. They would know, she bet.

Heather wanted to stay at the Barn Room instead of a hospice home, so a hospice worker was supposed to make twice-weekly visits now, but Kathryn had never called to set up the appointments. Heather seemed to be doing okay for the time being, and calling in hospice just seemed like it would jinx her health somehow. Bring death closer.

Kathryn took another sip of tea.

She heard her name from the barn and turned to see Kyle flying outside in bare feet and pajamas.

"Kathryn!" he yelled.

Kathryn dropped her mug and ran toward the barn.

64

Kathryn

KATHRYN RAN INTO THE ROOM, KYLE AND THOM behind her.

"Oh my god. Heather," Kathryn whispered.

Thom took one look at Heather writhing on the floor and ran outside.

Heather gasped and groaned and cried out. So much pain.

"Oh my baby." Kathryn cradled Heather's torso and lifted her halfway onto her lap. She pushed down on the side of Heather's abdomen. Heather screamed.

"Okay okay," Kathryn said. She pushed Heather's hair out of her face. "I'm here, baby. I'm here."

Kyle bit his lips and hovered over them. His hands shook.

"Find out if Thom is calling the ambulance," she whispered to him.

He sped off into the dawn. The nautical twilight permeated the barn, casting light and shadows through the open Barn Room door. The dropping temperature made Kathryn wish for the door closed, but that felt cut off from the help that would surely arrive soon.

"Shh, shh," Kathryn cooed, rocking.

Heather sobbed in pain.

Kathryn sang. She sang "Hush Little Baby" and "Amazing Grace" and "Let it Be."

Kyle returned and nodded.

Kathryn hoped that Thom or Margie would be waiting at their front door for the ambulance so the paramedics would know where to go.

"Kyle," Kathryn said in a low voice. "Can you start gathering a couple of things we might need at the hospital?"

"I need to get dressed," he said. He looked around the room like it would tell him what to do.

"Do you think we should give her a pain pill right now? Or do you think the hospital will want to start from scratch?" Kathryn asked.

"Give her the pain meds. They can give her more at the hospital. It might even kick in before we get there." He retrieved a glass of water and four Advil and handed them to Kathryn.

"Heather, baby. Take this. It'll help with the pain." She put the pills between Heather's lips. Heather tilted her head forward, gulping the water from the glass. She arched backwards and twisted from Kathryn's grasp and cried out again.

Kyle kneeled on the floor and held Heather's hand.

"I'm here, Heather. Tell me what to do," he said.

Kathryn shook her head.

"She probably doesn't know, dear. She's just hurting," Kathryn said. "It's disorienting, I imagine."

They waited on the floor. Kathryn and Kyle both silent, but poor Heather not. Kyle looked scared, with wide eyes. Kathryn reached over and touched his arm.

"Breathe," she said.

He shuddered and squeezed Heather's hand.

Heather whimpered and panted.

They heard the sirens from afar, getting louder and closer. Kyle stood up and scrambled to get a sweatshirt over his pajamas, then pulled on his boots.

"The ambulance is almost here, Heather," Kathryn said calmly. She didn't want to leave Heather's side but needed to throw a couple of things into her backpack. A toothbrush, a book, her phone, and all Heather's meds. She contemplated taking the herbal supplements, too, but then the rushing footsteps of several people stayed her hand. She zipped up the backpack and grabbed her purse. She handed them over to Kyle.

"Here. Please take these."

"Help is here, sweet lovely," Kathryn said to Heather.

"Over here," Thom called out from the barn.

Two paramedics hurried through the door and visually assessed the situation. They checked Heather's vitals, palpated internal organs. They conferred together in low tones that Kathryn couldn't quite hear, and one of them left the room.

"How long has she been in pain like this?" the ambulance technician said.

Kathryn looked at Kyle.

"For about twenty minutes now. It was sudden. Woke her up. We gave her 800 mg of ibuprofen about fifteen minutes ago," he said.

The paramedic opened a bag that he'd brought in. He pulled out a syringe and a bottle of clear liquid.

"What's that?" Kathryn asked.

"Morphine. First choice for pain relief. This will take the edge off until we can find out what's troubling her," he said. He drew the liquid into the syringe.

"We know what's troubling her," Kyle scoffed. Catching his own rudeness, he lowered his voice. "She has cancer."

The technician looked up at him and then to Kathryn.

"What kind?" he asked and continued administering the morphine.

"Ovarian," Kathryn said. "But it's in her liver now."

"Well, this will feel real good, Heather. Just relax into it."

Heather's contortions visibly released, and she settled into a soft pool of *Heatherness* on the floor.

The second ambulance tech returned with the gurney. Kyle helped with the door and then the two paramedics slid Heather onto a stretcher, and lifted her onto the gurney.

They wheeled her out and Kyle and Kathryn followed.

There wasn't room for them in the ambulance, but Thom—thankfully—had anticipated this and his truck was already warmed up and ready to go. This simple act of compassion from one parent to another was what sent Kathryn into tears. Old Thom helped her up into the truck, and Kyle clambered into the backseat.

"Margie has sent along some tea." He handed Kathryn a thermos. She laughed and wiped her nose.

Heather

Heather blinked sleepy crust from her eyes and stared at the hospital's ceiling. She was weighted down by an iron ball of pain—pain so heavy it pushed her through the earth's crust, squishing her. The only thing that kept her from being swallowed by the gates of hell, was her anchor to Earth.

Kyle.

The thought startled her. He was the first person she expected to see—wanted to see—and he did not fail her. He sat beside the hospital bed in a chair, looking at her face, waiting. Her heart warmed.

"Hi," Heather said, her throat dry.

Kathryn looked up from her book at the window seat.

"Hey," Kathryn said softly. "How are you feeling?" She walked to the bed, and Kyle receded to give them space.

Heather watched him fade into the background and her tether to him tightened.

"I'm good now," she said.

"I bet that was scary," Kathryn said. "Scary for me to watch. Scary for you to feel."

Heather nodded again. She felt lethargic and not very clear. She remembered the pain from earlier, different from now, like ice hooks gouging her guts and scraping through them. She'd never felt that much pain before. Nor fear like that. She wondered why the pain had scared her. Such a strange reaction to pain. She supposed it was because she didn't know when it would stop. Or how bad it would get before it stopped.

But it was gone now. She still felt stabby twinges every once in a while, but mostly she floated in unconcerned normality.

"I feel kinda stiff and achy," Heather said. She shifted in the bed.

"I imagine that's from the muscle contractions. You were a tight little ball until the paramedics came."

"What happened?" Heather shook her head. "I mean, what caused the pain?"

"The tumor, love. It's grown big enough to push on some nerves that are taking umbrage with that."

Heather stared at her feet under the bedsheet and said nothing for the longest time. Kathryn laid her hand on Heather's shin. They sat in companionable silence and

Kyle went back to his book, though it didn't look like he was actually reading it.

At last, Heather sighed deeply, and Kyle looked up again.

"I guess this means pain meds until the end, huh?" she said.

Kathryn's expression was full of compassion. Heather drank it up.

"It's hospice time, my angel," Kathryn said. She grimaced and her eyes glossed with unshed tears.

Heather did the same, nodding her answer. Kyle walked around to the other side of the bed and hugged her.

The weeping wasn't loud. There wasn't any wailing or renting of garments this time. Only dripping sadness. And acceptance. It certainly wasn't a surprise.

Heather sniffed and wiped her eyes on the sheet.

"I want to go to Gordon Castle. Now. As soon as possible," Heather said. She looked at her mom. "Can you organize it? It is my final wish." She smoothed her hands across the sheet.

The room was silent with held breath.

Heather looked up and chuckled. The tension cleared visibly from Kathryn and Kyle's faces.

It *was* a pretty dramatic thing to say. Even if it was true.

Despite Kathryn's smile, Heather could read her mother's face like never before.

What if she dies during the trip? Or worse—before?

"Could I have a few minutes with Kyle, Mom?"

She nodded and left.

Heather and Kyle looked at each other. His eyes held the darkest brown compassion she'd ever seen. And something else. Something she couldn't bear to look at. She looked away and bit her lip, holding her breath.

A soft exhaled sob puffed out of him. He crawled into bed with her. She inched aside, making room, and curled around the swollen heaviness in her abdomen. She looked at his tears and touched them in bewilderment.

"Kyle."

She told him about the anchor. The tie to Earth. In wonderment, perhaps slightly induced by the morphine, she pondered if he was keeping her alive. That maybe he was the answer to her wellness.

Was it a sign?

"It's you I want to see when I wake up," she said.

He squeezed her hand and kissed it.

And then a wave of despair crashed over her and she gasped in a crush of pain. What a shitty time to fall in love and *know for sure* he was the One.

The weight of Kyle's hands settled securely on her arms.

"The anchor," he whispered. "I'm your anchor. I'm here."

She breathed through the wave of pain. He rubbed her cheek with the back of his hand.

"I'd do anything to keep you alive," he said.

They shook in each other's arms and cried their hopelessness out.

Kathryn planned everything in top speed. They were to stay in Courtyard Cottage across from the estate grounds of Gordon Castle—the castle of their ancestors. Heather wondered if they'd receive special treatment, being Gordons themselves. But then probably every Gordon wondered that.

It would take them an hour and a half to drive to Spey Bay where the castle was. They would drive the morning after Heather's release from the hospital. They'd get settled in the cottage and then tour the castle. The next day would afford a touring of the grounds and the estate. Then they would go home. Just one night. But a wish come true. And her mama would make it happen.

The night before they left, Heather woke in her bunk to Kyle sitting beside her. He'd lit a candle, which cast just enough light to see his face. He held Heather's hand and cried soft huffing sounds while Heather struggled to come out of the morphine fog.

She raised Kyle's hand to her lips and kissed his knuckles. She knew he could see her love for him in that moment because she could feel it welling up inside her and pouring out of her eyes. So much love for this crying man in front of her who loved her unconditionally, and always would. Always had. There was no time for wishing what couldn't be. There was such a deep love kindled in Heather's breast, that she wished she could live longer just to bask in its glow.

Heather

While Kathryn drove the rental car, Kyle skimmed a printout from the castle's website. He read aloud the interesting tidbits.

"There's an eight-acre Victorian Walled Garden in the center of the grounds—"

Kathryn squealed. "*That's* where I'm hanging out," she said. She smiled at Heather through the rearview mirror.

"—And there's a fully restored Victorian Greenhouse. And," Kyle read off the paper, "we'll be seeing some ancient famous holly trees."

Heather raised her eyebrows. "Famous holly trees?"

He winked at her.

"There's this ballad written by some famous Scottish

poet, referencing a Highland 'laddie,' the Marquis of Huntly—the guy who lived in this castle. He was the Colonel of the 92nd Gordon Highlanders. The song goes, 'Where has your Highland laddie gone? He dwelt *beneath the holly trees,* beside the rapid Spey.' Turns out this Marquis went to campaign against Napoleon in Holland. That's what the song is about." He grinned. "I love shit like this."

Heather smiled from the backseat.

She napped then and when she awoke, they were there.

The Courtyard Cottage was constructed of large tan stone bricks, bleached by the sun. A strip of grass and flower beds lined the house. When they checked in to the two-bedroom cottage, they saw that all the rooms looked out on the castle garden. Inside, there was a quaint sitting room and a large kitchen. Too bad they weren't staying longer. The cottage wouldn't be fully utilized with their one-night stay.

Heather felt so weak that she was content to stay in the wheelchair for the whole tour. She didn't suppose anyone would mind. She chuckled from a haze of oxycodone.

The castle was exquisite.

She breathed in the opulence and imagined living there. She imagined her ancestors living there. As Kyle pushed her in the chair, Heather looked at the sitting room in pure blissful envy. She laughed at the array of little tables and decided she knew why most of the period movies she'd watched had characters with little lap dogs.

A big dog would knock down four tables just walking in.

There were eight bedrooms in the castle, a drawing room—the one with all the little tables—a billiard room, and two large reception rooms. The reception rooms must have been for the balls back in the day.

Kyle pushed Heather back to the cottage, and she marveled at the beauty of the gardens. She breathed in the fresh air and couldn't wait for the next morning, when she too would be fresh and could explore them more fully, before they headed home. But right then, Heather felt exhausted.

"Heather, my darling. You look positively gray, baby. Are you in pain?" her mother said.

Heather nodded, hugging her middle. She didn't want to push into it because that hurt, but somehow *not pushing* it seemed to hurt worse.

Kyle rifled through the houndstooth rucksack he bought at the gift store, found another oxycodone, and handed it and a water bottle to Heather.

He and Kathryn looked on somberly.

Heather remembered the hand-holding on the day they took pictures of themselves on Church Street in Inverness. It had been a Good-Bye Day, of sorts.

Heather took Kathryn's hand and gestured with her eyes for Kyle to take her other. She squeezed their hands and hoped they were remembering that day, too. She nodded and breathed deeply.

"Let's go home to Oregon," Heather said. "I want to say good-bye to a few friends."

Her mom squeezed Heather's hand again. There were

a few things Heather wanted to give away—her banjo would go to Kyle. Suddenly she wanted him in her room back in Oregon. In her bed. She wanted to revel in her love of him. To feel his skin on hers. To feel him inside her.

She could picture him at the house playing with Mica, as he often did, and she felt swarms of gratitude buzz around her. This trip had been monumental. It was what brought them together.

She *had* to live. It wasn't *fair* to die now. Her head sagged and she almost swooned into depressive darkness, but Kyle's quick hand on her shoulder steadied her. *Her anchor.*

67

Kathryn

When they returned home from the castle, Heather went to bed early and slept for most of the next day.

The following morning, in the dark before the milking, Kathryn awoke without knowing why. Sophia jumped down from Heather's bunk and shook herself. She padded over to the air mattress and crawled into the crook of Kathryn's arm.

Kathryn scratched under Sophia's chin, sniffed the air and listened hard. The kitten purred. There was a difference to the room. Was it colder? Darker? Could it be that it *sounded* different? The space heater wasn't clicking on or off. There were no refrigerator noises. Kyle's breathy snores were the same as ever.

Kathryn shifted the kitten out of the way, rolled off the air mattress, and approached her daughter's bunk—a dim nightlight slanting on her face. Was she breathing? Kathryn held her own breath, straining to hear, limbs heavy with dread. Forcing herself forward the last few inches, Kathryn touched Heather's hand and jerked away.

Heather was icy.

Kathryn hesitated. She touched her again. Shook her. Tried to rouse her. But nothing. Heather was rigid. *Dead.* Kathryn shivered, hair prickling, goosebumps rising. Her breath ragged. Sharp, like the grass that cut her ankles when she'd run through fields in search of grasshoppers and wildflowers as a child. Kathryn had never touched a dead body before.

She sat back on her heels, steadying herself, palms on the mattress. The flannel sheets were soft under her fingers. She pulled back the covers and crawled into bed with Heather, the painful coldness pressing against Kathryn's body. She ignored it as best she could and traced Heather's hairline with a finger. She smoothed her hair back like she did when Heather was little. Kathryn held the stiffness in her arms and wept.

"I love you so much," she whispered in Heather's shell ear. She squeezed the coldness, begging Flora, God, the faeries—anyone—for the power to warm her daughter. She rubbed Heather's arms and pulled at her wrist, stuffing Heather's stiff hand under Kathryn's own arm, wanting to transfer that living warmth to her baby's knuckles and fingertips.

Heather's arm slid out from Kathryn's embrace and thumped on the mattress. A sob escaped from Kathryn's throat. Kyle shifted above her in the top bunk. Her heart stabbed and she couldn't breathe. She knew this had been coming, but the pain of it startled her—scared her—and for a few minutes she thought she would die of it. Right there. Next to Heather.

And then Kathryn *wished* for that death. They could be buried together. The obituary would say they lived together and died together. Kathryn waited and fruitlessly hoped, hysteria rising.

But breath came and went. Her heart continued to beat and despair covered her nostrils, drowning her.

She was left to live without her rock. Her other half. To exist without the blood of her blood. She would never again make Heather a smoothie or a cup of tea, or listen to her play the banjo.

She pushed the blankets down and sat up, wrapping her arms around her knees, organs warming extremities. She rocked forward and back, and shook. Her teeth rattled and waves of shivers rushed up her spine. Kyle turned over in his sleep again, sending the top bunk swaying, and Kathryn quieted herself to a silent sob, wanting a sliver of more time alone with Heather.

She lay back down and stayed there with no sense of time—touching, smelling, hugging—telling herself it hadn't happened, yet seeing with her own eyes that it was true. She mewed her sobs and the kitten, back on the bed again, pushed against her face. Kathryn shuddered out her last sob and slid off the bunk. She pulled the blankets back up around her daughter and set Sophia back on Heather's stomach, but she wouldn't stay—knowing, perhaps, that something was wrong.

Kathryn stood, touched Kyle's sleeve, his elbow. He rolled to face her in the dim light, eyes blinking awake. Then Kathryn experienced the second hardest thing in her life. She made the first thing real. Cemented it in the annals of history. Spoke it out loud.

"Heather has died." She choked and shook her head.

Kyle launched out of bed and was by Heather's side faster than Kathryn could even see how. It was like he beamed directly there. He knelt reverently, holding his breath. He seemed to change his mind then and crawled on the bunk, straddled Heather's knees and bent to touch their foreheads together.

"I see you," he said, beginning to cry. "Be at peace, my love." He slid down next to her, as Kathryn had done.

Kathryn's throat closed and she turned away from his grief, awash with her own. She couldn't handle his, too. Not right then.

She turned around in the room, gathering her thoughts and breathing through the crusting of her lungs. She was altered now. Her daughter was dead. There was no way Kathryn could ever be who she used to be. Never again. Her eyes settled on the desk they used as a table. There was a candle there, and matches. It was too soon for the brightness of a lamp. Let them live their numbness by candlelight for a little while. She groped around in the dim room, lit a match, and placed flame to wick.

Still averting her eyes—giving Kyle as much privacy

as she could in the tight quarters—she slowly pulled on clothes over the top of her pajamas. Sweaters and socks and fingerless gloves. She put on her hat, but her teeth still chattered.

The rooster crowed outside. Thom would be milking soon. The hens would need to be fed. Kathryn put on her coat. Life was intruding, but how could it? *At this moment!*

The candle cast a fuzzy-edged golden circle around Heather and Kyle.

She sat down with her boots. She had to call the coroner. But then she stopped.

One boot on, one off.

68

Kathryn

She wasn't going to.

Not yet anyway.

She didn't want the invasion of medical examiners, ambulance drivers, or even the McVays.

Kathryn caught Kyle's eye and they stared at each other a moment. He heaved a sigh and laid his head next to Heather's on her pillow, looking all the world like he just wanted to sleep next to her one more time. His shoulders shook and he gripped Heather's shoulder in a manic hug. He wept through gritted teeth—the quietness of his weeping in contrast to the raw sharpness of his pain.

She knew he was in pain. She could see it. She felt it. The whole room hurt. The air mattress cried, too. And

Sophia sat like a statue, her ears flattened back against her head.

Kathryn put on her other boot and left the room. She stuffed her hands into her coat pockets and walked around the perimeter of the barn, the dirt solid and frozen under her feet. The skies were clear of clouds that morning, and Kathryn watched the still-present moon, absorbed its light into the pores of her face. She wanted to be washed clean in the moon's rays, but she didn't felt anything but stagnate sadness.

She filled a barn bucket with water from the hose and brought it inside. She filled the electric kettle and set it to boil. She gathered Heather's favorite soaps and lotions and fished Heather's kimono out of her suitcase.

She turned to Kyle and gestured him off the bed.

"I want to wash her," she told him.

He nodded, looking at the floor.

"Do you think we should move her to the air mattress?" she said.

He nodded again.

She pulled the top linens off the air mattress in readiness and turned to the bunk. They first stripped Heather of her pajamas and then wiped away body fluids with a towel. She was heavy and awkward and stiff, but they lovingly adjusted her onto the air mattress and Kathryn brought the warm water and soap.

Kyle gathered the dirty sheets and pajamas and put them in a garbage bag to be dealt with later. Kathryn washed her darling with all the love and fear and hope and devastation she had inside her.

"Put on some bluegrass music, Kyle," she said suddenly.

He complied and then they worked together to put Heather's kimono on her.

They sat back and looked at her. Kathryn covered her with blankets for the last time.

"Would it be gross if I took her picture?" Kyle said, his voice shaking.

Kathryn looked at him. At Heather.

"No." She shook her head. "Do you want one of you together?"

He bit his lip and squeezed his eyes shut. He shrugged helplessly.

After Kathryn told the McVays and made the proper phone calls, she went back and sat with Heather and Kyle. Margie came with some freshly baked muffins and a thermos of tea and sat with them, too.

Thom came over after milking the cows. He brought whiskey. Just in case.

Where should I bury Heather? The funeral people were going to ask her and she needed an answer to give them.

Kathryn tucked her hair behind her ears and rubbed her hands on her jeans. She paced in the Barn Room. She vaguely missed her land in Veneta and thought it odd that at that horrible lost time in her world she didn't crave and yearn for it. But, then again, perhaps it was obvious that she didn't—or wouldn't—want that right then.

Kyle lay on the floor next to the air mattress with his left arm slung over Heather's middle. Snuggling. Kathryn looked away, blinking fast. She felt swollen, but hollow. Dried out, but full of a spongy wetness that hadn't been rung out yet. She was a contradiction. Would she always be?

Margie sat solemn on a wooden chair near the desk-turned-dining table, her hands in her lap. Kathryn was oddly comforted by her silent presence. Thom had gone out again to start work and to look out for the mortician.

Kathryn abruptly stopped her pacing and went to Heather. She kneeled down on the floor across the bed from Kyle and touched the iciness of Heather's forehead. She cupped Heather's earlobe and she held her breath to stem the tears again.

"I need to walk. To go outside," she said. A guilty sob later, she said, "I'm sorry, Heather." If Heather was watching them somewhere above the Barn Room's ceiling, Kathryn didn't want her thinking that Kathryn was trying to run away from her.

She pushed herself up, not bothering to hide her tears now. Who would even care that she was crying? It would be more odd if she wasn't. She pulled on gloves and stumbled out the door in her haste. She steadied herself on the other side of the threshold and closed the door. She leaned into it, rested her forehead to it.

Heather. Was. Gone.

Never to return.

She lifted her head and stared at the woodgrain of the door, following the stained lines into another realm.

Flora? she called out from inside the casing of her own skin. Calling out to her like she did in the forest behind the chalet. *Flora? What should I do?*

There was no answer. Maybe Kathryn was without

Flora now, too. Alone. Just as Flora's husband was. Kathryn turned and walked out of the barn, her face numb, tears frozen inside, unable to fall anymore.

The sky was gray and surprisingly not rainy. She had hoped that the sky could cry for her. Her breath puffed out and she walked the fields, bundled against the wind, boots crunching in the frost.

The fields were barren in winter death. She knew that they would grow green again, hope emerging in the spring. But Heather wouldn't return with spring's buds.

Kathryn sighed, deep, from the bottom of her rib cage. Sometimes she forgot to breathe, or wouldn't. Now that Heather wasn't alive, there hardly seemed a strong enough reason to breathe. But her body betrayed her and she'd gasp in a breath, heart pounding.

Still she walked. She was on her second circuit of the enormous farm fields before she allowed any thoughts of burial again.

Where would she bury Heather? Here? Or would she ship Heather home and bury her in Eugene? A funeral would be good. More ritual to make sense of the impossibility of her child dying.

Did she even want to go back to Oregon? She'd been able to connect so deeply with Heather here in Scotland. And it was the land of her parents, her ancestors. She actually *did* have some family around here somewhere. Cousins in other regions of the country. Some in England. Some in Wales. She could contact them.

But it felt too exhausting.

She didn't really know them. Just peripherally. Christmas cards. The knowledge of a birth or wedding through the familial vine of grapes.

She could fly home with Heather and live the rest of her days in a house that would be too big now. And with a farm that would be ever increasingly difficult to manage alone.

Alone.

Kathryn's numbness intensified with the chilled air. She didn't want to walk anymore but didn't want to be in the Barn Room with Heather either. Guilt twisted in her sternum, and she grimaced out a dry sob. She wondered if the coroner had been by yet.

She looked out across the fields to see if she could spot a hearse or ambulance—whatever they would send. *But wait!* What if they'd left already? She didn't want Heather to be taken away before she could hold her hand one more time. To kiss her hair one more time.

Resolute, she speed-walked back toward the barn, worried now that she'd lost her chance. But the back of her brain reminded her that even if she had, she'd see Heather at the funeral, and she slowed her step imperceptibly.

She'd stay with Heather. That was certain. If she buried her there in Scotland, then Kathryn would stay. What else would take her back to Oregon? Her parents were dead. Tonya was a dear, dear friend, but she was young and would find another man someday. Who knows where she'd end up? Leaving Kathryn alone once again.

She couldn't tell if she was nauseated or hungry. The barn loomed in front of her. The *Uniforms* hadn't come to take her child away yet. She stopped in front of the barn door, willing herself to go in again, yet not wanting to until she'd made up her mind.

What a horrible thing to have to decide at a moment like this.

And it was a life-altering decision. Potentially. What would she do with herself if she stayed in Scotland? Why was she even thinking of that? She loved her land in Oregon, had been there by choice for thirty years.

The longer she waited outside, the more blank she became. The emotional numbness was easing up enough for her to recognize the physical numbness and the painful cold of winter.

Shivering and shaking and suddenly terrified, Kathryn walked back into the barn. She hadn't thought of Kyle. If she buried Heather here, how would Kyle react?

She trudged into the drab hallway of stalls to the Barn Room. Her hand on the door knob, she filled her lungs, and pulled open the door.

Margie and Kyle looked up, but Kathryn could only look at Heather. Her daughter's pain was gone. The poison had left her body. She hoped Heather was at peace.

Kyle needed to use the bathroom in the Main House, and Margie offered to make some sandwiches—no one had eaten in some time.

"Would you…sit with her, Kathryn?" Kyle said. "I'll be back in a flash. I don't—" His face crumpled. "I don't want her to be alone."

Be alone.

Kathryn's only fear. Come true.

She nodded, her face rubber. Margie held Kathryn's

elbow, guiding her into a chair. She wrapped a blanket around Kathryn's shoulders and started for the door.

"Sophia!" Kathryn said. "Where's Sophia?" She hadn't thought of the poor little kitten at all. Had she been fed? Was she all right?

"Here," Margie said. She scooped up the kitty from the end of Heather's bunk and set her in Kathryn's lap. Gentle. Then left with Kyle.

Kathryn snuggled Sophia into her breast, beneath the blanket, and rubbed her face into her fur. The warmth to her lap thawed Kathryn. Only a little. But it was enough to breathe for the moment.

Heather's red hair looked brittle now. She looked like a discarded glove, fallen from a pocket. This wasn't Heather anymore. She knew that. Just a reminder of her.

A snapshot.

Like the ones Kyle had taken.

Like the ones they'd all posed for in Inverness.

A picture of a time that used to be.

Kathryn closed her mind and called out to the dark realm again. But this time she didn't call Flora. She called Heather.

Crushed, it was like before, at the door. Flora didn't answer then, and Heather didn't answer now.

I must decide alone. Without the help of others.

She thought of the experiences that she and Heather had shared. The Tiny Tot Tea Times, the soccer practices, feeding the rabbits and chickens together, Heather graduating high school, the depression diagnosis, the cancer diagnosis, the fights about the farm business, listening to Heather play the banjo, watching old movies on the couch together.

Kathryn's throat squeezed. It was all passing before her eyes. Only she wasn't the one dying. Arguably, though, a part of her *was* dying. A part of her *life* was dying.

What better place to start fresh and anew than the last place Heather had been? Heather had opened Kathryn's eyes to a place that belonged to Kathryn—even though she hadn't been born there. A place where Kathryn fit.

A tingling sensation wormed its way up her spine and her arm hair stood on end under her sweater. A truth.

She'd already made some heartfelt friendships here. And she had a job. Sort of.

And then she knew with a sudden heat.

She couldn't go back to Oregon. Not to all those memories. And yes, there were memories in Scotland, too. And a lot of them were not so nice. Some were terrifying and desperately sad. But it was a place that Heather had scurried to for something new.

Heather had known something that Kathryn didn't. Maybe she had come here to bring Kathryn here. Maybe that was her purpose in dying so quickly. She'd only lived three months past her diagnosis. Maybe Heather brought her here so that Kathryn wouldn't be *alone*.

Flora would be here more and more, and Kathryn did have some remote family here. She'd made friends quicker here than any other place or time in her life, not having anything else to distract her.

Kathryn breathed a sigh of relief and the numbness wore off completely. Tears spilled out. She ruffled Sophia's fur and looked at Heather's body again. Her face on the pillow. Her hair splayed out in contrast to the pale fabric behind her.

I will stay in Scotland and find my old connection to the land. It's almost there. I feel it growing stronger. I can belong here. And Heather is so very much here. I don't want to disregard that.

THE FUNERAL WAS SMALL. ONLY THE PRIEST, KYLE, THOM and Margie. And Jill. Kyle had called her the day Heather died, and she flew over immediately. Tonya and Bailey managed to come to the funeral, as well, and they brought Janet and Mica.

At the McVay's house after the service, they supped in silence. Thom played a mournful tune on his fiddle. And Kathryn introduced Sophia to Mica and Janet. Mica was indignant and haughty, stomping to the corner and swishing his tail. Janet was curious, but more interested in table scraps.

"What will you do now?" Kathryn said to Kyle.

He smiled, tired and sad.

"I was going to ask you the same thing," he said.

They smiled and dried their eyes, now sharing a bond forever formed in grief and tragedy.

"You will always be welcome in my home, wherever I live. And Heather's grave will always be here whenever you can visit. I know it's not much. But it's all I can offer." She embraced Kyle, squeezing, siphoning his strength and wishing he'd been her son-in-law.

69

Kathryn

THE AIRPORT WAS DARK AND CHILLY. IT WAS TIME for Kyle to go back home. They promised to stay in touch and exchanged contact information.

"I'll be coming back at some point to get some things and pack up the house. I'll probably be in Oregon for a month or two, getting it all ready."

"What will you do with the farm?" he said.

"I'm not sure yet. Sell it? Rent it out?" She shrugged. "I'll certainly have some loose ends to…" She dwindled off in midsentence.

Kyle nodded. She thought he understood. They both had things they would need closure on in the coming months. And for her, even years. Though maybe that was true of Kyle, too. She had no idea of the depth of his relationship with Heather before her death.

It had probably been fairly complicated. As love, under the best circumstances, could be.

"I'll get in touch before I leave Oregon again. I expect I'll have one or two things of Heather's I'll want to give you." Her eyes filled and she stuffed her hand into her coat pocket.

"In the meantime…" She sniffed. "I'd like you to have this." She handed him Heather's hat. The alpaca wool one that she'd knit just last month.

His fingers curled around it, and he looked at it with an expression Kathryn found hard to identify. There were too many layers to it, but in its crudest form, it was probably old-fashioned grief.

He nodded, took the hat, and walked inside the airport.

Tonya and Bailey would be leaving, too. But not for two days. Kathryn was glad all of them weren't leaving at the same time.

After dropping Kyle at the airport, Kathryn drove back toward Reelig and the Barn Room. She'd continue to stay there until she was back from Oregon with the things she wanted. She'd want her own place, some small cottage she could keep up by herself, and a yard big enough for herb and flower gardens, but not acres. It was just her now.

She didn't need to hurry, though. Thom and Margie had made that clear.

Mostly she wanted a room with windows.

But that could wait. For now.

For *now* she was on her way back to Tonya and Bailey and the last of their visit. She pulled into the driveway of Thom's farm and parked Margie's car. Kathryn waved to Margie through the window and walked back to the barn and her Oregon friends.

When Kathryn walked in, darling Janet bounded to the door, barking in merriment. It was so good to have her back. She'd missed the little furball. She scooped her up and scratched behind Janet's ear.

Tonya was eating leftover muffins from the funeral. Margie had made scores of them to have around. Convinced that they were the perfect hand-held snack, she'd made savory cheese-and-ham corn muffins, and sweet honey pecan, and lemon poppyseed. Tea and muffins seemed to be Margie's main comfort food.

Far from complaining, Kathryn was grateful to not have to think about eating. There was just food, available without thinking about it.

Bailey was enraptured by Sophia and played elaborate and extensive aluminum ball games with her, keeping them both occupied. Only Mica seemed miffed. He didn't like the tight space of the Barn Room with nowhere to hide, though he did make almost constant use of Kyle's top bunk—high above other's heads. And it probably still smelled a lot like Kathryn, it having been hers up until a week ago.

Mica would be happy when they got their own place. Kathryn was afraid to let him outside now when he'd only just got there. She worried that he'd take off and get lost. And there could be no more loss in her life right now, thank you very much.

"Tonya," Kathryn said, taking off her coat and hanging it on the back of a chair. "I wanted to talk some things out with you. I had an idea on the way home from the airport that I need to…" She turned her hands in circles at the wrists. "…to process out loud."

"Okay," Tonya said.

"I'm just going to spit it out, and then we can digest it together." Kathryn's heart raced a little, wondering if she was making a huge mistake. But she'd known Tonya for many years, and they understood each other—understood how each other communicated. Even if she said something she'd need to "take back" later, after thinking about it, she felt sure that Tonya would not take offense.

"Sit," Tonya said, gesturing at a matching dining chair. She moved so she was facing Kathryn. "Should I be taking notes?"

Kathryn smiled. Tonya was teasing, but not too far off the mark. They had often brainstormed together, making lists and mind maps until a challenge was understood better and a Plan of Action was initiated.

"Maybe. But not yet. Let's just bounce some ideas around first. We may never get to the planning stage. It might fizzle out before then."

Tonya nodded and picked up her tea mug.

"Spit it out then," she said.

Kathryn took a deep breath. "Here it is. Me spitting it out."

Kathryn swallowed.

"I want to give you Herbal Junction Farm."

Kathryn

With the Barn Room empty, Kathryn relapsed.

Here she was, all by herself, in a foreign country with no land, no farm, no daughter, no parents, and no friends. Well, not many.

Three. She had three friends here.

But while she *knew* lots of people in Oregon and was a part of a couple communities, she wasn't close with anyone except Tonya. She wasn't sure how that happened, but the important part was that she was satisfied and grateful for Tonya's friendship. She didn't need anyone else's.

So three friends were an improvement over Veneta, she supposed, but it didn't feel that way now. And even

Flora hadn't been around as much as she had been in Oregon.

What will happen to me?

She was going to die alone, just like she was afraid of all along. Just like Flora's husband did. She remembered the grave he had dug himself, and shivered.

Kathryn went back to work with Thom. Routine was merciful.

She had lunch with the McVays not long after the funeral.

"Do you have any family?" Kathryn asked, vaguely recalling a son who used to milk the cows.

"We have a son. His wife and their three children live with him in the city," Thom said.

"Edinburgh," Margie said.

Kathryn nodded.

"What are your plans for the farm?" she asked.

"Our son will run it. And his family," Margie said, bustling at the soup pot again, ladling out seconds.

"Kathryn, if you want—I trust you—you can use the plot of land to the west of the potatoes. I used to plant corn there, but I decided not to this year," Thom said.

Kathryn basked in the glow of new friendship and the kind of abundance that sometimes appears small to the giver but is enormous to the receiver.

She could plant her flowers and herbs here this year. She'd try the Barn Room one season. Maybe she could do without windows if she was working her fingers into the soil again.

"One worry I have," Thom said, "is that he won't

stay—my son. He'll just sell it when I'm gone. Or worse, that he and his family won't come after all. I fear he might just ship us to the city where he can look after us." Thom scowled.

"I think it's sweet," Kathryn said, wishing that Heather were here to look after her.

"But I can't leave my land! This is what I know, it's in my blood!" Thom was quite animated, the lines on his face creating a map.

"I did it," Kathryn said with an even voice.

"But that's different. You came because your daughter was here. Dying. You had to come," he said.

Kathryn

"WHAT HAVE I DONE?" KATHRYN WAILED TO TONYA on the phone. "I've moved away from everything I know, everyone I know. I'm alone over here."

"You don't have to do it. You can come back anytime. You'll always have a home with me and Bailey. It's *still* your home, Kathryn," Tonya said, sternly. "As long as you are alive, this will be your home. We talked about this. And Bailey and I will always help you out. You and I have always helped each other out."

That stopped Kathryn. Tonya and Bailey *were* family. Even Kyle was closer to her heart now, with all the help he gave.

"But I can't leave Heather here. I just buried her."

Kathryn looked wildly around the Barn Room, cell phone held tightly to her face.

"You wouldn't be leaving her behind," Tonya said. "You can still visit her whenever you want. Go every year. Make it a pilgrimage."

"I'm getting old, Tonya. I'm poor. I'm not good for much but a farmhand job, and I don't have many years left for that. With what income would I be traveling every year to Scotland to visit my daughter's grave?" Her voice was harsher than she intended. "Sorry," she said.

"It's okay. Just brainstorming. You don't have to do anything you don't want to do. I just want you to know that despite what it might feel like in an empty house at night, you aren't alone. You have me. Always."

"Thank you, Tonya. I'll see you next month." Kathryn felt tired and ended the call. The next day she was going to start cataloging—by memory—all of her belongings and deciding what she wanted to ship over, what she wanted to sell, and what she'd give to Tonya.

In an impulsive—yet perfectly sane—act, Kathryn had given Tonya Herbal Junction Farm. Tonya had worked on the farm with her for so many years that she basically knew what to do anyway. And Jack was there if she wanted to continue hiring him on.

Tonya might not even want to run an herbal business.

Waiting for the indignation or sadness to flare up in her chest at that thought, Kathryn was surprised to feel neither.

Herbal Junction Farm was her past. A lovely and meaningful past, but one that she was willingly putting behind her. Scotland lay in front of her. A smaller way of living. She felt gratitude for the simpler times ahead.

More flowers, fewer carrot weevils.

"I had to mortgage it to pay for Heather's treatments, so I can't offer it outright," she'd said to Tonya after the funeral. "You'd have to pay the mortgage. But I'll transfer the deed to you. It's yours, if you want it."

When Tonya had left, it was to go home and think seriously about it for the final say, but as of then—in the Reelig Barn Room—her answer had been yes. Yes with glee, yes with immense gratitude, yes with love and a desire to be the best friend Kathryn could ever want.

"Well, you're already that," Kathryn had said to Tonya at the airport. They had hugged fiercely and made plans to talk about it again in two months' time when Kathryn returned to start packing up.

THAT NIGHT FLORA VISITED. IT WAS REALLY A RERUN, YET Kathryn had a strong sense of her being in the room, filling it with warmth and love. The rerun was from when Heather was still alive, before Kathryn had gone to Scotland. The dream with only one visual.

Old hands. And the warm scent of apple tea.

Mostly, the dream left Kathryn with a secure and homey feeling. Of growing old and safe in her home.

Before Scotland, she'd thought Flora's dream was about her Veneta farm. But Kathryn had been wrong. It was her *Scottish* farm. Thom's farm.

She would grow old and safe *here*, in Inverness—where, perhaps, she should've been all along.

Kathryn

"MAMA, COME AND SEE WHAT I'VE MADE FOR YOU."

Heather led her to a cottage garden of tall floppy flowers and a beehive. There was a comfortable lounge chair flanking a table with a glass of lavender lemonade and a Territorial Seed catalog on top. Beyond the flowers, there were three tiny raised beds with soil ready for planting. Heather handed Kathryn a seedling start, its roots bare.

"Let's plant this one first. I'll help you." Heather smiled at Kathryn.

She looked different to Kathryn, somehow. But she knew all the same that it was Heather.

Valerie Ihsan

WHEN KATHRYN WOKE, HER HEART RACED.

Heather could visit her. Like Flora!

There was a lot that Kathryn had to feel grateful for. Indeed, gratitude seemed to be a daily occurrence in the past couple of weeks. And here was the number one reason.

Heather wasn't gone.

Heather was *with* her.

And she always would be.

They say our lives flash before our eyes when we die, and if that were true, then Kathryn *couldn't* be alone. Whenever Kathryn died, Heather would be there, in every memory. Kathryn scrunched the blankets under her chin and held her breath.

Maybe that was the way it was for Flora's husband.

Her breath rushed out. Oh, she hoped it was so. For if that were true, he hadn't died alone after all.

And neither would she.

Kathryn

In the turmoil of the past six months, Kathryn hadn't noticed that the neighboring farmers had a ten-year-old daughter named Meg.

It was high time that Kathryn stepped out of her grief shell and began breathing and living more. Late spring was a perfect time for it, too. Everything was blooming, the threat of frost was mostly over, and new growth promised a harvest worth living for.

Kathryn knocked on the neighbor's door on a bright Saturday morning. It was late enough Kathryn figured it wouldn't bring them to the door in their pajamas, but not *too* late that they'd be working in the fields already. She held a potted herbal plant that she'd started in Thom's

     Valerie Ihsan

greenhouse the month she'd gotten back from Oregon.

Meg answered the door, her mother a few steps behind.

"Hello Meg. I'm Kathryn. Your new neighbor." She grinned at Meg's mother and handed the plant to Meg.

"It's an herb called lavender. It can get big and the bees really love it, so when it gets bigger, you can plant it outside. I can show you if you like. Later."

Meg nodded, shy, and held her mother's hand, pulling her to the door.

"Back in America, I had an herb farm," Kathryn said to the woman.

"Welcome. My name is Mary." A man wandered up from behind, wiping his hands on a dish towel. "And this is Mark." She gestured toward him.

"Nice to meet you," he said, extending his hand.

"Mary, Mark, and Meg," Kathryn said, grinning hugely.

"Yes," Mary said. "We quite like it."

"What made you move here?" Mark said.

Kathryn's Cheshire grin melted into a soft smile.

"My daughter brought me. And when she died, I didn't want to leave," she said.

There was a small silence. Kathryn could see it was awkward for them. She smiled to lighten their embarrassed discomfort.

"My family was actually all born here," Kathryn said. "So, really, I haven't moved here. I've come home."

THE END

Acknowledgments

From its inception, *The Scent of Apple Tea* has had many helpers along the way to its publication. I'd like to thank, in order of appearance: my critique group members—Terry, Tiffany, Anna, Ann, Susan, Daryll Lynne, P.C., and Julie (especially Anna for helping at the developmental stage and providing me with a writer's retreat, and Daryll Lynne for helping with plot structure); the folks at Indulge Antiques in Springfield, Oregon for providing me space away from the housework I seem to procrastinate with when I work from home (especially Penny, Bill, Montana, and Brad); Rodney Hutchinson and Shannon Spencer, for allowing me to interview them as experts on matters I knew nothing about; my editor and proofreader Stephanie Amargi; my beta readers Kate, Rebecca, and Shelby; Kristen James for writing the book blurb; Christa Holland of paperandsage.com for the cover design, and Patricia Marshall of Luminare Press for the layout design.

Whew! Thanks team! Of course, there have been others that provided support and kindness and helped me in non-specific ways that made a lot of difference to me. Thank you all.

And finally, a special thank you to my husband, Ali, and to my teenagers, Aubrey and Robert. Thank you for all you do, and for making a difference in my life. I love you.

Hello!

Thanks so much for reading *The Scent of Apple Tea*. If you enjoyed it, please leave a review at your favorite retailer's website and/or on Goodreads or LibraryThing. Even just a star rating and a sentence or two helps spread the word. Your review makes a big difference.

If you'd like to read Deleted Scenes from the original manuscript, you can go to my website to download a free pdf at valerieihsanauthor.com.

If you'd like to join my Advanced Readers Team, find out when my next book is coming, and get a chance to read it before anybody else, please go to my website valerieihsanauthor.com and sign up.

Have a great day!

Book Club Questions

1. Describe the dynamics between Kathryn and Heather. How has the past shaped their lives? Do you admire or disapprove of them?
2. Do Kathryn and Heather change and mature by the end of the book? What do they learn about themselves?
3. Are their voices genuine and believable? For example, does Heather seem younger than she really is?
4. What main ideas—themes—does the author explore? Does the author use symbols to reinforce the main ideas?
5. Is the ending satisfying? If so, why? If not, why? Or how would you change it?
6. Does traveling to Scotland have any effect on Kathryn and Heather? How?
7. Do you think the book cover does a good job of indicating the type of story in it? Would you give the book as a gift? Is this book a "keeper"—one that you'd keep if you needed to downsize your book collection?
8. How did the book affect you? Do you feel changed in anyway? Did it expand your range of experience or challenge your assumptions? Did reading it help you to understand a person better, or even yourself?

(Versions of these questions are attributed to bookbrowse.com and litlovers.com.)

About the Author

Valerie Ihsan is an author, freelance editor, and licensed massage therapist living in Springfield, Oregon. She's served in the United States Army, owns land in Costa Rica, and lives with three dogs, two kids, and one Turk. She loves olives, chai, and Honey Mama's Paleo Lavender Red Rose bars. She can be found on Facebook and Instagram. She blogs at valerieihsanauthor.com.

www.ingramcontent.com/pod-product-compliance
Lightning Source LLC
Chambersburg PA
CBHW051213120726
47905CB00004B/1103